D1806399

Our Dan's 5th Column

Ron Walters

Published 2009 by arima publishing

www.arimapublishing.com

ISBN 978 1 84549 403 2

© Ron Walters 2009

Printed and bound in the United Kingdom

Typeset in Garamond 11/14

Swirl is an imprint of arima publishing.

arima publishing

ASK House, Northgate Avenue

Bury St Edmunds, Suffolk IP32 6BB

t: (+44) 01284 700321

www.arimapublishing.com

This book is a sequel to the book "Our Dan", published in 2008 (ISBN 978 1 84549 239 7).

CHAPTER 1

Dan Green was walking down the path leading to the park bench by the lake, where he had arranged to meet Fred Wharton, his friend and business partner of many years. They first met in the infants school when Fred had protected Dan from being bullied and taunted by other children because of his deformed left leg and they had been friends ever since. They started in business together and they have built up a thriving company, which, is now mainly controlled by their children but Fred and Dan still have the last word on any decisions made regarding the company.

This morning they had arranged to meet in the park to discuss new projects they were toying with. Fred thought it would be better out in the open air, too many interruptions took place when they were in the office. They had arranged to meet in the park to toss around a few new ideas. When Dan arrived, Fred moved along the bench to make room for him to sit down, he smiled to himself, Dan did not appear to have aged over the years, while he had put on a little too much weight and his fair hair was almost white, his wife Mary, who was Dan's sister, said, it was down to good living. Ah! Well, she could be right. His thoughts turned to the business on hand. Unfortunately, their future plans were to be interrupted by events from the past, which, not only threatened the business but also the lives of their immediate families.

Over the years, Dan, Fred and their co-director Frank, had disagreements but it did not leave any bitterness to spoil their friendship and this would have seriously harmed their business. The first and main business formed was D.F.F. Furniture Ltd. This was started up in 1938 in Liverpool and it had a very difficult beginning. Frank being the cabinet maker, he received a salary but the other two worked in different fields, Fred as a bookies runner and Dan as a lather boy in a Barbers Shop to enable them to finance the business and to keep it solvent. When the war came along the government work kept their factory very busy and created a springboard to launch into the big time. Although it helped their business, they in turn, helped the war effort. Anything asked of them, they did, working very long hours; Fred often said that their families would not work the hours they had worked during that period. All three are so disappointed that the family members who have taken over the various businesses cannot work together. Dan often says that the businesses should not have been given to them until they were more experienced.

Apart from the furniture business, there are the Hairdressing and Training Group, Window and Interior Display Company and Hairdressers Sundry Supply Company; a member of the family by birth or marriage controls each of the companies. Dan finds it difficult to understand why they cannot work together as there is no reason for any jealously. After discussing the problem, it was decided that the three retired friends together with their wives, would arrange a meeting and thrash the problem out until they come up with a solution.

Dan Green, Fred Wharton and Frank Belcher are still the founder directors of the Furniture Company and Margery Green, Mary Wharton and Bella Belcher are the founder directors of M.B.M. Display Company. Any discord within a company seeps into the market place and affects its trading potential; they know this from a previous situation.

*

Fred's daughter, Salina and Dan's daughter Lillian had grown up together and attended the same art college and on completion of their education they joined their mothers M.B.M. Company. They had a different outlook with regard to displays from their mothers; they found they got a lot of work from the younger couples, mainly interior work. Being younger, it reflected in the modern contemporary interior layout of furniture, lighting and wall colourings. They were very much in demand, which pleased them greatly. Their mothers assisted by Gwen, Bella's daughter in law, concentrated on dressing store windows, asking advice on any modern colourings, if needed.

Salina and Lillian both lived at home with their parents, just two doors away from each other. They spent many evenings together discussing, preparing and planning how to deal with a job they were working on. An exhibition was advertised dealing with display work, they all decided to go but as the date approached several cancelled so the visit was called off and accommodation was cancelled.

Salina and Lillian were very disappointed and at the last minute they decided to go by themselves, Exhibitions held in Blackpool are always well attended and accommodation is at a premium, so when they arrived in Blackpool, they visited the tourist centre. They were offered one room in a two star hotel; it was within walking distance from the Exhibition, which helped. They went to the hotel and booked in and headed straight back to the exhibition hall leaving the car in the hotel car park and their cases still in the boot.

They walked around visiting various stands and they were very impressed how the various colours had been blended; in fact, they were delighted that they had made the effort to come along. Of course they talked to the people on the stands and were able to discuss various points about the exotic displays. They arranged to meet up with several of them for a meal during the evening, which pleased them, as they were not sure where to eat. They went into the hotel with their luggage and were shown to their room. It was so small but it had its own toilet facility with a shower and a double bed.

When they had unpacked, Salina said, "Who is first for the shower?"

"Me" said Lillian, pushing past Salina

"Oh! no you don't."

They both ended up in the shower.

When they were dressed they went out to meet up with the people they had arranged to eat with, every one enjoyed the meal and the company was good, the talk was all about work, so it went well. The evening came to a close and they all went their different ways, Salina and Lillian went back to their hotel and then to their room, Salina made a cup of coffee and they watched television for a while before going to bed. They agreed the visit was worthwhile; they gained knowledge as to how various colours can be used against each other to create a greater effect.

*

When Salina and Lillian attended another Exhibition in Manchester they met two brothers who were also involved in interior design and when they took the brothers to meet their respective parents they were made most welcome. The families immediately took to Arne and Richard. They enjoyed the boy's company over the next twelve months.

Salina and Lillian decided to arrange a dinner party in the house of Dan and Margery; the guests were to include Arne and Richard. The food was now all on the table; the girls went round refilling the glasses with either red or white wine. The two girls remained standing.

Salina said, "Meet my future husband" dragging Arne to his feet.

"This is my future husband," said Lillian pulling Richard to his feet. The table erupted with the respective parents offering their congratulations followed by toasts on the couple's engagement.

Margery and Mary were mentally arranging the weddings, when Mary spoke to Salina about the future arrangements; she was taken aback by Salina saying she wanted a low key affair, as she was pregnant.

CHAPTER 2

Dan contacted his retired bank manager, Mr Blake. When they met, Dan realised how time had flown by and Mr Blake had changed considerably. He no longer had a round cherub face and black curly hair, the most noticeable thing was, he had lost the bright sparkle from his eyes, they were now a little dull. Dan had booked a table for lunch, as they sat down Fred walked in to join them and told Dan that Frank would not be joining them, as Bella, his wife is not too well, so he felt that he should stay with her.

During the lunch Dan outlined the problems with their families being jealous of each other, at least, that is the only way I can understand the unpleasant atmosphere. Mr Blake could see that both Dan and Fred were concerned with the situation, which could result in the loss of customers and the company falling apart, which would be a tragedy after all the hard work that had gone into making the company so successful.

Mr Blake thanked Dan for inviting him to lunch,

"I will ring you when I have the answer to your problem, in fact, I have an idea mulling around in my mind now but I do think that all three of you must take a firm stand, please or offend your family and friends."
Fred and Dan said they were aware of this.

"Just to clarify, you three still hold the controlling shares?"

"Yes, we have not passed any share control to anyone."

"Good, I will be in touch."

True to his word, Mr Blake contacted Dan inviting him to join him for coffee one morning a week later. He went through several ideas' he had thought of but left it to the three directors to decide which road to take.

*

It was decided to call a family meeting in the canteen of the D.F.F. Factory. Dan pointed out that he meant all the family including those joined through marriage. The problems to be discussed at the meeting had been chewed over by all three of them. They have become very concerned with the unrest that has crept into the company; naturally, their wives were invited, as they too had worked hard to achieve the company's success. Counting up, they decided that the family present would amount to nine apart from themselves. Dan's sister Ruth's son, named Alan, had been included in the number, at present he was studying a Business and Marketing degree at Nottingham University. This young man is Dan's favourite nephew; he has the same outlook on life and yet it was Alan's father who gave Dan such a terrible time at school, bullying him because of his disabled left leg.

However, over the years, his father Charlie and Dan had become firm friends due to them both being hard workers. Dan is hoping that when Alan obtains his degree, he can be groomed to take full control of the company. Mr Blake had suggested giving each member of the family 5% of the companies share capital, this would put them all on an equal level; no one would have more influence than the next. Fred, Dan and Frank would still control the remaining 55%, providing they retained the control, the company shares cannot be sold without their authority. Mr Blake had pointed out that if a predator managed to purchase a certain number of the shares they could launch a take over bid. To prevent such a thing happening, a proviso should be included; no shares can be sold without the direct authorisation of the board of directors.

After a long deliberation the three directors considered Mr Blake's idea to be sound and they would adopt it in principal. Dan expected opposition from Frank's son Simon and in view of his dishonest action in the past when he got hooked on gambling and embezzled company's money. Dan would be more than happy to have the shares legally controlled. Simon always considered himself far more important than the rest of the family, it is hoped and this move would create a level playing field.

*

The day of the meeting came around; a long table had been erected in order that they would be able to watch the facial expressions of each person present at the meeting. The three partners sat at the head of the table and at the opposite end sat their wives. Coffee and biscuits were made available before the meeting, this encouraged chitchat.

They all sat down, Dan opened the meeting.

"We are disappointed with all of you present because of all the silly arguments you keep having between yourselves and this creates a most unpleasant atmosphere within the company. Let me point out, not one of you is indispensable; if you are not satisfied with the management of this company, you are free to leave. We do not intend to allow this unpleasantness to continue creeping into the company, if it persists, the person, or persons responsible will have their employment terminated, this of course would be our last resort. You might object to my being so blunt but the company has been in business for many years and in the past our employees have enjoyed coming to work. If any member of our staff thought they were being unfairly treated, they knew that they could approach the person in charge and their grievance would receive a fair hearing. If their complaint was considered to be justified, it would receive prompt attention."

"The unpleasant part of this meeting has now been dealt with; I will draw your attention to the names on the list in front of you. We are considering reducing the number of shares held by we three and transfer 5% of the stock to each named person on the list, it will still leave we three in overall control of the company even if you combine your total. At this stage, it is only a proposal being considered, if however, one of the named person decide to sell their shares, they will have to be offered back to the board, this will be written in the legal transfer document. Each of the named will become a director; this would mean putting all the businesses under one umbrella of the parent company D.F.F. Bear in mind, this is just a proposal being considered, we will have another meeting to debate any changes to take place."

*

"Right, the floor is now all yours, to prevent you all speaking at once, you must go through the chairman, and Frank is acting as chairman today."

The first was Jenny,

"Mr Chairman; does that mean that I shall lose control of my Hairdressing and Training Company?"

Dan said, "Mr Chairman, may I answer that question, No Jenny, you will continue to trade as you do now, in charge of your own company, you will also have 5% of D.F.F. stock to whom you will be answerable as a parent company. You will not lose any of your authority; we are talking with the future in mind."

Jenny replied, "My three sisters and I formed and run our group without any financial help from D.F.F. Why should we be taken over by that company?"

"That is a very valid point Jenny; we will have to have further discussions."

Simon spoke up, "Mr. Chairman, I am responsible for the finances of the company and I feel that I should be on a higher salary scale than the hairdressers and the factory workers. One name on the list Alan Oates how does that come about?"

Frank looked across at Dan to reply, as Simon is Frank's son.

Dan took the hint.

"Simon, you are on a very good salary, you have a company car with all expenses paid by the company, we will not dismiss your comment out of hand, all of the points here today will be very carefully looked into. You ask about Alan Oates name being included on the list, he is my nephew and both his parents helped this company to succeed and prosper, on many occasion they both worked a seventy-hour week to help your father and Fred to complete government contracts in order to keep the company up and running. The inclusion of this young man's name was discussed at length before it was added and we decided that when Alan achieves his degree in Business studies and Marketing, he could be an asset to the company."

"The object of this meeting is for any one of you to air a subject, which you would like to discuss." The Chairman looked across at Alec, who had taken over Dan's Barbers Shop.

"Have you anything to talk about?"

"Mr. Chairman, I am more than happy with my little lot."

"I am delighted to hear you say that Alec, for the benefit of you all, Alec is marrying my youngest daughter and is already considered to be a member of our family, hence his name is included on the list." The look on Simon's face said otherwise, obviously he did not agree.

"Sam, you look a little hesitant, what ever is on your mind, let us join in your thoughts?"

"Roy and I have kept up with the required production in the factory but here and now we would like you to make the decision, Who is in charge, Roy and I can no longer continue working under the present conditions of not knowing who is answerable to whom?"

"Thank you Sam, we appreciate your frankness but will you bear with us today, I promise this matter will receive our urgent attention not just put on the back burner. As I said before, this is why we are all here today, to thrash out any problems you might have."

"They cannot be any bigger problem as when we visited several second hand shops with a borrowed handcart to buy any old oak furniture, as we did not have the money to buy new wood. Hours were spent cleaning the wood, ready for me to use to complete an oak desk, which had been ordered, happy days; the friends looked at each other and smiled.""Roy, the floor is yours."

"Dan, when you said that you were considering allocating 5% to each of us, does that mean D.F.F. is going public, This would necessitate electing a Managing Director and a Board of Directors which would consist of those holding sufficient shares."

"Whooo-aa, Roy. This is a very delicate matter and we are entering uncharted waters. We intend to investigate every possible advantage and disadvantage relating to this meeting. When we think we have arrived at a satisfactory conclusion, we will have another meeting to lay all the facts before you before going ahead. Our main objective is to get the company running smoothly and see every one smiling at work rather than working in an unpleasant atmosphere?" "Mr. Chairman, why aren't Salina and Lillian included on the list?"

"It is an oversight Mary, it will be dealt with."

Fred turned to Dan, "How did we make that error?" Dan just shrugged his shoulders.

CHAPTER 3

The girl in charge of the office came out on to the shop floor looking for Sam, when she found him, she handed him two letters to read, each letter was complaining of the poor quality furniture delivered to them.

"You had better show these letters to Fred urgently."

"Yes, I will, he is coming in this morning."

When Fred arrived, he was presented with the two complaint letters, having read both letters; he called Sam and Roy into the office away from the shop floor. Fred read the two letters out to them and asked for an explanation.

Sam looked at Roy.

"Come on," "What is going on?"

Neither of them could or would offer an explanation.

Fred was very angry. "Both of these company's are our oldest and most regular customers."

*

"The warehouse of one of these complaints is only 15 miles down the road, I am going and you are both coming with me, we will call for Dan and then we will visit this gentleman and clear this mess up." They called for Dan; he too became very angry when he read the letters. This being the first time they have received complaint letters. Driving along, each one was wondering what sort of a reception they would be given.

Fred brought the van to a halt close to the loading bay at the rear of the warehouse, as they entered, a man wearing a fawn smock said,

"Can I help you gentlemen?"

"Yes you can."

"Will you kindly ask Mr Ball, if Dan and Fred from D.F.F. Furniture can speak to him?" he walked away smiling. Several minutes later Mr Ball came down the stairs into the warehouse, he smiled as he shook hands with them.

"There was no need to have brought your minders with you, I am not that vicious." He was introduced to Sam and Roy as their factory managers amid the laughter.

"Now Eric, what is the problem?" Eric led the way to the back of the warehouse and pointed to a Table and a Welsh Dresser.

" These are the two items." The joints on the table legs were partly open and shakes (splits) in the timber on the pot board of the Dresser. "This is not your usual standard," Dan and Fred were appalled at the condition of the furniture; they turned to Sam and Roy.

"How on earth has this happened, how the hell was this rubbish despatched bearing the name D.F.F. Furniture?"

The items were carefully scrutinised and they looked at Sam for an explanation. Sam was upset.

"I cannot understand how this has happened, these items were put into the seconds room, I am sure of this as I personally put the Dresser in the room because of the splits in the wood. As you know a Mr Bowen buys the furniture from the second's room as a job lot to sell off in his second hand shops."

"Eric, will you ask your young gentleman to load these and any other items you are not happy with on to our van and I will personally ensure you will receive replacements tomorrow. Also Eric, you will receive an additional 5% discount on these items for the inconvenience you have been caused."

When they got back in the van, Sam turned to Fred and Dan.

"I did not want those items included with the order to be sent out but I was told that I had no authority to decide what was sent out."

"Right, who told you this?"

"Simon said the company could not afford to pay overtime money to complete the order, so, he sent these items. Simon had remarked that it was ridiculous; to sell off the seconds so cheaply, he made the point that he was in charge of the company's finances. Several times I remarked that the items were inferior, he replied that I was in no position to question his decision."

"You are telling us, Simon instructed that these items were to be despatched to our customers?" Roy and Sam together said, "Yes."

Fred and Dan agreed that they should speak to Frank before taking the matter any further. They contacted Frank and put him in the picture, he was most upset, this was the second time his son has caused him problems. Simon was called into the main office, as he walked in; he looked around.

"Now what"?

"We have received complaints from our customers about the poor quality furniture that has been delivered to them and we have been told that you authorised the substandard goods to be despatched." Simon looked most indignant,

"Yes, I did, I am responsible for the company's finances. I consider it ludicrous for the items in the second's room to be sold off so cheaply."

Dan said, "We will discuss this matter, a little later."

They called Bert into the office; he is the despatch manager.

"Bert, nothing leaves this factory if you have any doubt about them being below standard."

They all met up in the works canteen two days later. The canteen lady provided coffee and biscuits for them hoping it would take the look of concern off their faces; it was new to her to see worried expressions.

Sam stood up, "I would like to refer to a speech made by Fred just after the war had finished in this very canteen. He addressed all of the staff explaining that we would have to excel to compete in the market place and he continued by saying, if any member of the staff saw any furniture they considered inferior they should bring it to the notice of the management, not for any one person to be chastised but just to maintain our high quality furniture."

Frank then asked Simon, who gave him the authority to send out furniture that had been placed in the second's room. These items are put in there because they are either damaged, splits in the wood, shrinking or the polishing is below standard.

"I think it is ridiculous to sell off furniture so cheaply."

"Simon, you have no authority in this factory regarding production, Sam is the production manager and what he says goes, if he is not available Roy must be consulted, no goods from the second's room must ever be sent out to our customers, we have spent years building up a good honest customer relationship."

Dan turned to Roy, "Will you check if any of our other customers have been sent rubbish, if you find any, pass the details to me."

"Simon, your responsibilities are in the finance and wages department, just keep away from the production side of the business." Simon stormed off,

Dan turned to Sam, "I take it, this is the matter you brought up at the meeting,"

"Yes Dan that was the gist of it. The furniture was sent out to complete an order, its condition was queried several times by Bert but Simon told him that he was completely in charge and his employment would be terminated if he failed to carry out instructions." When the meeting was over, Dan went into the despatch room to speak to Bert, Dan told him that his job was safe and only Fred had the authority to dismiss any member of the staff. A look of relief came across Bert's face.

"If you think any of our goods are below par, speak to Sam or Roy, if however, there is still a doubt, take it up with Fred or Frank, cheers Bert," Dan left Bert smiling, which was the object of the exercise."

CHAPTER 4

Frank and his wife Bella visited their son Simon and his wife Gwen; the main reason for the visit was for Bella to spoil her granddaughter Julie, as grand parents like to do. When Gwen opened the door her face lit up with a big smile, she and her in-laws were very close.

As they sat down, Gwen said "Tea?" to which they both nodded. Simon came down from upstairs to join them, "Hello you two, nice of you to call."

His father got up from his seat, "Shall we take our tea into the next room Simon, I want to talk with you." Frank turned to Simon, "I am very concerned with your attitude towards the staff at the factory and I just cannot understand why you insist on being so unpleasant. They are all hard working people, why are you so difficult Simon, come along now what is the problem? You were never like this when you were growing up."

"Your mother and I have tried all ways to ensure that you and Gwen were never left wanting for anything."

Simon looked at his father, "Now I suppose you are going to remind me of when I embezzled money from the company's funds when I got hooked on gambling."

Franks face flushed red, "No, I am not and I think you are unfair to mention that hiccup because the people you appear to dislike forgave you, helped and trusted you enough to get you back on even keel."

Simon snapped, "I am going to leave the company."

"In that case, you will need to hand in your notice to Fred; incidentally, you will have to leave the company car at the end of your notice."

"Why should I lose the car, Mark kept his when he left the company, in fact, he was very surprised when it was given to him."

Frank angrily retorted, "Mark did not just leave the company, he retired and the car was fitted out for a disabled driver. The main reason he was given the car was because in the early days, he carried out a lot of work without getting or expecting payment. On occasion we gave him the odd £1 when we were able. His dedication and loyalty deserved recognition, which, we have been able to give over the past few years. Simon, you do not appreciate how lucky you are and what good friends you have around you, if only you would take that chip off your shoulder and accept the fact that we all working for a living."

"However, your mother will be disappointed when she is told you are leaving the company, as I told you earlier, you must speak to Fred tomorrow, I have given up on you son, I had hoped you would see sense and start to enjoy life. One thing you must think about, you have a wife and baby to support plus a heavy mortgage. Let us rejoin the ladies, have you told Gwen of your decision?"

"No, not yet,"

"Okay if I tell your mother?"

"Yes if you must."

When they went back into the lounge, Bella looked up.

"Are you both okay?"

"No," said Frank, "I am very disappointed, Simon has told me that he intends leaving the company and seek employment elsewhere."

Bella shouted, "Whatever for Simon, why"?

"I am fed up being treated just like one of the flock, instead of one of the bosses."

"You are not one of the bosses Simon, your domain is in the financial and wages office, Sam nor Roy would enter your office and tell you how to do your job, why try and interfere with their jobs, it is all a matter of teamwork."

Simon replied, "My mind is made up to leave."

"Make sure you speak to Fred in the morning as arrangements will have to be made to advertise for your replacement, by the way, make sure you take all your personal goods out of the car as it will most probably go to an auction company."

Gwen sat in her chair with tears streaming down her face. Frank and Bella said their good byes and left.

Bella gave the car keys to Frank saying, "Will you drive, I cannot concentrate." As they were going home, she asked the real reason for Simon wanting to leave.

"I will tell you Bella, he wants to be in charge of the whole factory. I do not think he is capable of withstanding the pressure nor does he have the leadership qualities."

*

The following morning, Frank contacted Fred and put him in the picture with regard to Simon's decision but asked him not to mention that he had been told. Fred, just look surprised when he tells you, I told him that he must speak to you. Fred made a point of going into the factory and wandering around, when he saw Simon go into the canteen, he followed him, when he arrived, Simon was seated with a cup of coffee in front of him, Fred collected his cup of tea and went over.

"Good morning Simon, May I join you. How are your family, has Gwen got over the birth of Julie?"

"Yes thanks Fred, they are quite well, that is until two o'clock in the morning."

"Yes, we have all experienced that in the past."

"Have you got over our little disagreement last week, I do hope so, we all make mistakes Simon."?

"Fred, I want to give my notice, I have decided to leave the company," Fred looked up surprised, "Surely you are kidding Simon, does your father know?"

"Yes he does."

"Have you been offered a job paying more money?" "No, I have not got another job as yet."

"You have shaken me Simon, you realise as a company executive you will have to work one months notice."

"Good lord, as long as that."

"It is in your contract of employment; this is to give the employer time to arrange a replacement." Fred looked at Simon; "I am not going to try and stop you leaving or even offer you more money to reconsider. I can see your mind is made up, however, I would like to know the reason for your decision, you are the first person to leave this company to join another employer and that dates back to 1939."

Simon looked at Fred, "I feel like a small fish in a very large pool which makes me feel insecure."

"Good lord, whatever makes you feel that way? As you know when your father Dan and myself started out, I was a bookies runner, Dan, was a lather boy in a Barbers shop and your father was the furniture maker. Dan and myself paid money to keep D.F.F. up and running, Dan picked up some share tips, which helped. I was a Mr Nobody but I kept doing what I thought was right and finally I studied and designed some of our beautiful furniture. I feel I have succeeded. Simon, I was as small as an ants egg in a fish bowl, it is the faith in oneself that brings success. You do a good job and the rest of the factory could become your friends but only if you treat them as you would like them to treat you. Anyway, I will arrange for an advert for your replacement." "You say that you have told your parents?"

"Yes, I told them last night."

"What was their reaction?"

Simon raised his eyebrows; "Both said they thought me to be mad, they claimed to be disappointed."

"You realise you will lose your company car; it might go out to be auctioned or placed in the car pool. Simon, will you keep this conversation to yourself for the time being, I think it would be advisable, don't mention it to the office girls, we do not want any rumours running around the factory"

Fred and Dan made a point of visiting Mark, he is still very mentally active but he struggles physically, he is not as active as he would like to be. They explained the full situation concerning Simon, Mark was quite upset, he had thought that Simon had learned his lesson and had buckled down and was doing a good job when he handed over the reins on his retirement.

"We do not want him to leave, he is a likeable lad and he is good at his job, still, you know that as you trained him. We hope he does not leave for Frank's sake; he always thought his son would be an asset to the Family Company. During Simon's one months notice, do you think you could come to the factory just for one or two days a week, just to give the impression that he will not be missed, just a psychology exercise."

Fred told Mark, He had sat and talked to Simon and gave him the impression, you are leaving, so!

"Yes Dan, I will come in for a few days, it will do me good to have something to do again, will you arrange transport for me, I am not happy driving just at present, my legs are very troublesome."

"Yes, Fred or one of the girls will pick you up but you must behave if it is one of the girls who transport you," this created a chuckle.

"I will ask Simon to bring me right up to date on all the new orders; this will enable me to pass on the information to his replacement. It is a shame that we are planning to use psychology pressure to make him rethink his decision, you will explain to Frank what we are up to. We don't want him to think we are pushing Simon out, we are just trying to make him realise what a good job he has and what friends he has around him, if only he would accept this."

Fred went to visit Bella and Frank that evening; they made it so obvious that they were pleased to see him. Fred explained the strategy. "We do not want Simon to leave but we cannot allow him to take complete charge of the factory in view of his attitude at present, as he gets older, he may change. Are you both quite happy with my approach to the problem?" They both nodded, "You are, good." "Just keep it to yourselves whatever is said; otherwise we might lose Simon, which would be a great shame to us and disaster to him and Gwen." Both Frank and Bella were happy with the way Fred was going to handle Simon's problem; they were beginning to despair in view of the many upsets Simon has caused them.

*

Simon was very surprised and suspicious the morning Mark arrived, "Good morning Simon, I have come in for you to update me on all the latest orders etc. It is a while since I retired and need to know everything to pass on to your replacement, tell me everything that goes on in this office as far as the office staff are concerned, I have come to work as I am going mad at home" When Mark mentioned the word replacement, it shook Simon, it was obvious he had given in his notice but he was not too sure about leaving the company, he stood to lose too much.

The canteen lady made a fuss of Mark; she brought tea and toast to his office, as he was unable to negotiate the steps leading to the canteen. Simon brought his coffee down to the office and sat at the desk with Mark, he tried to make light conversation but Mark craftily brought the conversation back to the work in the office but Simon was reluctant to go down that road. The third week into his one months notice,

Simon appeared to be very subdued; "I will be a little late coming to work tomorrow morning as I have an interview for another job." He arrived the following day just before lunch, Mark had changed his plans, he intended to stay at home but in view of Simon's interview, he had come to the office.

The canteen lady brought Mark a plate of sandwiches and a cup of tea into his office. Mark looked up as Simon walked in carrying his lunch; he pulled up a chair and sat beside Mark.

"He quietly said how did it go Simon?"

"Not too good, three directors interviewed me; their real aim was to find out the reason for my leaving this company, which, they understood to be a happy and efficiently run company. They asked, was it me that could not get along with them or was it them who could not get along with me? I must admit Mark, I got a little ruffled at some of the personal questions they levelled at me and I don't think I made the right impression. They said they would write to me within the next two days as they had four more applicants to interview."

Simon sat looking completely lost. "I will have to enquire if any other jobs are available."

Mark looked at Simon saying, "You will have to look sharp, you told me that you are leaving next week." Simon looked sick. With just four days to go, Mark had got to grips with the office routine, this left very little for Simon to do.

When Simon arrived home, he had just four days before the completion of his notice. Gwen handed him a long white business looking envelope, Simon opened the letter, he was disappointed with the contents, his application and interview had been unsuccessful, he was surprised, he has such an ego, he thought any employer would jump at the chance to employ him. He handed the letter to Gwen for her to read.

"Now! what Simon?"

"It looks as if I will become unemployed or ask if I can withdraw my notice, which, I will do."

Gwen was in tears, "I am so pleased that is your plan. Who will you have to approach?"

"I gave my notice to Fred, so it is he I must speak to and grovel."

"I think you are unfair to Fred, Dan and your father, they worked so hard to set up a company for their children and you continually throw it back in their face, you should be grateful to them."

The following morning, Simon asked around and he eventually found Fred.

"Fred, I have made a big mistake, is it too late to withdraw my notice?"

"I am not in the position to give you an answer today as we have been carrying out several interviews for your replacement. I will have to discuss it with Frank and Dan this evening when we meet but we cannot have you saying you are going to leave then changing your mind. If we should decide to keep you on, I am not saying we will, you will have to sign a contract to safeguard ourselves, would you be prepared to do that?" "Yes Fred, I would."

"The one big problem is how you treat other members of the staff; in fact, if the decision is made for you to stay, you will have to change your attitude. The first contract will be for one month's probation before signing the final contract."

Fred felt awfully mean treating Simon in this way but he felt it was to Simon's benefit. That evening Fred and Mary went round to visit Dan and Margery to enjoy a social drink, during the evening Fred brought up the subject of Simon's position, he outlined exactly what had transpired between Simon and himself.

"Give Frank a ring and tell him exactly what you have told us. Of course we want Simon to stay with the company but your approach has been the right one, I am sure Bella and Frank will agree."

Fred went into the next room to telephone Frank; he was delighted with the news that Simon wanted to stay with the company and he thought that Fred's strategy had been correct and agreed with the probationary period. "I know he is my son but I hope this will bring him down a peg or two. He discovered when he went for an interview what a good job he has working for this company, once again Fred; I appreciate your help with Simon."

*

The following morning Fred called Simon into his office and told him that at the meeting last night it was decided to give him another chance, providing he accepted the one-month's probation and subject to your behaviour, we will offer you a contract to continue your employment with this company. Simon agreed readily, he had found out such a job as he has, is not easy to find. He went back to his office and told Mark;

"You have made a very wise decision Simon." "You have a very good position with this company and very well paid a company car with all expenses and people in charge who care for you."

"Go home and tell Gwen that you have come to your senses and you realise what a wonderful life you have with such a caring wife and baby." "I think you are right Mark; I will go home with a bunch of flowers, hoping we can overcome our differences in the past."

"I will be a little late coming in tomorrow morning Simon; it will be about lunchtime, okay?" When Simon had left, Mark telephoned Bella and told her what had taken place, please do not let on that I have phoned you but I thought you might have been worrying. Gwen will get a surprise when Simon arrives with a bunch of flowers." He heard Bella sobbing with relief at the other end of the line.

"Don't forget Bella, you must act surprised when you are told." That evening, Simon, Gwen and baby Julie visited Frank and Bella.

Simon faced his parents and said, "I have decided to stay with the company, at least I am on one months probation. Mark has convinced me, instead of complaining, I should appreciate what I have and what a wonderful life I have, thanks to you both and Gwen, I can assure you, that you will have no more trouble from me, I promise." Bella and Gwen were both in tears.

"Gwen, if I take Simon into the next room to enjoy a drink will you drive the car?" "Of course I will, can't have a drunk driving his wife and baby home." This broke the ice, smiles replaced the tears. Bella turned to Gwen, "Do you intend to carry on with the M.B.M. Company?" "I will but not for a few weeks, at least, not until I get the all clear from the hospital saying I can return to work."

CHAPTER 5

Dan telephoned Frank and Fred asking them to join him the following morning in the factory canteen for coffee; they both agreed but felt a little surprised. "Right Dan, we are here." "Before I put my idea forward, do you mind if Roy, Sam and Simon join us?" They both looked at each other a little bewildered but nodded their agreement. When the boys joined them, they all sat looking at Dan, wondering, what next. "Simon's mistake last week set me thinking about the retail side of our business, Simon looked a little uncomfortable, I am not getting at you Simon, in fact, I should thank you for putting this idea into my head.

I have this idea running around in my head, should we open up a retail store selling our own furniture, making use of the expertise of M.B.M. to deal with the displays and incorporate a lighting department. Do not go thinking too far ahead as we will have to consider this move very carefully, it has to be a viable proposition. I suggest, you all take this idea away with you and we will have another meeting later to go into the idea in depth. One thing I am not too sure about, how will our own customers we supply react, will they consider it unfair trading, perhaps we will have to call the outlet by a different name from our own. Should we start off with a small unit or chance a larger unit with plenty of display area. Simon, if we do go ahead, you will have plenty on your plate, in fact you might need more staff, we will rely on you to cost out business rates, lighting and the staffing level with regard to wages." "I need to have the figures to work from, I think you will find that the rent and rates will be the greater expenditure, however, we shall see". "Sam and Roy; Fred will come up with some new furniture designs, so, no doubt you will have to put up with Frank back in the fray." Frank and Fred just smiled at each other.

"The retirees will be returning to work."

Both Fred and Frank said, "What a wonderful idea." Dan was delighted to see Sam, Roy and Simon chatting together with the future in mind.

*

That evening Dan and his wife visited Fred and Mary, as they sat down.

Fred said, "Dan has come up with a brilliant idea; you explain it to the girls Dan." "This is what I discussed this morning, he then outlined his idea, and really this is just a toy to give three retired gentlemen something to do." This was greeted with laughter, the two girls got really excited, what a great idea, "Cool down" said Dan, "This idea is only in the melting pot." In spite of this, the girls were making plans and offering suggestions,

"What a challenge" said Mary, "I must phone Bella," just as she said that, the phone rang, it was Bella and she was so excited?

Mary tried to calm her down, Bella started by saying that the girls will have to meet in their workroom at the factory.

Dan took the phone from Mary and laughed as Bella was going on, "May I speak to Frank?" He took over the phone. "The girls at this end are just as bad as Bella, before we go too far I suggest we three go for a wander around and look for some suitable premises, with good customer traffic and affordable overheads."

"We must not go into this venture without a lot of planning, not like we did when we first started, our planning was none existent." He could hear Frank laughing at the other end of the line.

Dan, Fred and Frank met up and went into the Liverpool City Centre to look for a suitable site around the shopping area, they found some units to let or for sale but they did not consider them to be in a prime busy retailing position. They decided to have lunch and discuss what they had seen, after lunch they were on the way back to the car park when Fred spotted a small-disused cinema. The roof had been damaged during the wartime air raids but it appeared to have been repaired and retiled but the entrance was all boarded up so they could not assess the interior.

They noted the estate agent's telephone number and called him from a phone box, the agent must have had the cinema on his books for a while and keen to sell, he offered to join them in ten minutes. He arrived with the keys, when he opened the door, the interior looked vast; all three went in to look around, the agent flipped the lights on, each one became uncertain in view of the vast floor space. A lot of work would be necessary but when the agent told them the cost of the lease they became very interested and thought this might be the answer to their plans.

Frank looked at Fred, "Nearly as bad as the unit, we rented from a Mr Benson," and they both chuckled. A large number of seats had been removed; perhaps, Frank had bought several at the auction when he was fitting out Jenny's Salon but the carpet looked as if it might be reasonable when all the rubbish is removed. The boxes either side of the screen were very ornate and in need of a little TLC, to bring them back to their former glory. The ceiling was also very decorative but that too will need some attention.

Looking around, Frank said, "This interior reminds me of The Grand Theatre in Blackpool."

One of the first questions put to the agent, what was the length of the lease? They would need a long lease to recoup their monetary investment.

The agent put their minds at rest by saying it had another 99years to run.

They were aware that the repainting of the ornate plasterwork will take time and could be costly as scaffolding will be necessary to carry out the work.

Dan turned to Fred; "You will have to design some colonial furniture verging on to antique to blend in with the beautiful old style plasterwork," Fred just smiled.

Frank told the agent they would give the property some consideration, he replied,"

"I might get the owners to lower the asking price of the lease."

"We will contact you later." They left the cinema and went across the road to the Co-operative store; the number of shoppers inside the store amazed them. They spent a little more time wandering around the area, weighing up the customer traffic, they still wondered if there was enough traffic to warrant their investment in the cinema.

After two more visits, they decided to go ahead as it could be a good investment. When all the legal papers had been signed, they organised a contractor to go in and clear all the rubbish away and then they engaged an industrial cleaning company to go in and really blitz right through the building. They were all surprised to find the fresh water and the sewerage system in working order. The boys visited the cinema after the contractors had finished; they were amazed how vast and attractive the interior of the old cinema had become, the only disadvantage was the sloping floor but not enough to bother them.

Having got this far, it was agreed to invite the family to a meeting to be held in the old cinema the following Sunday afternoon. As they arrived, each was given a clipboard, pencil and paper to write down any suggestions they might have. The boys were hoping to form a concrete plan in order to submit to the City Planning Dept. Richard was the first to come up with an idea, the front of the unit will have to be reconstructed and replaced with two large display windows left and right, taking the windows and the central arcade right into the shop and that is where the customer will be looking in the window, "In the shop." A steel roller shutter will need to be installed at pavement level to keep the store secure.

*

All the family kept wandering around and writing away, the M.B.M. group were taken with the boxes either side of the screen, which still showed a little gold leaf on the plasterwork but any replacement will have to be gold coloured paint.

Margery said, "May I point out to you peasants, it is not called plaster, its real name is Baroque," this caused a lot of leg pulling. On the left-hand side of the screen was the remnant of an organ, which appeared to be damaged beyond repair but Dan, insisted that it was for him to sort out. The pipes were still intact and he intended to have them cleaned and painted as an additional focal point.

The ornamental plasterwork was also at the front of the Balcony, in fact, it could become a very interesting unit. The structural engineers went through the whole building and found it structurally sound, which was a relief as the stairs leading to the Balcony had been repaired. When the family was looking at the Balcony wondering how to make use of it, Margery said, "Make it a café come restaurant," What a good idea but it will have to go to the bottom of the spending list, until some money is available. It would prove to be a very expensive job to level the floor. Jenny was the next with an idea, "Why not incorporate a Hairdressing Salon, three chairs would fit down at the front on the right hand side of the screen, they would have to pass the furniture, which might wet their appetite."

"Thanks Jenny, another idea to play with."

Arne said, "Can I come in now with my suggestion, just so as you can mull it over. Leave the two front rows of seats, reduce the size of the screen, make a video picture describing how a tree is selected to be felled, sawn into planks and then show how the timber is stacked for a year or so to dry out and mature. The matured planks arrive at the factory; show Fred with drawings and design sheets on a desk, Simon in the finance office. Then, this is the important part, show the care and attention the furniture receives going through the process of the machine shop, assembling in the cabinet area, finishing, polishing and scrutinising before being sent out to the customer. I would suggest that it is produced professionally with a very good voice over." They all agreed that it was a very good and novel idea but it might have to wait depending on the cost.

Arne said that he had a contact working in that field, he would ask for an estimated cost with the future in mind.

When the council offices were contacted, they only required plans of the structural window frontage and facia signs submitted, indicating the change from a cinema to a retail store. They were soon supplied and they were up and running.

*

Several days later Dan visited the cinema and he found it to be a hive of industry, the decorating was almost complete, Fred had been fortunate in getting Nigel Rogers to assemble a team and the painting was promised to be completed in one week, Nigel had worked in the factory during the war and he and Fred had become very good friends. The reason for Dan's visit was because he arranged for an audio engineer and a surveyor to meet him in the store; the surveyor was to supply a correct floor area for Simon to work out the cost of square footage of the sales area in the unit. They had been approached by an Upholstery Company to rent a space, their own property had been condemned due to bomb damage to the foundations during one of the wartime air raids and the building movement had only been noticed recently.

The audio engineer arrived and Dan explained that he wanted to play taped organ music with speakers behind the pipes, which had now been painted and they looked very attractive. The organ had been repainted in its original colours and it looks as if it could be played but it is so badly damaged that it was beyond repair, the painter had blended red and gold beautifully. The engineer had the audio system installed in about one hour; he left Dan several tapes of organ music recorded by the top people in the business. The tapes were inserted at the front of the machine but the volume control at the back of the organ, he gave Dan the invoice and left. The surveyor finished off and told Dan that all the details would be forwarded to his office, the workmen left with the surveyor leaving Dan to lock up.

He locked the doors and switched on the organ music and relaxed in a chair, this was his toy; he decided to increase the volume to make the sound fill the cinema. He went round to the back of the organ, as he put his weight on his good leg, he felt a movement, he investigated and he rolled the corner of the carpet back, and found that there were three loose floor boards. The boards were not nailed down, when he lifted them; he saw a solid stepladder leading down into the basement. He did not feel confident enough to venture down the steps with his deformed leg and it was very dark.

Dan was so intrigued, he immediately telephoned Fred and Frank asking them to join him and bring a good flashlight. They too were intrigued, they were with Dan in about half an hour, Dan opened the door, they both asked if he was okay? They thought he was ill.

"I am quite well, follow me." He took them to the back of the organ, lifted the carpet, and removed the floorboards exposing the steps in the basement.

"Good lord," Fred switched on his flashlight and went down the steps, when he reached the bottom step he looked around and spotted an electric light switch. He pressed the toggle switch, which illuminated a long narrow passage. "Heavens above, you should both come down here." Frank helped Dan down the steps and they were aghast when saw the long passage.

They walked down the passage and the first door was unlocked, when they entered the room, they could not believe their eyes, on the left hand side was a long rail with civilian clothing, all on hangers, on the right hand side was a similar rail containing German Army uniforms, Hats and Leather Top Coats, again beautifully arranged on shaped hangers all thick with dust. They all stood with their mouths open.

Fred said, "This must be what Mr Churchill meant when he referred to the dangers of the Fifth Column."

Dan said, "That is the name of our store, The Fifth Column."

"Not yet but I agree with the name." They found another door unlocked, this room was filled with rifles, machine guns with boxes of ammunition. Underneath a metal canopy were boxes of hand grenades,

"What do we do now"?

"Firstly, let us continue looking around," said Dan. At the bottom of the passage, a large room had been set up as a canteen with a long table and twenty chairs positioned around it, on the surrounding shelves were canisters containing water, tea, coffee, powdered milk, tins of soup, meat and packets of dehydrated vegetables. Nearby, there was another table with a large map of Liverpool with all the strategic points in the city ringed in coloured pencil, such as the Police Station, Electrical Sub Station, Local Radio and the Railway Station, in fact, all the relevant positions to control a city. Pinned to the wall was a large Nazi Flag, no doubt it was in preparation to be placed outside.

"This is no Nazi sympathisers meeting place, it is a well organised operation." Frank said, " We must contact the authorities,"

Dan did not agree, "We open in two days time, let us keep quiet just for a few days, yes, I am mercenary but think of the publicity we will receive, do you both agree? We have not touched anything and everything is coated in a thick dust." They all agreed because the authorities will close the store until the guns etc have been removed. Right, next Thursday morning we will discover the loose floorboards and then go to the Police Station.

CHAPTER 6

Dan and Margery were up bright and early: today was the opening day for the start of the new venture. They were leaving their house when suddenly Mary and Fred joined them and there was a lot of leg pulling on the way to the cinema, which house will have to be sold if this venture should flop.

On arrival, they were surprised to see people milling around, long before the advertised opening time of 9.30. They walked into the store and the first thing to catch their eye was the screen in front of them on the stage, the screen was illuminated with D.F.F. Furniture being the top line in large letters, below to the left was an oak tree with large oak leaves, on the right was a silhouette of an elderly gentleman, it could be Mr Pickwick, wearing a woodworking apron and round steel rimmed glasses, chisel in his left hand and a mallet in his right. They all agreed it must be the work of Arne and Richard. On the left hand side of the stage on the floor was the organ, it looked magnificent now the painting had been carried out and they looked at Dan, they knew that this was his pet. The organ music was playing through the speakers behind the pipes, not too loud, just gentle to the ears. Then the dark polished colonial furniture, which looked really elegant.

Nearer the door the Upholstery Company had several three-piece suites on display, they had been persuaded by M.B.M. to display light coloured carriage cloths and a coloured imitation leather suite. The other side of the showroom, near the stage was Jenny's small Salon consisting of three chairs with partitions to provide a little privacy. Jenny did not have any clients booked in but she had persuaded several of her customers to come along for a free wash and set to look busy when they opened. Behind Jenny came the lighting department, there were Standard Lamps, Centre Lights, Wall Lights and a selection of Lamp Shades. The lighting industry was just getting to grips with the modern customers demand. In the right hand window leading down into the store itself, was D.F.F. own designed dining room chairs and table together with a Welsh Dresser made from Beech Wood, the colour and grain makes it look so attractive under the carefully placed lights.

Dan swelled with pride as he walked around the store, he felt so proud to be associated with this group of talented people. He had engaged a Jazz Band to play just outside the shop for one hour during the morning and one hour in the afternoon. Two reporters from the local papers were snooping around hoping for a story. Fred and Mary were very impressed how the lighting and the decorations had been carried out,

Mary turned to Fred, "We have created an Aladdin's Cave," Fred just laughed but he thought, Mary was right, it looked wonderful.

The Balcony had been advertised hoping to attract a catering company to invest but no enquiries had been received. The trading on the day had been phenomenal but there was a big demand for credit facilities, when this was told to Dan, he realised that it must be addressed urgently. He made a note in his little book to invite Mr Blake out to lunch, to glean his knowledge in the world of credit trading.

Dan had arranged transport for Sally and Mark, to attend and enjoy the opening of the old cinema, Mark just looked around in wonderment and he turned to Dan, "This is a long way from our pulley problem in our first unit." This caused laughter but it made each one realise how lucky they all were.

*

Thursday morning the three friends met at the cinema, they went to a nearby café bar to enjoy a cup of coffee and decide on their next move. It was decided to open up the floorboards to ensure nothing had been interfered with and it was Fred who was elected to go to the police and Dan and Frank stayed behind to make sure no one went near the basement. Fred entered the local Police Station and spoke to the officer on the front desk,

"Is it possible for me to speak to a Senior CID officer?"

"Kindly take a seat sir and I will enquire if one is available." Fred had just got himself seated when a tall pleasant looking gentleman came out of the office,

"Just come with me sir" and they went into the interview room.

"Yes sir, how can I help you?" Fred explained how they had discovered the steps leading into the basement and what it contains. The officer opened a notepad, "Kindly give me your name, address," he then wrote down exactly what Fred was telling him, after explaining about the ammunition. "Would you mind waiting here and I will get my boss, then, we can decide on the next move." A tall heavily built man walked in, shook hands with Fred, "From what my officer has told me, we had better take a look in the basement for ourselves."

"We must ensure nothing is touched or removed before this is reported." Four plain clothed policemen went along with Fred, on arrival, Frank and Dan were introduced, each of the policemen had brought a flashlight with them, Fred said, "May I go down first, I know where the electric switch is?" The policemen got to the bottom of the steps and looked along the illuminated passage they just gasped. The senior officer called, "Turn the lights off, replace the boards and the carpet and I will contact The Home Office, this is very serious." Dan made the point that he was hoping that the unit would not be closed but he was told it would be up to the powers that be.

The customers in the shop were trying their utmost to see what was going on. One hour later six men arrived in white overalls carrying cameras; they proved their identity to Fred, he had been delegated to deal with this as he had served in the army, he knew how to deal with these situations. Nothing must be touched until the whole place has been photographed, in fact, not then; it appeared that they still had to wait until the top brass arrive. When they did arrive and saw the volatile hand grenades etc, they declared that the store had to close all day Friday to remove the armaments from the basement but it is hoped to allow normal trading on Saturday. Fred, Frank and Dan were introduced to the big wig; my name is "Major Goodchild," his face had been badly disfigured during the war.

After a while he approached Fred, "Haven't we met before"? "Not that I can recall." "I could have been Lieutenant Goodchild when we met," he looked down and saw Fred's left hand, "Yes, I remember now, Dunkirk Beach, you helped to move some injured soldiers before you and your fellows were lucky enough to get on a boat and get home. I caught a bomb blast in my face, not a pretty sight; still, I got away with my life." The Major took Fred out for a cup of coffee, as he wanted to speak with him.

The Major then proceeded to tell Fred about a similar situation in Birmingham but on a much smaller scale than here, had been found.

"If you come across anything you consider suspicious, ring me direct, here is my card, don't bother going to the police. The real reason I wanted to speak to you in confidence, when one of the boxes of hand grenades was moved, we found a pair of binoculars in a leather case, inside the lid of the case was a small photograph of a German Officer receiving the Iron Cross from Hitler. This particular officer was never traced; the last time he was seen in the field was as we left Dunkirk. He was given the job of removing the dead and wounded allied soldiers from the beach. It was reported that many of the wounded personnel were never seen or heard of again, that is the reason he should have stood alongside his colleagues at the Nuremberg trials, could he be in this country, Fred"?

When they arrived back at the store there were several reporters from the local papers trying to find out what was going on. It was arranged that the bomb squad could have access to the basement at 6.30 Friday morning to enable them to shift most of the armaments before the streets got busy but it was not to be, the photographers were snapping away with their cameras as the rifles were being loaded in the army vans. The photographs were plastered across the front pages in the evening papers. Some papers reported that twenty rifles had been shifted; another paper said one hundred had been taken out. All the volatile ammunition had been moved by Friday lunchtime, so the store was allowed to open Friday afternoon.

The store became crowded with people, one couldn't say if they intended buying or being nosey after reading the newspaper reports. Dan had been right; Saturday was a fantastic trading day. The people from the Home Office are going to return on Monday morning to investigate how the basement could have been set up during the war. They had discovered, that the date it was reported the building had received damage during an air raid, which, needed three weeks spending on repairs was incorrect, the date referred to, the city had a visit of one aircraft dropping a few incendiary bombs. It must have been constructed when all the so-called building repair work was carried out but the puzzling part is that all the guns and the ammunition had been made in Germany, how had they got into the basement?

The three Directors were interviewed separately, why did they lease this property, did they know of the existence of the clothing, food and explosives within the building? No, it was only found on the day it was reported. To whom do you the rent or lease or whatever you prefer to call it? The directors had not been aware that the money they paid to the estate agent was channelled through to a Swiss Bank. The investigation was very thorough, so much so, they found that the back door had been bricked up, when they broke through into the next shop, it had been a German Pork Butchers shop but the tenants have long gone, the original owner was Mr Finkle and two sons but no longer traceable. The people interviewing came across as if Dan and friends knew about the contents of the basement and had rented the cinema to remove the evidence.

*

When the intelligence men removed the metal canopy protecting the hand grenades they found another door that had been closed up, it led to a small alley down the side of the cinema, Fred told them that the kids would have used it to get into the cinema for free until the manager had an iron bar fitted across the door on the inside. It was proven, that it was the door used when fitting out the basement.

CHAPTER 7

Jenny spoke to Dan at the cinema asking him if he would arrange a family meeting as she and her sisters wished to put their plans into operation. The meeting was duly arranged to be held at the house of Bella and Frank, Bella had made coffee for those who would prefer coffee to drinking Sherry, very little coffee was taken.

Jenny stood up. "The reason we wanted to have this meeting, is that we did not agree with what was said at the last family meeting, about us all coming under the umbrella of D.F.F. However, I must point out that apart from Uncle Dan kindly allowing three months rent-free for our first shop, we have received no financial support from D.F.F, at any time. Through our own hard work and prudence we have opened three shops, four if we include the cinema, they are all quite successful, also, we have opened a small training centre to teach Hairdressing and this too is proving to be very successful, the demand is so great we are considering expansion. The hairdressing sundry supplies were very haphazard, so we have opened our own supply unit. This again has turned out to be fruitful, so much so, we intend to widen our area and we are going ahead with our plans to employ a driver for our own delivery van.

I have outlined what we have achieved through our own efforts; we wish to remain a completely independent company and we are prepared to pay rent for the space we have at the cinema" Jenny sat down. The room erupted with laughter and they all started clapping, well done Jenny, her three sisters were beaming. The three friends looked at each other and smiled, Dan started laughing, "You are certainly a go ahead girl, the way you have presented your case in such a forthright manner, I think you are right." Frank or Fred could not vote against Jenny's request. Frank said, "Jenny, you must contact Mr Blake, he is retired but he will deal with your request, he will put in place all the safeguards for all three of you."

Dan telephoned Mr Blake; who said he was more than happy to guide Jenny through the minefield of forming the girl's own company. You will need a company secretary to deal with company house; Frank suggested, they should pay a visit to Mark with a view to persuade him to act for them. He will probably relish the task of dealing with another company. He is once again housebound, this could be a lifeline for him," Jenny took all this information on board and noted Mr Blake's telephone number. Dan, Fred and Frank went off to a small café for lunch and to discuss the meeting. "Jenny is quite right about not taking money from D.F.F. so good luck to them," said Dan, Frank joined in, "if ever they need help anytime, we are here for them."

*

Fred was wandering around the store waiting for Dan to arrive; the meeting this morning was to discuss the applications received from three catering companies who were interested in renting the balcony. A group of five gentlemen walked into the store, just looking around, they did not appear to be focussed on one particular sales section. When Fred heard them speaking he knew straight away they were German and from the body language the taller one of the group was in charge. One of the salesmen from the Upholstery Group told Fred that the men had been in the store almost every day since it opened, they just wander around.

Fred was very intrigued, this could be something or nothing but it made him curious. Dan arrived and they went off to the local coffee bar. Having got their coffee, Fred turned to Dan. "We have known each other for many years and I feel positive we can trust each other with confidences.""I do hope so Fred, which road are you taking me down?" "Dan, I am going to break a confidence and share it with you, which, must stay with you." Fred then told him about the S.S, Nazi Officer Kayberg who was delegated with the job of removing the dead and wounded allied soldiers from the Dunkirk Beaches, the wounded were never seen or heard of again. A lot of effort was spent trying to trace him but unsuccessfully, he is a war criminal. However, when one of the boxes of hand grenades was removed they found a pair of binoculars in a leather case, inside the lid was a small photograph of this officer receiving the Iron Cross from Hitler himself. There are five Germans wandering around the store, I have been told that they have been in the store every day since we opened, I am very curious.

When they returned to the store the five gentlemen were still wandering around, Fred went up to them and asked if they were interested in any particular item, the man in charge said, "Why do you ask?" "I wondered if you are with a catering company deciding whether or not to invest in the balcony as a café"? "Certainly not, it is the beautiful architecture that attracts me. Good day," He stood upright, bowed and clicked his heels together and left. Dan had witnessed this encounter and he was amused.

The local newspaper photographer named Jack Green was standing on the pavement outside of the store, Fred went out to speak to him, "Jack can we talk?" "Of, course Fred." "If I said that I will take you into the basement to take photographs of the canteen and one of the other rooms, will you snap those five fellows and if possible a full face of the taller one but this must be strictly between us, agreed?" "Agreed Fred, I know that I can trust you to keep your word." That evening Jack was in his dark room developing the snaps he had taken for Fred, a knock came on the door, he turned off the outside lights just leaving a dimmed red light on. His daughter, Helen, came in to develop snaps she had taken of her children. As Jack was taking his photographs out of the tray of fixing liquid, his daughter said, "That man came into the planning office this afternoon, not asking but demanding a copy of the plans of the old cinema now called The Fifth Column," "Are you sure Helen?" "Yes I am positive but he was told he would have to wait two days." Jack telephoned Fred straight away and told him what his daughter had told him.

*

Fred arranged to meet Jack and collect the photographs the following day, "Jack, Do impress on your daughter to keep quiet about these photographs. The powers that be will put you in the picture later but in the meantime please keep quiet about the whole situation." Fred then telephoned Major Goodchild on his direct number as shown on the card he had given Fred. He became very excited, "Tomorrow morning I shall be wandering around the store as if I am a customer at approximately ten o'clock. I will be dressed in civilian clothing and my name is Lance, not Major, Okay Fred?" Fred then asked him if his security guys could enhance the small snap that was found inside the binocular case, in other words add a few years to Kayberg's appearance.

The following morning accompanied by Dan, Fred strolled into the store, looking round, he saw that Lance had already arrived, "Good morning Lance, will you join me for a cup coffee?" When they were seated, Fred explained to Lance that there were five Germans wandering around the store, in fact, they have been in the store each day since it was first opened, what they are looking for, is any one's guess. I told you on the telephone that the taller one of the group called at the city planning office demanding a copy of the plans and general layout of the cinema, he was told to call back in two days. They went back to the store and true enough the five were wandering around, Lance could not be absolutely sure but he could see a likeness of Officer Karl Kayberg in the taller man. Fred then accompanied Lance to the City Planning office; they approached the enquiry desk and asked to speak with the manager or whoever is in charge of this department.

They were taken into a large office; Lance produced his warrant card to confirm his identity and asked if his name was Mr Gerald Snaith, the manager confirmed it was his name. "The conversation we are going to have is very sensitive and confidential, the security guys have already checked you out and you are considered trustworthy?" This brought smiles to their faces. "A gentleman called here yesterday requesting plans of the old cinema now trading as The Fifth Column, now, what I would like you to do is to fax your copy of the basement to the number on this card and they will make certain changes and fax it back to you and this is the copy he will be given when he calls. I want a true copy without any adjustments. Right, Gerald will you do that for me?" "Certainly, in fact, I can do it straight away as I have the copy of the cinema plans to hand." Two days later Officer Kayberg called to collect his copy of the plans, he was indignant when a payment was requested to cover the cost of photocopying, materials and time taken by a member of the staff. When Lance and Fred called at the office Gerald had their copies ready for them and he had arranged refreshments. Armed with their plans they went straight back to the store, Fred suggested that they should wait in the balcony; from there they had a clear uninterrupted view of the ground floor.

The five gentlemen entered the store and wandered to different areas of the store while consulting a page of paper, Lance looked at Fred, "I wonder what they are looking for, or what are they up to." Dan arrived; he was put in the picture of what was happening. "Bring your plans to my house tonight Lance, we can study them over dinner. We can go through them step by step, there must be something we are missing." Frank and Bella were invited but unfortunately Bella did not feel well enough to come out and socialise. "Thank you Dan, about seven," "No, make it six then we can have a drink before dinner." Fred phoned Frank telling him that he would be put completely in the picture.

When Lance arrived, they went into the larger room so they could lay the plans on the floor, all three stood looking at them. "Dan, have you seen these plans before?" "No," "In that case you can take us through them, you might spot something we have missed." He started by the door, which went into the German Butchers shop, travelling into the canteen and the two rooms. The overall outside measurements corresponds correctly with the interior sizes, leaving no spare space.

After dinner, again they all stood looking and puzzling, where and how, Margery got off her knees where she had been studying the plan. "How about the space in the loft, have you investigated there yet?" "No." "According to the plan a man could stand upright in the centre." Lance looked at Margery, "What a clever girl." Lance went on to describe his plans, the clever boys at the Home Office are going to place small cameras throughout the building which will record any activity on tape for us to view later. The main door will have the normal alarm system connected to the police station; we will have to investigate access to the loft space.

CHAPTER 8

Dan telephoned Mr Blake asking if he if would join him for lunch, so a date was set. "Dan, Will you please call me Ben, in the first place, we have known each other long enough to be on first name terms but the real reason is, you make me feel old calling me mister all the time." "Right Ben, our driver Ted, will pick you up eleven o'clock on Tuesday morning, does that suit you?" "Yes, Tuesday morning will be fine." Dan worked in his office dealing with an odd letter or two to clear his desk before Ben arrived. The office girl rang to say that Ben had arrived, Dan asked her to bring him into his office, he entered and they shook hands saying how pleased that he was able to join him. Ben just looked around, "What a wonderful office," "Yes Ben, all three offices are identical, so Fred and Frank feel at home whichever room they are in." The room is very spacious, the walls panelled in light Oak wood, a matching desk with two large swivel chairs. In the far end of the room are two armchairs with a small table between them. In the centre of the room is a dining room table with four chairs and a Welsh Dresser with drinks on the pot board. Dan invited Ben to sit in one of the armchairs and then poured out two Sherries, He knew sherry was Ben's favourite tipple; Dan had telephoned and asked Ben's wife his likes and dislikes. Ben's favourite food is Lamb and mint sauce. When they were seated and comfortable, Ben said, "What a life you lead now Dan". They sat talking for a long time about nothing in particular, just sat at peace with the world, trying out different brands of sherry, "Are you ready to eat now Ben?" "Yes, where are we going?" "I thought it would be okay to sit here and have lunch served, are you comfortable with that Ben?" "I am, as long as you are not the cook."

The office girl knocked on the door; "Julie wants to know if she is to serve lunch now?" "Certainly, she can set the table." Table set and they sat at the table, soup was served as a starter and then Julie brought in the Lamb roast, it looked fantastic and it must have tasted good because nothing was left. Julie then brought in another of Ben's favourite, Spotted Dick with Custard. "What a wonderful meal Dan," they finished off with coffee and Brandy.

"Do you mind if I call my young man in who deals with the finances of D.F.F?" "Not, at all." Dan buzzed his girl on the desk outside, "Ask Simon to come to my office." Simon arrived, he looked a little perturbed. "Don't worry Simon, Ben has been advising on credit trading. Would you like a sherry?" "Yes please," Dan placed a glass in front of him. "Right Ben, the floor is yours." "What I would suggest, is this, The Fifth Column should set up a complete separate account with the bank, arranging an overdraft figure at an agreed interest rate. The other thing I would suggest is that the store should become a separate company to safeguard you should anything go wrong. If the D.F.F. can afford to defer payment for the furniture they supply for the next three months, you will find that with the weekly payments the store should remain solvent and would not need the help of the bank's overdraft facility, this would save interest charges. Simon, I have printed it all up for you to digest, just think about it very carefully, Dan has told me that 60% of your customers ask for credit. You will need extra staff to cope with this operation; I would suggest that the store finances are kept independent from the factory accounts."

"If they do decide to form another company, they will need a company secretary, if you take on that job, just call me and I will guide you through what is required by company house. There it is in a nutshell Simon." "May I study these papers and come back to you?" Simon sat studying the papers. "Of course, just give a ring if you have any queries."

*

Lance again explained to Fred that cameras were being placed inside the store and normal cameras positioned around the outside of the building, you might think that the Home Office is over reacting but they are determined to get to the bottom of how and when this was all set up, this could not have been organised without local help. Two days later Fred received a phone call telling him that the outside camera had photographed a group of men walking round the property pushing what looks like long steel probes into the wall. "My bosses and I are at a loss to know what is going on, or what they are looking for. Was something of value left behind, or is there some damning evidence for a local person who could be charged with treason."

It was arranged that a team of scientist would visit the store on Sunday morning to check out the store with the latest x-ray and metal detectors to find if there could be another room between the outer and inner walls. The equipment was set up and they spent the next two hours checking every part of the walls on the ground floor but without success. The stairs leading up to the balcony became suspect when they saw the amount of repair work that had been carried out, claiming it to be bomb damage.

Another hour was spent checking the stairs and the balcony itself but not a thing could they find to give them any encouragement, so it was decided to break off for lunch. Lunch over, they decided to take all the scientific instruments above the balcony into the projection room, again it took quite some time to set up.

All the walls were checked without success and then, as one of the scientists was carrying an instrument past a large deep cupboard used for storing the reels of film, they heard a very faint blip, turning and putting the probe against the cupboard they got a definite reading. They opened the cupboard doors and it was just an empty cupboard but surprisingly deep, the right hand side was wider than the left, on a closer inspection the shelves were just resting on rails, not screwed or nailed. Major Goodchild must be contacted, he is staying at a local hotel, he will want to know that our boss is confident they have found what he was hoping to find, a room or space. At this stage, Fred telephoned Frank and Dan as he thought that they should be in on the operation in view of the money invested in the building.

Lance arrived, accompanied by two other gentlemen dressed in overalls, they immediately removed the shelves and the back panel, as they did this, it became obvious why the cupboard was so deep, between the outer wall and the back of the cupboard, stairs had been erected on the right side leading up into the roof space. When one of them went up the stairs and shone his powerful flashlight he could see a pile of boxes partially covered by a tarpaulin. He came down the stairs and suggested to Lance that he should take a look, when he did, he said, "No one, I repeat No one, will go into the roof space until I have contacted the bomb squad, I have seen piles set up like this before with a booby trap bomb."

He telephoned his boss and within the hour an officer and three specialists arrived with their technical equipment and protective clothing. They went up into the roof space to start their dangerous mission, every one else was ushered to the ground floor as a precaution, Frank said, "We might be safe but how about the poor souls in the loft." Forty five minutes later the officer came down to speak to Lance, "You were right, a booby trap had been set up but it is quite safe now, if I may suggest sir, I would call the special security team in before you allow any person back in the loft," "Why do you say that?" "There is British and German currency and more important, Gold Bars." The security officers arrived and brought down boxes of British £1and £5 notes, they could be counterfeit and a load of German Marks all in small denominations.

Everyone stood open mouthed when they saw the amount of Gold Bars they brought out of the loft, each with the German Eagle on the one side and the Swastika on the other, there were thirty in total. Lance turned to Fred, "We now know what they were looking for, come with me," they went into the loft and they found a large folder with correspondence, one of the letters referred to a prominent business man who was also a councillor. Fred recognised the address so Lance decided to call on that address the following day. "Will you come with me Fred?" "Yes of course, before we go, I promised Jack Green that I would give him the opportunity of photographing the canteen in the basement as he helped us out with the earlier photographs," "Why not take him upstairs to snap all the rubble that is left and tell him what was under the tarpaulin but I do not want to be part of this, it is a scoop, a very big scoop for him."

Fred phoned Jack inviting him but telling him to be careful coming into the store, do not let too many people see you come in. Jack arrived with camera and his notebook at the ready, Fred gave him all the details of what had been found in the loft and the basement, Jack could not believe his good luck. Having filled his notebook and taken many snaps he said "I am going straight back to the Editor, I am most grateful Fred, this is a wonderful break for me, Cheers," and off he went.

*

The following morning, Fred called at Lance's hotel, to collect him and pay a visit to the gentleman at the address found in one of the letters in the folder. Lance got in the car and sat beside Fred, "Just look! at this, is he your man"? The headline of the local paper showing Jack Green who had been attacked on the way to the local newspaper office, his face had nasty gashes and black eyes; he certainly looked in a bad way. Fred was devastated, he immediately did a detour to the newspaper offices, at the main desk Fred asked to speak to the Editor and they were invited into his office. Fred related how he was the person who helped Jack to obtain the photographs and all the information for him to get a scoop that is what he called it, "When they attacked him, did they get his camera and notebook?" "No, he must have thrown his bag over the hedgerow, the police found it this morning and brought it into the office. I plan to use the whole of the front page; it will be devoted to Jack's scoop that should make him feel better."

Fred looked at the Editor; "I feel awful about Jack's attack I feel responsible." Fred decided to visit Jack in hospital, he was confident that the authorities would allow them into the ward and they did. As they entered the ward Fred thought that Jacks face looked a lot better than in the newspaper. "A policeman found your bag containing the photographs and your notebook this morning; your Editor is going to use your information and snaps on the whole of the front page in tonight's edition."

"Did you recognise the person or persons who attacked you?" "No, they were more interested in getting my bag; they had just started punching me when four young lads came to my assistance and the attackers ran off. Just think of the publicity I will get from my attack and the story Fred." "Cheers for now Jack, in future I bet you will keep me at arms length." Lance looked at Fred, "We have opened a large can of worms."

CHAPTER 9

They set off to find the address they had found in the attic, they rang the doorbell and a tall, attractive elderly lady opened the door. "Can I help you gentlemen"? "I do hope so, my name is Major Goodchild and this is my assistant Sergeant Wharton. We would like to speak with your husband," "May I see your identity please," having satisfied herself they were who they said they were, she said, "You had better come in. My husband died very mysteriously a few years ago, you must know he was a prominent business man and a councillor, he attended a council meeting the night he died, after the meetings, he always walked home because the council chamber was filled with smoke, either cigarette, cigar or pipe smoke. He did not smoke; he would walk home to clear his lungs and attempt to get the tobacco smell from his clothes. He helped to improve a hydraulic system to raise the undercarriage of an aircraft after it had taken off and to lower for landing."

*

"In 1938 he visited Stuttgart in Germany, a company wanted to produce his invention under licence, he had protected his invention by taking out a patent. A family named Kayberg ran the hotel he stayed at for his visit, their son Hans was a troop leader in the Hitler youth movement. Harry said, he was a vicious young man and he worried for his future. My husband was either drugged or drunk and during his conversation with an engineer who was also staying at the hotel he divulged the details of his invention and the improvements he was working on, obviously the engineer had been planted. When he came round or sobered up, he was told that unless he did as he was told, his government would be told of his treasonable action. When he returned from that trip he was a changed man. They had convinced him that for such treason he could be hanged."

"Prior to his death, he went to the secret service people and explained the situation and told them the full story, which they accepted. They listened and asked him many questions and they prepared to catch the next person to contact him, in fact, several of the secret service personnel stayed in this house hoping that Harry would get a visitor. There is not much more I can tell you, one thing I do know, through Harry a trap was set but he was killed before the trap could be sprung. There was a big internal investigation as some one had leaked the information, which resulted in the death of my husband and one of the secret service operators whose body was found washed up on the beach at Formby Point. In both cases they were murdered by a person or persons, unknown, that was the coroner's verdict. Now I have told you all I know, would you like a cup of tea?"

They sat drinking their tea, "Going back to the patented hydraulic undercarriage, who has received the royalties for making them under licence?" "I have no idea, after Harry's death his partner took over the engineering plant and I suppose they produced the parts as required." "If Harry patented his invention in his name you should have received some money. You think how many aircraft have been fitted with this invention during the war, naturally you can forget about getting any money from Germany but there should be some from this country." "Is the plant still open and working?" "Yes," "In that case we will pay it a visit just to make enquiries. Before a visit to the engineering plant is made, I will contact the patent office to make sure we are on solid ground."

*

Major Goodchild reported back to his superiors, they in turn suggested a meeting with a senior member of the secret service present. The patent office confirmed in writing to his office, the Hydraulic Patent was in the name of Harry Blythe and they pointed out that the patent was still in operation so royalties should have been paid and written permission must have been obtained from the owner and this office to produce under licence. Lance contacted Fred and gave him some of the information; he thought it unwise to tell him too much, it might put him in danger.

A secret service agent visited the engineering plant, he enquired relating to the patent but all the owner did was to shrug his shoulders and said, "Harry invented it but I am now the owner of the plant and I can use this information." "How is it, that Mrs Blythe has not received any royalties as the patent is registered in Harry's name not the plant?" The man again shrugged his shoulders, "She is not entitled to any money." "I can tell you, Mrs Blythe has instructed a solicitor to look into Harry's legacy." The agent then left the plant, jumped into his car and drove away but he left a colleague watching the plant.

The partner named Bill Russell, came dashing out of the offices jumped into his car and drove off at a very high speed, he was not aware that he was being followed, eventually he pulled up outside a large house on the outskirts of Liverpool. He walked down a long pathway to a large beautifully polished wooden door and rang the door bell, a man came to the door and it was so obvious that he was annoyed to see his visitor, he started waving his arms around as if he was shooing an animal off his lawn. Bill was not invited into the house; in fact, the door was slammed in his face. Bill paced up and down the drive, unsure what to do he looked completely lost. The operator took several photographs and noted the address. He forwarded a copy of the snaps to his and Lance's office plus the address.

An investigation was carried out and it was found that the German Embassy owns the house in question; the occupants are employed in the embassy. In view of this information it was decided to put the house and Bill Russell under surveillance. Lance rang Fred and told him about the owners of the house and its occupants, one of which, he was sure was in fact Officer Kayberg. I cannot leave this alone now and one of our secret agents on the case is the nephew of the man whose body was found on Formby Beach, he is very keen to catch those responsible.

Fred and Mary visited Dan and Margery that evening. Fred said, "What I am going to tell you is very confidential;" he then related the whole story to them right up to date. Lance is positive that one of the occupants of the house is SS Officer Kayberg; he is wanted to face charges of war crimes carried out on the beaches of Dunkirk. He has passed the snaps and information to Interpol and the War Crimes Commission; he is sure they will deal with it."

CHAPTER 10

Salina and Lillian decided to have a double wedding, they planned the date and time at the registry office and the Wedding Breakfast is to be held at the Adelphi Hotel. Mary and Margery spent quite a long time going round the shops looking for suitable wedding outfits, Fred and Dan kept out of the shopping expeditions. The two brides were having excursions to town looking, trying on and then leaving the decision till a later day. Salina was having difficulty finding a suitable dress as her pregnancy was beginning to show. Fred and Dan went to the tailors in London Road and bought their new wedding suits, this took less than an hour and they were quite pleased with themselves.

The day of the wedding, it was arranged that they should all meet up at the registry office, all with their best bib and tuckers on and with the flowers in the button holes and of course the brides beautiful bouquet. The bride's mothers both had a large corsage selected and approved of by their daughters to be worn on the lapels of their smart tailored costume jackets. The bride's fathers were there to carry out their duties and there were plenty of people present to act as witnesses. Leaving the registry office they had to undergo the orders from the photographer, stand here, stand there, look this or that way, "Good job we only have one child Dan." When the photographer had completed his routine they all started to walk to the taxis.

On arrival at the Adelphi they were handed a glass of sherry and of course there was a lot of chatting. Mark, who is now looking his age, was present; the necessary arrangements had been made for him to receive help with his wheelchair. His sister, the bride's grandmother would have been proud today. Lillian never knew her grandmother; she was killed during an air raid before Lillian was born. Sally, Marks wife, was still the chatty jovial person, getting a little more rotund as the years go by.

When they were all seated at the large oval shaped table, Dan was concerned because the two chairs allocated for Bella and Frank were empty. After the meal they had the usual round of speeches, Richard and Arne's father's speeches were very humorous and they went down very well. Each couple cut their cake while having their photographs taken; the cakes were then taken away by a member of the hotel staff to be cut up and handed round.

A member of the hotel staff came into the room, asking for Jenny, as she is required at the reception desk. On her return it was obvious that she was distressed, she went to Dan and told him that her father, Frank, had suffered a heart attack while in the taxi on the way to the hotel, the taxi had taken him straight to the Royal Hospital. Bella is with him, his condition is stable and he is comfortable. When Fred was told he was quite upset but not altogether surprised, Frank failed his medical for the forces during the war due to a heart condition. Frank is only five feet in height and he has put on two stone in weight over the past few months, Fred had warned him but Frank loved his food and disregarded any advice.

*

A taxi was called and Jenny and her sisters went off to the hospital promising to telephone later. Unfortunately, this news put a damper on the celebrations, Lillian and Richard went off on their planned honeymoon and Salina and Arne went back to her parent's house, Mary had suggested that they stay with them until their baby is born. Salina readily agreed she would like her mother near to advise and help. They have their own house all ready to move into when she feels confident enough to manage by herself. Fred was surprised by their choice of kitchen furniture, not D.F.F. but chromium chair legs and a table with a glass top. Salina said her father was old fashioned if he didn't like the ultra modern furniture.

Later that evening, Jenny telephoned Dan, telling him, that Frank had been lucky as it was just a minor attack. He will be allowed home tomorrow but he must lose at least two stone in weight otherwise the specialist will not treat him. Dan and Margery visited Fred and Mary to pass on the news and Dan proposed that they drank Fred's booze; the motion was carried by three to one.

CHAPTER 11

Dan, Fred, Sam, Roy and Simon met up in Dan's office. They all started laughing when Fred said, "Now what is it professor?" "Suggestion, modify the steel plate which is covering the steps to the basement behind the organ. The Pork Butchers Shop is available to rent, we rent it and open up the basement to the public on a Sunday. Make the entrance on the left-hand side of the shop but the exit on the right and on leaving they would have to pass through a craft shop. Fred you will have to speak to Lance asking if he can obtain permission, also, if he can find any old rifles and hand grenade or ammunition boxes and can we leave the clothing and the canteen exactly as we found it

A charge to enter could be made of perhaps two shillings; this can be decided on at a later date.

Now, this is my main thought, the look on faces present was a picture, Ruth and Charlie's little girl Daisy had a terrible affliction being born with her right foot going the wrong way, with the skill of the surgeon Sam Stromsburg and the financial help of friends, that little girls foot was corrected. A charity will be set up in the name of Daisy Oates to help finance any operation required by any other child born with such a problem, the money coming from the admission charges to the basement. At the present time, I do not know how one goes about setting up a charity such as I have outlined. That is my idea but at present keep it confidential as some stuffy council body might throw a spanner in the works, well what do you think?" For the first time the lads gave Dan a round of applause, Dan was pleased with their response.

*

Fred went straight off to telephone Lance and explained what the plans were and if he can obtain permission from the Home Office, he emphasized, that it is for charity and explained about Daisy's operation. Lance promised to phone Fred the following day. He then went to visit Maurice Stromsburg, asking if his Uncle Sam Stromsburg, the surgeon who operated on Daisy, still had any photographs of a foot such as Daisy had, preferably before and after the operation. I realise he must now be retired, Fred then explained their plans but asking Maurice to keep it under wraps, he too thought it a wonderful idea.

Fred suggested to Dan that they should have dinner together and invite Mary and Margery in on their latest proposal; a woman's view might be useful. That evening the suggested plan was put forward to their wives asking their opinion. Their response was positive, it is a great idea and so the idea went into the think tank for further discussion

Lance contacted Fred the following morning as promised and told him that the Home Office had no objections to their plans at all; in fact Lance said he would call at the store to discuss the question of empty ammunition boxes etc. The Home Office insists that if they should see any suspicious activity to telephone Lance straight away, which Fred promised to do.

Fred contacted Dan and passed on all that had been said. Dan went off to visit the Estate Agent who was responsible for letting the butchers shop. The figure requested was far too high, Dan explained that they were going to fit it out as a charity shop and the shop would be completely redecorated to a high standard and the owners of the property would be shown as a sponsor. The agent agreed to telephone the owner. Dan was asked to call in the following morning and be given his decision, Dan realised every thing would now be on hold until the following day.

The following morning Dan left the store to walk round to the Estate Office, walking very slowly tapping the pavement with his walking stick; this has become a habit of his while he was pondering over a problem. He had spent the previous night puzzling what to do if the agent cannot get a lower price, instead of sleeping. Arriving at the Estate Office the man gave him a cup of coffee and told him that the owner has offered to lower the rent by 50%, Dan was delighted but the agent insisted that the owner of the shop must be acknowledged as a sponsor, to which Dan readily agreed.

That evening Dan and his wife, visited Frank and Bella, he was most surprised to see how well Frank looked and he had lost a little weight in such a short space of time. Dan proceeded to explain what he, with Frank's approval was planning with the basement but he insisted that it is kept under wraps until they all agree on the plans. Bella immediately suggested that she, Mary and Margery should organise and run the craft shop as they are getting a little old for jumping in and out of windows, this brought smiles to their faces. Frank, "Don't you even think about helping with the shop fitting, I am sure Sam and Roy can cope with that side of the business, I would not be surprised if they come to you for advice and opinion but under no circumstance do you do any work."

Sunday morning the staff from M. B. M, Roy and Sam came to the shop to discuss and plan the lay out. Sam had brought some tools with him and made a start to make the large wooden main door secure with new fitted locks. The next step was to plan the craft shop, making the left hand side a narrow entry; this would allow more room available for the craft shop. They all looked around, Arne and Richard were arguing, this is a good sign, their compromise could be interesting.

There was no decision made that morning but it was obvious that several plans were being mulled over in their heads. Dan told Sam that he was not to skimp on the quality of wood used for the counters, he wanted it to look a high-class establishment, any problem with the cost Dan said, he would pay for the timber.

Thursday evening, they all met up at Margery and Dan's house, Frank and Bella insisted on coming along. They all had their own ideas of how the shop should look. The plans and measurements were agreed upon and Sam and Roy took them away with them to machine the wood to size, hoping it would all fit together like a jigsaw. Before the get together broke up, Sherry, Coffee and Tea was on offer, it turned into a real social evening. It was agreed that they should all meet on Sunday morning at the Butchers shop.

*

Margery turned to Dan and told him that he had not approached Daisy asking if she will allow her name to go forward to be used for the charity. "Yes Margery, he answered, we must visit her tomorrow." When they arrived at Ruth and Charlie's house they were made most welcome. Dan explained what his plans are and he is hoping that Daisy will put her name to the charity. They telephoned Daisy asking her to come along, she only lived in the next street and she was with them in five minutes. When she saw Dan she threw her arms around him giving him a big kiss, she knew who had helped her.

"I must apologise, I have taken you for granted" and he then proceeded to explain how he wanted to create a charity using her name and collecting money to help pay for treatment for any child who had been born with such an affliction," her reply was spontaneous, "Of course Uncle Dan, look what a difference it has made to me." She was wearing high heel shoes, of the latest fashion. "I will do all you ask of me but I do not want to handle any money." "That is great, perhaps Mark or

Mr Blake will take the treasurers job on but I would like you to open the Basement and the charity shop when all is ready," "I'd love to." "It will be known as "Daisy's Charity." That is, as it will be shown on the facia on the craft shop.

Fred had been most fortunate in getting an electrician and Ian the decorator to fall in with his plans, firstly he wanted the large cold room disconnected and a different type of wall and ceiling light fittings in place before Ian decorated. The lighting was to be organised by Bella as this is where she excels. The most important thing was, Fred wanted it all finished by the weekend, Ian put up little fight but Fred won the battle, Ian and his team worked very late in the evenings to get the job completed.

Sunday morning they all came to the shop as planned and they were delighted with the transformation that had taken place in just a few days. Again Ian had excelled in his colour schemes. Ian called into the shop and he was surprised to see so many willing hands to put their plans in operation. Ian sought out Fred, "Why did you send those five men in to check on me yesterday?" "Who do you mean Ian?" "They said they were looking around and wanted to know what we were doing and what for," "I told them that I had no idea; I was just employed to decorate as instructed." "Was one of the five, tall, blue eyes and blonde hair?" "Yes Fred; you have got it in one." "Thanks Ian, they are troublesome and several people will be pleased that you mentioned it to me."

There was knocking on the door. "There is a man and a woman at the main door," Fred went to investigate and who should be standing there but Lance and his wife Pat, Lance introduced his wife to them all. "Mary, will you make Pat, a cup of tea while I talk with Lance," Mary turned to Fred saying, "Chauvinist," this was enjoyed by the woman present. "Fred then went into detail of the five men who came pestering Ian, wanting to know what was happening to the shop but Ian told him that he was only employed to decorate, other than that he had no idea what was happening to the shop." "Fred, my bosses were afraid this would happen, there is still a mystery surrounding this building."

"Plans have already been made thinking this might happen, the idea is, miniature cameras will be installed in every nook and cranny in the basement the rooms and of course the store, these are apart from the main camera's we have installed. Not only will they record on tape but also they will be connected to a central security office locally and watched twenty- four hours each day and seven days each week. They are determined to find out why this building is still attracting the Germans"

*

"The plan is this, you will be sent two or three boxes, each containing the special cameras to your factory and then you will transport them to your store on the normal delivery day and how do we get our technicians into the store without being seen to carry out the full installation Operation?" "I suggest that the technicians wander in separately just prior to the closing time and stay behind when the store is locked up, I will stay behind with them" said Dan.

Bill Russell was kept under constant surveillance as planned but apart from his frequent visits to the Embassy House on the out-skirts of Liverpool, all his actions appeared to be legitimate. When he does visit the house he is never allowed to enter, in fact, it is obvious they do not want his visits and ask him to leave. Bill is beginning to look very distressed.

A meeting was called with a senior secret service person present; he suggested that Bill should be made aware that he was being watched. Lance agreed, this might force Bill to make a move and break cover. Bill did suddenly become aware that he was being watched even when walking or followed when driving his car. The pressure was really getting to him and his wife felt sure he was on the verge of having a nervous breakdown or even a heart attack. His wife Ursula was very concerned, so much so, she asked the local doctor to help but the doctor told her that only Bill could help himself.

One evening on his arrival home from the plant, Ursula took a glass from the cupboard, poured Bill out a good measure of whiskey and handed it to him; he took a mouthful, not a sip. "Now Bill, are you going to tell me what is going on, if not, I am going to leave you, I cannot stand your moody attitude any longer?" "Right Ursula, I will tell you, In 1938 Harry invented a hydraulic system, which revolutionised the aircraft landing gear systems for which he took out a patent. He went to Stuttgart to meet with a German company who wanted to produce his invention under licence, for which, he would receive money known as royalties.

During one evening he was drugged and he divulged all the details of his invention and further improvements he was working on to a German engineer, who had obviously been planted for this purpose. When he came round sufficiently, they told him that he had given his countries secrets away. If they should leak this to his government he could be hanged for treason. He was told that when he was approached to help any of their agents in this country, he would do so, if not, they will contact his government. This is the hold they had over Harry; he was told that he must do whatever they asked of him to keep them quiet."

"Harry discussed this with me on many occasion, he was frantic with worry and he did not know what to do. I suggested that he should go to the secret service people and tell them every thing that had happened, which he did. A British secret service operator was planted in Harry's house 24 hours each day waiting for him to receive a caller; they could then arrest the agent. It was at the time that our son Bobby was in need of medical treatment, for which, we were unable to find the money. A gentleman called at the plant asking to speak to Harry. As he was not available, he just chatted away to me. He gradually brought the conversation around to Harry's visit to Germany and then he enquired about Bobby's health, I told him that we were unable to finance the specialist's treatment which the doctors think might help but with blood problems, they are working in the dark. He said he would help me. The following day he called and gave me £500 to fund Bobby's treatment but we still sadly lost our son. I told you that I had sold some stock to get the money. Foolishly, I told him that Harry should be safe as a secret service man is holed up in his house hoping for a visitor to arrive and they could arrest him or her whoever the agent was. Three days later Harry and the secret agent were murdered."

"One week later I received a visit from the same man telling me that the plant would be receiving several crates. He told me to take them in and they would be removed later the same day. I refused to accept this but I was told that I had accepted £500 bribe for information about Harry's lodger. Several RSJ'S were selected from my stock and I had to cut them to the sizes they asked for, I was told they were to be used in the basement at the Town Hall and it was confidential knowledge. I now realise that these RSJ'S were used to construct the tunnel in the basement at the old cinema as reported in the press."

*

Ursula said, "I know someone who will help you, the husband of my friend Mary is still in touch with the Army, shall I ask her for help?" "Yes but insist that it is confidential." Ursula went to see Mary, before she started to explain; she insisted that it was all very sensitive. A meeting was arranged at Fred's house and Lance was also present. Bill explained all the details right through from Harry's trip to Germany right up to the present day, everything he knew. Bill did not leave anything out at all. "Why do you keep going to the house belonging to the Embassy?" "I wanted to speak to the boss to tell him not to visit me again but they said that I accepted money for secrets and supplied materials to create the tunnel, the fate of my wife is in my hands." "Thank you for telling us all the details, we will keep an eye on you both to keep you safe". "Why me after all these years?" said Bill.

CHAPTER 12

"Dan contacted the company solicitor instructing him to get in touch with the Charity Commissioners and apply to register a Charity in the name of "Daisy's Charity". It was decided that the Trustees would be, Dan, Fred, Ruth and Daisy, if more trustees are required further names would be submitted. Frank did not feel well enough to offer his services. Mr Blake and Mark will handle the finances but nothing can happen until a charity number has been issued and attached to the Banking Account to benefit from the tax breaks available to charities."

"Mark is anxious to get the charity number as he is holding two undated cheques from donors to start the charity off. One is from Maurice and the other is from Samuel Stromsburg the surgeon and he has also sent several large pictures showing a child's deformed foot facing the wrong way, as it was in the case of Daisy's foot and a photograph showing the same foot after corrective surgery carried out by Sam Stromsburg, help could be offered but not available to all. It all depends on the severity of the affliction and the bone structure. It has not been decided yet whether to display the photographs on the wall of the canteen in the basement, in the craft shop or as one goes through the payment turnstile." Dan made a note in his little book to invite the donors to the opening when it takes place. Samuel Stromsburg called to meet up with Dan, he pointed out that the charity would be swamped with calls for help. If Dan should need any help in selecting whom to help with the payment for the operation, he would be available to advise, it is not possible to correct the affliction in every case.

*

Dan's solicitor contacted him saying that another member of the public must be named as a trustee to make it an odd number. Dan approached Charlie, Ruth's husband and Daisy's father and asked him if he would serve as a trustee, it was not a question of persuading him; he was delighted to be asked. Several days later Dan was informed that the charity application had been approved and a registered number had been issued. It will be known as "Daisy's Charity", Mark was so pleased to get the number which now allowed him and Mr Blake to open the bank account and deposit the cheques they were holding.

On the Sunday morning all the family met up, Sam is holding the keys until he is told how many keys to get cut and for whom. Dan and Margery entered the shop and they were absolutely astounded, Sam and Roy had fitted the counters and the shelves, they had been beautifully polished in a deep burgundy colour. As with the original plan, the left hand side was narrow to enter but the right hand side had been opened up as a craft shop, the girls had filled the shelves with merchandise. As with this type of exhibition, the customers must pass through the craft shop to leave the premises, hoping to promote sales.

It had been arranged that a new facia would be delivered and fitted this morning, the facia will be painted cream with the lettering standing out in brown, the letters are painted in such a way that the "Daisy's Charity" appears to be 3D, most impressive, another M. B. M. touch. The family wandered around but no one could offer any suggestion to improve the lay out. "Right! Next Sunday will be the Grand Opening," they all cheered.

The council inspectors had paid a visit several days earlier to view the display and they insisted that all the dust should be removed from the clothing and they wanted the canteen cleaned up, paying particular attention to the food and water containers on the shelves and the map showing the strategic points of the city. They were a little disturbed when they saw all the ammunition boxes until they were shown to be empty. The room with the German army uniforms had several large photographs of German officers wearing this type of uniform with leather top coats and peaked caps, however, eventually they were quite satisfied and would allow the opening to go ahead on whatever date was decided.

*

Fred telephoned Lance telling him that the opening was planned for the following Sunday. He told Lance if he wished to inspect before the basement is open to the public, just give me a call. He then telephoned Jack Green to tell him that the opening was planned for the following Sunday and if he wished to take his photographs without the hustle and bustle, give me a ring and I will open up for you. I am hoping that the paper will promote the opening and cover it on the day of the opening. Jack said "I would not miss it for the world; my editor will come along to make sure we miss nothing."

Lance came back to Fred and arranged to visit on the Monday morning; Fred collected the keys and opened up for Lance to look around. When Lance entered the shop he was most surprised and very impressed how it had all been set up. Lance told Fred that there was a possibility that his bosses from the Home Office would attend the opening; they were still puzzled by the Germans interest in this building. There had not been any definite activity recorded on the cameras sited in and around the building but there had been a few little unexplained specific movements by men wandering on all sides and looking at the building, weighing up as if for a break in. Lance offered to arrange a replica of the tarpaulin covering the pile of currency and the gold found in the loft with the booby trap that had been attached. Fred asked if it could be arranged before Friday.

Sunday morning, Dan and Margery were out of bed and raring to go, Dan calmed Margery down and they enjoyed breakfast. Today was the day to prove that all their work at the charity shop had been worthwhile. It was a beautiful bright sunny morning, the opening was planned for 11am but when they arrived at 10-00am a large crowd was already milling around just talking and looking, in fact, just passing time till the opening ceremony. Drinks and refreshments were arranged within the store for invited guests who had donated money or who had helped with getting the charity underway. The floor opening behind the organ had been made larger and the rickety ladder replaced with a proper stairway and safety rails thus enabling the guests to enter the basement from the store. The opening had been made safe with a lightweight steel cover that could be locked for security. Jack Green and his Editor had made an excellent job of promoting the opening in their local newspaper; they had created a lot of interest.

To add magic to the atmosphere a jazz band began playing, Dan wondered who had ordered the band and who is going to meet the cost. The leader of the band came across to speak to Dan when they had a break, it was the same group that Dan had engaged when the main store was opened and he explained that they were not booked nor did they expect any payment. They considered it to be a worthwhile Charity; they came to add to the occasion with their music and their colourful uniforms.

By the entrance Arne had set up a public address system with a microphone on a platform, as the time was approaching 11am Daisy stepped on to the platform and proceeded to thank the people who had come along to support the opening. Daisy made a point of thanking Dan who had helped her to overcome her affliction and said it is his idea to set up this charity to help any other children who should be unfortunate enough to be born with such a deformity. One must realise that not all cases can be corrected but if one is successful we have achieved our goal. This is now a registered charity so you will see collecting boxes around; I hope you will be tempted to make a donation. At any time you wish to know where the money is, or how it has been spent, ask and you will receive a full explanation, this I promise." Daisy then leaned over, cut the ribbon and declared the Exhibition open; the loud applause was quite surprising.

The people queued up to enter the exhibition paying their two shillings for adults and children six pence; oddly the first five people to enter were men. Dan was not sure whether they were the Germans or the people from the Home Office. Fred and Lance wandered around watching the visitors, twice they had to ask a gentleman to refrain from moving objects and it was with a reluctant nod of the head as he moved away. The craft shop had a very busy time, which pleased the girls, especially when they counted the takings at the end of the day.

Jack Green was busy taking photograph of various people thronging around the entrance and inside the Basement. He knew that Lance would want copies for his team to study. One of the gentlemen he snapped, was the same man who had gone into the city planning office demanding a copy of the plans of the old cinema, he went into the exhibition but he stood and looked at each item as if he was in a different world. Jack persuaded his editor to include this gentleman's picture on the front page of the newspaper with the article covering the opening of the charity shop.

The opening of the charity shop certainly got a good write up in the newspapers; it stated how much cash had been taken on the day and how the public were absolutely fascinated. The visitors found it all very interesting but could not understand how the place had been built and this had taken place during wartime. The armaments had been made in Germany and brought into this country; the unit had been set up as a real fifth column in readiness for an invasion of this country. The so-called security people had been sadly lacking because someone must have been suspicious, this had all been carried out under their noses.

The Home Office has been ordered to carry out a full investigation as to how this was allowed to happen while several sections of the armed forces were stationed around this area during the war. Dan was a little perturbed that his venture should cause so many problems but on the other hand, the publicity certainly paid off. The following Sunday the numbers going into the exhibition had to be regulated and queues formed outside waiting to enter. Mark had notified Dan that they had been inundated with calls for help as predicted by Samuel Stromsburg, so the publicity is not all good.

CHAPTER 13

Sunday afternoon Simon saw Mark and his wife Sally arrive by taxi, he went out to help Mark into his wheel chair, "You feeling okay Mark?" he smiled, "Yes thanks, I am fine." Simon went to have a word with Dan, "Look at Mark do you think he is experiencing a health problem?" "Goodness Simon, your right he does look ill, we must consider taking some pressure off him. We will meet in the factory canteen on Tuesday morning." They met up as planned in the canteen, "Simon made a point that in his opinion Mark was doing too much and his health is beginning to fail, he is company secretary to D.F.F, Jenny's company and now he has taken on the job of treasurer with Daisy's Charity. I feel that we are expecting too much from Mark especially as he retired two years ago but recalled to help out."

"While we are all together, can we talk money? It was agreed that the retail store would not pay for any furniture delivered and then sold on credit within the store to enable the credit system to get off the ground. The store owes the factory £2500, the credit payments taken each week at the store will now enable it to pay for any future deliveries of furniture and start paying the outstanding balance."

"The Fifth Column bank balance is increasing and it is becoming difficult to run both companies in tandem, in my opinion the two companies need to be restructured." "They are two separate companies." Simon smiled, "I am company secretary of the store but who is in charge of what." Fred came in saying, "You are right Simon, and we should have a manager completely in charge of all aspects of the store trading also the Franchise of people renting space. Alan has now completed his degree; why not appoint him to be Managing Director, Simon, Financial Director and the three of us on the board. "Do you think you could hold down both jobs without neglecting either, Simon?" "If you decide I am to go ahead, I will report back after six months." "That is a fair comment"

*

Fred and Dan arranged to visit Frank in his own house; he appeared to be progressing very well after the heart attack and he had lost a lot of weight in such a short space of time. Bella is doing exactly as the specialist told her to do, Frank is fighting her all the way as he does like his food but like it or not Bella is keeping him on a strict diet. The reason for their visit is because of Simon's statement saying the whole company is in need of restructuring; bringing in modern equipment which is lagging behind present day's technology. We have been giving it a lot of thought and he might well be right.

Dan said, "Firstly, shall we deal with D.F.F. this is the one business we have grown up with. Let us discuss changes. Make Sam and Roy bosses in the furniture production and Simon the finance side of the business." Frank came in saying, "What you are suggesting, is that we make the three boys directors in their own field but we three should stay on the board as consultants?" Fred then joined in, "Yes that must be the plan." Dan said "My suggestion is, Sam is made Managing Director, Roy to be Production Director and Simon to become Financial Director." The discussion ceased as Bella came into the room carrying a tray with a pot of tea and cups and saucers, which they were very pleased to see. They were deliberating in their own minds as they drank their tea. The tea break finished, all three agreed to go ahead with the plan but we must make it quite clear, we are staying on the board to encourage them to keep on the right tracks, not to interfere with the running of the company. Frank looked at Fred and Dan, "Painful handing over isn't it?" to which, they both nodded.

"Now we have decided the future of D.F.F. we come to the store management. Alan has now finished his degree in Business and Marketing, should we give him the opportunity of the manager's job, after 12 months if he is managing the store and remains in complete charge of the staff and reaches the sales targets, we would then consider his promotion. The other thing we are faced with is the setting up of an office within the store, Simon says that the two companies cannot run in tandem and there should a separate finance office to deal with payments to D.F.F. and any other creditors who supply the store, electricity, rent and rates. At a previous meeting it was said that Mark is doing too much and he is not enjoying the best of health. I would suggest that we approach Mark and ask him, if we advertise for office staff, would he be willing to interview the applicants and make the choice of who is to be engaged, set up an office and select who is to be in charge. Once he is satisfied the office is running smoothly and correctly he could leave them to it, he can go and enjoy his retirement with our blessings and with any financial help he might require. That is my thinking," said Dan. "Do you agree?" They both nodded in agreement.

*

Jack Green gave Fred two sets of copies of the 30 photographs taken at the opening of the charity shop. Karl Kayberg telephoned Jack's Editor complaining that he had displayed his photograph in the newspaper without asking his permission. The Editors response was to print it in the paper again offering the paper's apology for printing his photograph without first obtaining his permission.

Karl Kayberg was photographed talking to the same man in various parts of the basement, by the look on their faces neither one looked very happy. When Lance saw the photograph he was taken aback, the man with whom Karl was in deep discussion is a senior member of the Home Office team sent to cover the opening. The copies sent to Lance's office for his team to study had all been numbered but when Lance was checking through he discovered that six copies were missing. Whoever had removed the copies must have thought that six from thirty would not be missed. Lance contacted Fred, asking him to send the missing copies, just as Lance had thought; the missing copies were the ones showing the official named Horace Hester in deep conversation with the German.

Lance telephoned the main office asking for an interview with his superior, which was granted. On entering the office, the man said, "What is bothering you Lance?" "It is this sir," Lance laid the six photographs he had obtained from Fred and he went on to explain how someone in his office had removed these copies." "Lance, on the surface it looks a very serious situation. What I will do is to delegate Horace to keep an eye on the Charity shop and the Embassy House and send me a report every third day, this will continue for two weeks. I will send one of my top men who Horace does not know to check on his movements. No one, I repeat no one apart from you and I will know this is taking place."

The meeting over, Lance decided to make his way home, he was sure that Pat, his wife, would make him very welcome as he had spent a lot time away from home over the past few weeks. Pat was pleased to have him home early for a change; she was a little bothered, he looked so tired. Pat made Lance his favourite meal and opened a bottle of wine. Lance really enjoyed it all but no sooner had he sat in his chair than he went to sleep. Later that evening he told his wife that he was going back to Liverpool for a few days, why don't you come with me, there are some excellent hotels and we can make it a break for us both, Pat readily agreed.

Lance telephoned Fred the following day telling him that he was returning to Liverpool in an attempt to find the missing pieces of the jigsaw, he heard Fred chuckling at the other end of the line. "Incidentally, I am bringing Pat with me to give her a break," "Great, Mary will be delighted, they got on very well together the other Sunday when you came. Ring me and tell me when and where to meet you both, why don't you stay with us rather than going to a hotel. We have plenty of room, it is just Mary and myself in a four bedroom house," "Thanks Fred, if you think it will be alright with your wife," "Lance, she will be only too pleased to have company, are you coming by train or car?" "We shall arrive at Lime Street Station at 12 noon" "Right, we will meet you off the train. I will book a table for lunch, see you soon."

Fred and Mary were at Lime Street Station to meet Lance and Pat, the train pulled in on time, most unusual these days. They met them off the platform, taking the cases from them and putting them in the boot of their car. Fred had booked lunch at the Adelphi; it was obvious that Pat had not been out socialising for a while, she was thoroughly enjoying the outing; Mary created laughter by telling them about their first visit to this hotel for Dan's birthday.

Mary suggested that she should take the men to the store then she and Pat could have a wander around town, Pat immediately agreed to this idea as she had been told of the large stores in the city. She told Mary that she enjoyed shopping but Lance would do anything to get out of it; she looked across at Lance, he just smiled.

Mary dropped the men off at the store as planned; they were surprised by the number of customers in the store, as Fred was passing the Upholstery department the salesman said, "They are here again". Looking around, the five Germans were seen wandering around and there was a sixth member with them, Fred recognised him from the photograph, It was Horace Hester, Fred said to Lance, "I thought he was going to observe them, not join them", "Yes Fred, puzzling isn't it."

He was a little surprised that Fred should say that Horace was here to observe the Germans; did he know of the plan? if so, how did he find out. He asked Fred what made him think that Horace was here to observe the Germans, Fred replied, "He was one of the team that arrived to cover the opening," Lance felt at ease with that explanation. Karl and his crowd spent a further ten minutes looking around and then they left, Horace going with them.

Lance spent several days wandering around but he was still puzzled over the visiting Germans. Fred took him to visit the furniture factory with which he was very impressed; Lance was introduced to various members of the staff as Major Goodchild who was with Fred on the Dunkirk Beaches. After a few more days in Liverpool, he thought he should go home and spend some time in his office but Pat had other ideas. She was enjoying going out for lunch and then window shopping with Mary and Margery, Lance lost the battle, so they stayed.

Lance telephoned his office to advise them that he was staying in the city a little longer, if you should need to contact me, here is the number during the daytime, giving them the store number for daytime and Fred's number for the evenings. A couple of days later they all went out to dinner with Margery and Dan, on the way home Fred insisted that they all went to his house for drinks, which they did and the evening became very jovial. They were all sat about laughing and giggling when the telephone rang out, Mary answered the phone, as she picked it up the voice of a man said "Is it possible to speak to Major Goodchild?" "Certainly, one minute please." Mary went back into the room; "You are wanted on the telephone Lance." He picked up the phone saying this is "Major Goodchild," "Lance I am the gentleman you met last week, he didn't mention his name over the phone, Horace has not submitted any report, Three days ago, he was photographed arguing with Karl by the front door of the Embassy House, he entered the house and has not been seen or heard of since. There is nothing you can do but I am just keeping you in the picture, the agent does not know you or that you too are investigating.

CHAPTER 14

Dan called all the family together in the store after it had closed and the doors were locked. Dan said, "I am going through the management reorganisation of both D.F.F. and Fifth Column, this may not affect some of you personally but Frank, Fred and I, like to think we are all family in business together, although some have become independent. Dan went on to say that it has been decided to make Sam Managing Director, Roy would become Production Director and Simon Financial Director; the people concerned have been interviewed and have decided to accept the positions offered.

The store management position is being given to Alan now he has completed his University Degree Course, he was offered the position and he has accepted. Providing he controls the store, staff and meets the sales targets, he too, could be offered promotion at a later date, we shall see. Mark has been interviewing several applicants to be employed in the new office at the store to deal with the credit and the cash side of the business. The office will be set up and controlled by the Chief Cashier named Betty Brant who I understand is a first class bookkeeper; she was engaged by Mark but answerable to Alan. It has been brought to our notice that it is necessary to know who is ultimately responsible, not as we have been running the company."

"The intention is that Mark will spend the next three weeks in the office, if and when he is happy the way the office is running, he intends relinquishing the various offices he holds and return to his retirement, with one exception, he will remain treasurer for Daisy's Charity shared with Mr Blake. I understand that the jungle drums have been heard with regard to M.B.M. I understand that they are considering going it alone. That is what all the plans are, we thought it only right that as a family you should all know what is happening, rather than sending it out in a newsletter."

*

Lance decided that in view of the recent developments he should return home and attend his own office; his wife did not raise any objections this time. He telephoned his boss, Mr Lee; He invited Lance to report to his office as soon as possible. On arrival at Mr Lee's office he shook Lance's hand and said, "What a mess, bring me up to date."

"I intend asking Bill Russell to visit the Embassy House in an attempt to glean any knowledge of Horace. While we have had Bill under surveillance over the past few months, he has not been allowed to enter the house, we shall see this time, one never knows." "You might be right Lance, it is getting very nasty, be sure it does not endanger his life; I do hope that Horace is safe, even if it is only for him to answer my questions."

"The tall blonde German to whom you refer to as Karl, is in fact Hans Kayberg and he was one of the stars who came up through the ranks of the Hitler's Youth Movement." "Now, that fits another little piece in the jig-saw puzzle, Harry was drugged while staying at his parent's hotel in Stuttgart before the war in 1938 and the son's name was Hans. They obtained the secrets of his patented hydraulic aircraft undercarriage while he was drugged and when he came round and had shaken off the effects of the drug they threatened they would expose him and he would be hanged for treason by the British Government unless he became one of their agents." "What on earth are they looking for; when the currency and gold was removed I thought the prowling Germans would go away, but no! I will visit the store tomorrow, when we meet there, call me Ken, if you call me Sir I might disappear, I am completely foxed."

Lance returned to Liverpool the following day as planned but this time he stayed in a Hotel, it was getting too dangerous and he did not want it to appear that Fred was implicated. He wandered into the store the following morning and asked if Fred was about, the office girl telephoned around until she found him and passed the message from Lance. Ten minutes later Fred walked into the store, he and Lance went off to a local café and treated themselves to tea and toast.

Lance put Fred in the picture what he was going to ask Bill to do, Fred was very uncertain about the plan, because if they or any of their compatriots had been involved in the wartime killing of Harry Blythe and the secret service agent, they would have no hesitation in killing again to preserve their cause. Lance appreciated Fred's uncertainties.

Fred invited Bill Russell and his wife Ursula to dinner and Lance was present, during the meal Lance put his proposition to Bill asking him to visit the Embassy House, He was very reluctant to agree to do as Lance requested. Bill then told them that he had a visit today by two Germans asking if the plant's gas furnace is capable of reaching a high enough temperature to deal with molten iron to be poured into moulds, I told them I would have to get the Gas Company to increase the gas flow, I could not think of any other excuse. Fred looked at Lance, his disfigured face looked ghastly and he had gone very pale, Fred thought, I hope he is not thinking the same as myself. However, when they were alone, it appeared that they were both on the same wavelength.

Fred arrived at the store as it was opening up, Alan was present, dressed in a very smart suit, polished shoes and a colourful tie and he looked every inch a store manager. He gave Fred a very courteous welcome, as a manager should to his boss.

Ten minutes later Lance arrived accompanied by a gentleman who was introduced to Fred as Ken Lee. Ken asked Fred if he could spare time to conduct him on a complete tour of the building including the Basement and the Loft. Fred collected the keys and they entered the basement through the "Charity Shop" rather than the trap door behind the organ. Ken was quite taken with the craft shop and he was very impressed with the layout of the exhibition.

The lower floor tour completed, Ken remarked, "How on earth was all this work carried out unnoticed, the construction of the passageway alone was a major engineering project, the R.S.J's were supplied by Bill Russell for the roof supports, that we do know but they had to be transported from the engineering plant to this building which would have been seen by many people and you would think it would have been queried."

"I have not seen the hiding place where the currency and gold was found." They went up the stairs leading to the balcony and then into the projection room, through the large cupboard doors and they mounted the stairs leading up into the loft, There was still a load of old newspapers but nothing to give any clues, the only thing Ken remarked about, was the newspapers are English, not German papers which he found disturbing. Ken thanked Fred for taking the time to conduct his tour; in fact, he put a donation in one of the Daisy Charity collecting boxes that were around the store.

"You are right Lance; this mystery is deeper than we thought, even after all these years since the war ended, why, oh why are the Germans still wandering around and what do they want?" "I am going ahead with sending Bill to the Embassy House; I hope it is not a mistake. Before you leave Ken, I must tell you of a puzzler; Bill had a visit from two Germans who wanted to know if his Gas Furnace could be made to reach a temperature to melt iron ore," Ken shouted, "Good God Lance, No." He too must have had that horrible thought.

"Fred, May I use your private office to make a phone call?" "Certainly, follow me," Fred showed him into his office, closing the door as he came out. Ken telephoned a number and when a man answered the phone, Ken instructed him to join him straight away. He then telephoned a Home Office official, he proceeded to bring him up to date and pointed out that the mystery is deepening, he too said he would join Ken as this is becoming to be a thorn in our side, too many questions are being asked. Ken came out of the office saying, "We have put the cat among the pigeons. Lance, whatever men or resources you need, just ask, that is the position now."

"Lance, how far is the house we requisitioned for the boys to watch the cameras from the engineering plant, is it in walking distance?" "Yes, I could walk it in ten minutes," "Good, are there any spare rooms?" "Yes, there are two large bedrooms, one with cooking facilities." "That solves quite a problem with accommodation, Henry will be here in a while, we will take him to the house and when his boys arrive he can sort them out."

"We will have to have a meeting to decide what action we are going to take, how and when. The only problem we might be up against is that a couple of officials are coming from the Home Office, they are qualified at a desk but not in the field and they can be impatient and fool hardy which can put other peoples lives at risk."

CHAPTER 15

Mark called a meeting of trustees for the Daisy Charity. "We have received twenty letters asking for help with their deformed feet. I have acknowledged their letters and have advised them that their application has been passed for consideration. Twenty people, how do we deal with that number?"

Samuel joined in the conversation by saying, "Sad as it might sound, are they all young children? from the operation point of view, the younger the better. When a person reaches adulthood the bone structure is set and difficult to manipulate."

Charles then suggested that they should go through the letters to ascertain the ages of the applicants and how many will fall into the very young child category. Checking through them, they found that seven children fell into the five years of age group. "The idea is to publicise the number of applicants and apply to the council for permission to have a street collection using the collecting boxes one Saturday. It is well known how generous the Liverpool people are when asked for cash for a charity." "What a good idea Charlie, I will write to the council today to get their reaction before we make any decision, or, we could go ahead with the seven children." It was decided by a show of hands to go ahead with the seven children.

Sam sat pondering, "The next step is for me to enquire the cost to use the X-ray machine for the children, do not forget we will have to meet the cost of transporting the children to and from the hospital. We could advertise in the children's local paper, looking for a Good Samaritan to help, when they realise the child's affliction, I feel sure a driver will be found to transport the child to keep their appointment." Samuel felt confident they would have no problem in that direction.

Permission was granted for the Daisy Charity to allow a team with collecting boxes, on the streets of Liverpool for one Saturday. Mark asked Jack Green if he would photograph one of the collectors and he would inform him of the amount collected. Mark did contact Jack with the total collected, the total was so good that the charity will now be able to go ahead and consider the other applicants who requested treatment. The charity is gaining momentum and people are beginning to give freely.

Mark sat reading through the letters again, he suddenly looked up, "One thing I have overlooked, eleven of the applicants will be unable to attend Liverpool Royal Hospital due to the travelling distance; two are living in Cornwall, three in Birmingham so it could be difficult. I didn't realise that the national papers had run the story." "We will contact their local Hospital asking them to carry out the X-ray and the charity will meet the cost." "That is a great idea Sam but sadly when we look at the X-rays we might find that we are unable to help." "We will have tried."

Samuel made the x-ray arrangements and the appointments sent out to the children's parents. The times of the appointments were arranged for the child with the furthest to travel to have the later times, as Samuel had hoped, drivers came forward to help with transport.

*

Mark received an invoice from the hospital requesting payment for the Radiographer and the use of the X-ray machine to deal with seven children. Enclosed in the same envelope was a letter addressed to Samuel Stromsburg. The surgeons had viewed the X-rays and in their opinion the feet of two of the children will not benefit from an operation. As the letter was open, Mark read it and was very disappointed but he had to accept the professional's decision.

Sam read the report but he did not altogether agree, he decided to visit the hospital and look at the X-rays himself. He went to the reception desk at the hospital and asked if he could go into the X-ray storeroom to study the X-rays of the two boys not considered for an operation. The nurse was quite hostile and said they belong to the hospital and they are confidential. Sam showed her the invoice requesting money from the Daisy Charity, her mood changed straight away. He was taken into the room and left to study the seven X-rays, he did not agree with the surgeons decision on the two boys put to one side.

Samuel decided to come out of retirement; he will find he has been sadly missed. He is an Internationally Respected Orthopaedic Surgeon and now he is available he will be sought after. His decision to return to work is purely as a volunteer for the Daisy Charity, for no fee.

The cost of hiring the operating theatre and its equipment really made them all sit up and wonder if they could go ahead, one thing which pleased Sam, two of his nurses came out of retirement and offered their services free of charge. Mark rang Jack Green; he explained that the cost of the X-rays for the thirteen patients was a lot more money than anticipated. We have the seven local children ready for their operation but we have not got the cash to go ahead. We have the country's top surgeon and his nurses ready to operate free of charge but no operating theatre.

If we got the seven children together, would you be willing to photograph them and put it in your paper with an article saying we would be grateful for any donation. I have told you we cannot afford to rent an operating theatre but if the public would make a donation it would put a smile on the little faces in the picture. Mark suggested the article should read something like, "Just send the form with your donation (no matter how small), Send it to the address printed below. Kindly "HELP." Jack agreed to speak to his editor. Dan contacted Mark and told him to go ahead with the operations; he will underwrite the cost until more funds are available.

Jack Greens Editor did not hesitate, his reply was "Yes Jack, you go ahead and deal with it, it will be a good PR job and will boost the circulation." Jack telephoned Mark; he was delighted, he felt sure the public would help. One thing you might like to know, Dan has told me to go ahead and if necessary he will underwrite the cost, a very kind gesture.

Mark telephoned asking Jack what day he would like the children assembled for him to take the photographs and suggested it be taken outside the Charity Shop, "Shall we say next Tuesday at three o'clock?" "Yes Mark, I will arrange that."

Mark contacted Dan to advise him of the arrangement, ask Fred if he could hire a small mini bus to transport the children and their parents from outside the city. Dan said, "He would have a word with Fred, Mary and I will collect the local children in our cars." Dan would have collected the small bus himself but it has a manual gearbox and with his deformed leg he drives an automatic car, his built up boot makes it difficult to operate the clutch.

The children were in the craft shop waiting for Jack, when he arrived he started to create a compact group, "Will you try and get the name of the bus in the photograph, if you can include it the owner will waive the hire charge." Fred did insist that Samuel and his two nurses should be included in the picture.

Jack called into the store the following day to show Fred the selection of photos he had taken, Jack suggested one particular photograph and Fred agreed with him. It showed all the children with Samuel and his nurses looking over them plus the Charity Shop and the name of the coach as Fred had requested. Jack and his editor discussed which evening paper to include the pictures. The editor decided to run it for two nights, Friday and Saturday's evening paper that should create a good impact.

The photograph was coupled with the written article pointing out the need for more money to hire an Operating Theatre to carry out the operations on the local children. The printed form was included, not only did it show to whom to send any donation but also Mark's home telephone number.

Sunday morning Mark received a telephone call from a private hospital near Chester. The caller offered their operating theatre for two or three afternoons free of charge but they would expect payment for any dressings used during the operations. "Our anaesthetist is willing to offer his services free of charge, if you should require him. If however, Samuel should want to keep any child in the hospital overnight, the charity will be expected to meet the cost of a nurse and the child's food."

"This is a most generous offer, May I ask your name and the name of the hospital?" "My name is Tim Pleasant and I will send you all the details of the hospital, Sam can then visit, in fact, Sam will remember working with me many years ago."

Mark called the trustees together and passed on the good news to them all we also have a bag to collect from the newspaper office, which should contain some donations. Samuel said, "When we have all the details to hand I will visit the hospital and make the necessary arrangements and what date will be convenient to them."

CHAPTER 16

Ken contacted Lance and asked him to arrange with Bill to take on two workers who will arrive in scruffy, dirty overalls and find them a job cleaning around near the furnace room. "If Bill is still going to the Embassy House, tell them the furnace has not been used for a couple of years and when he checked, it needs a new part to reach the temperature required. The new part has been ordered and will be delivered in ten to fourteen days; I will advise you when it has been fitted."

Bill went to the Embassy House, knocked on the door; a man opened the door, looking at Bill, "What do you want?" "One of your colleagues called at my engineering plant two days ago enquiring about the furnace." "Wait there, he returned, come in, go into the room over there, pointing to a large oak door which was slightly ajar." After a while a man entered the room. "Hello. You must be Bill Russell, now what about your furnace?" Bill explained that it had not been used for two years and on inspection it requires a new part which has been ordered and should be here in ten to fourteen days, when it is fitted I will advise you. The face of the man went purple as he shouted; "I want that furnace operational tomorrow night at the latest. My name is Hiene Spiers and no one messes with me. We will call tomorrow afternoon and you will take the necessary steps if you value your wife's good health."

He left the house and contacted Ken and Lance, Bill was very concerned with the threat to the life of his wife Ursula and he explained everything that was said. "We have put two men in your house and two armed men will be sweeping the floor around the furnace tomorrow, you will easily recognise them as they have a large white paint splash on the right shoulder. Make yourself known to them; you engaged them, so you must know their names. Bill, we are taking every precaution to safeguard you and your wife." Lance received a phone call from the camera room telling him that the usual group were wandering around the outside of the old cinema, When Lance told Ken, he scratched his head and smiled.

The following afternoon a car pulled into the plants car park and came to a halt. Five gentlemen got out of the car and walked towards the main entrance, as they entered the building a security buzzer alerted the staff. The leader of the group asked for Bill Russell, Bill came down the steps to meet them, without any hello's, Hiene Spiers stepped forward "Have you fixed the furnace?" the man shouted, Bill said "No, I told you, nothing can be done until I get the new part." That morning Bill had adjusted the safety switch to a lower setting to prove his argument. The man in charge insisted that Bill should ignite the gas jets and put the furnace on full power, which Bill did. The boiler was going for about five minutes when the alarm sounded and the gas automatically switched itself off. Hiene went berserk, he lunged at Bill to grab him but two gentlemen in scruffy overalls and carrying shovels stepped between Hiene and Bill.

The Germans went storming off, the leader shouting, "You have two days to correct the fault." Before Bill locked up, he disconnected the main gas supply to the plant. When Lance was told of the incident he suggested that a night shift should be put in place, to which, Ken agreed. The two Home Office agents suggested that new small High Tech: cameras should be put in place near the furnace and tuned in to the technical equipment in the house where the cinema is also being watched very carefully.

*

Fred contacted Lance, "Suggestion, Why not tell Bill to advise the Germans that he has made the part and the furnace is now fully operational and we can see what they are up to rather than keep stalling?" Lance thought it an excellent idea but first he must discuss it with his boss Ken Lee, Ken did not agree straight away, for some reason he was hesitant. Two hours later he telephoned Lance, "I have been churning your idea around in my head and after a lot of deliberation I must agree with you, go ahead with your plan but take care Lance it seems that we are dealing with a vicious crowd. Before you go ahead liaison with the tech men at the house to ensure that the cameras cover the furnace area, okay," "I will do that now." Lance did check with them, to convince Lance that all was well, a messenger brought him a print out, of one of the pictures showing the furnace area.

Lance visited Bill and told him of the plan, I will reset the safety valve setting now then it will not get over looked. Ken told Lance that as he was not trained in arms he would watch the proceedings in the camera house. Three men were put in the building each fully trained by the armed squad and they are armed with hand guns, Lance intends to watch from an attic window in an adjoining building, he still carries his service hand gun.

Bill visited the Embassy House leaving a message with the gentleman who opened the door, before he reached his car he was called back. Hiene called to him to return, he told Bill to ignite the furnace before he left the plant and leave the main door unlocked. "Where is the lever to increase the heat?" Bill gave him explicit instructions how it is operated. The plan was in place; Bill ignited the gas jets as he was leaving at seven o'clock to go home. When he arrived home he told Ursula what had taken place, "Bill isn't it intriguing, have you any thoughts?" "None whatsoever, the secret service agents must sort it out."

The local clock was heard chiming ten o'clock and the surveillance team was getting a little unsettled; they began to wonder if they had the wrong night. However, as the clock chimed eleven a large Mercedes car pulled up in front of the main entrance to the plant. Two men got out of the car and walked to the rear of the car and opened the luggage compartment and they lifted out a parcel in a large black plastic bag. Lance was watching the men lifting out the large bag, suddenly he saw a movement in the shadows and then he saw a man walk towards the car. Goodness!! It was one of the Home Office officials, what ever he said to the man we shall never know, one of the men dropped his end of the parcel and Lance heard a pop-pop, he knew it was a hand gun fitted with a silencer, the official fell to the floor and did not move.

The two men picked up the parcel and carried it through to the furnace room, one of them stepped up the gas burner by pushing the lever as Bill had explained and they then went back out and carried the dead official into the same room. The men kept checking the temperature gauge and after ten minutes they considered it to be on maximum heat, one man opened the furnace door, as he did so, an agent came around the corner shouting at him to close the door and put their hands above the heads. He went to close the door but while doing so, he pulled his gun and shot the agent in the shoulder, the agent shot the man at point blank range and he dropped dead. One of the other agents came running, by this time the intruder had got his gun out and fired at the second agent but the agent was a better shot and the other man fell to the floor. The driver of the Mercedes heard the shots being fired, he drove off into the night, in the chaos no one memorised the number plate.

Lance left his look out window and went into the furnace room; he was cross, what a mess and they had hoped to capture one of the intruders to be interrogated. However, Lance turned his attention to the parcel, he was hoping against hope that he would be wrong but no, it was the body of Horace Hester, he had been shot through the back of the head, it was an execution. Ken was devastated; he watched the happenings in the furnace room being recorded on the camera. He was very annoyed that the Home Office official had spoiled the plan but the poor devil had paid with his life. Ken phoned a special number, a black van pulled up at the scene and took the bodies away, all in twenty minutes, and the wounded agent was taken to hospital by car.

The two men who were killed were brothers and very well known to the authorities and to Interpol; it appears they were available for any job if the price was right. The wallets contained their details; their address was shown to be in Jersey and in each wallet there was a substantial amount of money, so they had been well paid for this job.

Ken asked Lance if he would visit Horace's wife and give her the bad news. He travelled by train to Newcastle and caught a taxi from the station, as he did not know the area; the taxi man dropped him off outside the address. He rang the doorbell and knocked on the door but he could not get a reply. The next-door neighbour came to her door and told him that Mrs Hester was in Stuttgart, Germany, visiting her parents; she could not tell Lance when she was expected back as Mrs Hester's marriage was a little rocky. She told Lance, Mrs Hester had visited her on many occasion in tears because of her husband's ill treatment, she was always covered in bruises. On one occasion her uncle Hans came up from Liverpool to try and talk some sense into Horace but he didn't change at all. Lance said, "Here is my telephone number, please telephone me when she returns, you can reverse the charge of the call." He had to report back to Ken to tell him that he had drawn a blank with Mrs Hester but he got excited when he told him about uncle Hans visits.

*

Sam made arrangements to visit the private hospital near Chester, when he went his two nurses accompanied him. He was delighted to meet Tim again after so many years, Tim proudly took Sam and his two nurses into the operating theatre, Sam was very impressed, it was right up to date with all the latest equipment, it was the finest he had seen for quite a while. The dates were arranged and the anaesthetist called to meet Sam, he found him to be a likeable level headed young man, a person Sam felt he could work with, the nurses thought so too.

Mark organised the parents to bring their child to the hospital on a particular date and at a certain time. The first day arrived, Sam intended to operate on three children on the first day, two on the following day in the afternoon and the two children the doctors thought might be difficult to correct on the third day, one in the morning and one in the afternoon. He requested with Tim that each child would stay in the hospital overnight after the operation and then he could check on the children before they left the hospital the following morning to return home. Tim agreed and allowed the parents to stay with the child and an invoice would be sent to the treasurer of the Daisy Charity to cover any additional expenditure.

Dan invited Sam and his wife to stay with Margery and himself for the week of the operations, Sam thanked Dan and explained that he and his wife would be staying with his Aunt who lived nearby. However, he said he would be most grateful if his two nurses could stay with them, the daily travel to and from Leeds would be very tiring for them. The nurses stayed and they were sorry when it was time for them to leave, they enjoyed the stay with Dan and Margery very much, they likened it to a holiday.

The seven operations were all completed in the one week, Mark contacted Jack asking if it was possible for him to photograph the seven children altogether showing them with their foot and leg in plaster, with a large caption saying "THANK YOU" above the picture. "Certainly Mark, my editor will be delighted to do this for you. The charity news and pictures is boosting our circulation." Dan and Fred collected the children and got them settled outside the charity shop, when Jack took the photograph the smiles were fantastic. The editor decided to put the photograph on the front page of the evening paper in Friday and Saturday editions. When the public saw the picture, they said, "To see the smiles on the little faces was worth every penny donated." Sam was now faced with the prospect of persuading the Liverpool Royal management to allocate a room for him to check on the children in a few weeks time to monitor the child's progress since the operation. The response came quickly, Sam was to go to the hospital a few days prior to the day he would like the room and then it could be prepared. The Charity Trust would pay for whatever dressings he used.

CHAPTER 17

Simon contacted his father, asking him if he could get Dan and Fred to attend a meeting as he has some concerns, which he would like to discuss. A meeting was arranged in Frank's office at the factory on the Tuesday morning, Simon arranged to collect his father, as he has not driven since his heart attack. Dan said "Sam, Roy and Alan should attend and as it is about money Betty should also be included." All present, Simon stood up and passed round the statement of accounts for the past two months. "You will see from the statements that our retail and wholesale figures have fallen by 15%, I realise that other businesses in the city are also facing a fall in trade but that is no consolation to us." They chuckled; at last the youngsters have got thoughts on business. "The fall is equal at the factory and the store, the store through lack of customers and the factory are not getting the orders from the various warehouses as in the past." They each sat back in their chairs and quietly toyed with the situation.

Dan stood up, right. "How does this sound? Fred, how about making the feet of a Welsh Dresser a Ball and Claw and a slight adjustment to the top shelf with a decorative plaque and increase the price of our dining room suite by 5%. What I am really saying is, make the kitchen table and chairs a little different to the ones we have on display. Then we will advertise it in the paper as a special new range, (calling it whatever name we come up with) it will cost the same if you pay cash or take advantage of our credit system. If a cash customer should start haggling, Alan knows that he can discount up to 5%. Frank, I know that you will be advising but that is as far as you go, you are not well enough to start working. Betty, you have the price, I would suggest you make the salesmen a list showing 2, 3, or the 5%, so if they are caught up in the haggling process the price is at their fingertips, this will make the salesman look more professional if he can reply to the customers offer quickly." Dan turned to Betty, "Congratulations, I understand you are getting married in about one year's time." The way Alan and Betty laugh together, touch and look at each other he thought, she is marrying the wrong man. Betty is a tall slim attractive young lady and very popular in the store and very efficient in her job.

Fred agreed, He thought it a good gimmick and if it should kick start trade it will be well worth the effort, the only thing now is to find suitable variations without upsetting the jigs and the machinery settings, Frank laughingly said, "You are more than capable Fred, you said you are good," this brought a lot of laughter. Fred joined the laughter too. "What you are saying Dan, is to advertise and promote the new suite as a special offer, right! I agree if the rest of you do," they all nodded their heads in agreement. "Will you all put your thinking caps on and come up with an attractive name for the new suite. There are so many choices, Cromwell Suite, Buckingham Suite or Windsor Suite. There are unlimited names we can choose from but we must find a name that catches the imagination of the public to create that "Must Have" feeling."

"We have had an enquiry from a local school asking to visit the Basement; one teacher has been explaining what happened during the war and how the enemy set up these sleeper units who will raise their heads in the event of an invasion. They would like to come on a Saturday morning as their parents are coming with them, I would suggest we allow this to happen but bring them through the store entering the basement down the stairs behind the organ. My thinking is this, once their parents have crossed the threshold to the store, they would be quite comfortable to call another day, they could be future customers." "You devious devil Fred Wharton, yes, you are but good thinking."

The visit was arranged for the following Saturday morning. The girls will have to build up their stocks of sweets and goodies that children buy as they leave the basement through the craft shop.

*

Dan was surprised to receive a telephone call from the company solicitor requesting him to ring and make an appointment to meet him urgently to discuss a situation, which has just risen. Fred and Dan were most intrigued and could not wait to get an appointment. Fred phoned Frank and put him in the picture and told him they would visit him when they had been to the solicitor's office.

They both went along to the solicitor's office, he had coffee ready for them and they just chatted about nothing in particular and then he took out a sheet of paper. "He shook them both by saying that the owner of the cinema is prepared to sell them the property but they must make a decision in three days. A German, Switzerland consortium wants him to sell the property to them, for why, he is at a loss to know why; He is being bombarded by them, so the owner's wish to sell to stop being harried by these people. In view of all the work your company has put into the building, the owner thinks you should have first refusal and it will not become a biding war, the price quoted to your company will remain the same whatever the consortium should come up with because he does not trust that crowd."

The solicitor said, "He thought it to be a very good offer and they should consider carefully before giving an answer, he contacted me as I dealt with the legal transaction when you first took the building over. The building is in a premium site for retailing, I do know, if I was in your position and could afford to take on a mortgage I would snatch his hand off." "We must discuss it with the other director but we will give you an answer tomorrow, at this moment in time I would think we would take up his offer."

Fred went back to his office and telephoned Lance and put him in the picture, "When Lance answered the phone and listened to what Fred had to say, he started stuttering, he couldn't get his words out. "What on earth is going on Fred?" "Dan and I are going to discuss it with Frank and we intend call on Mr Blake our retired banker for his opinion." Dan telephoned Mr Blake and arranged to pick him up on the way to visit Frank. Before Fred could put the phone down, Lance went on to say, "If you had owned the property when the gold was found, you could have fought the treasury for ten percent of the gold's value. What else is there I wonder?"

When they arrived at Franks house Bella made coffee for them and all the usual chit-chat took place, coffee finished, Bella got up to leave the room but Dan said, "You stay Bella, you were involved when we first started," from her facial expression she was pleased to stay. Dan told them all that had taken place at the solicitors, Fred brought out any points that Dan overlooked. They discussed the advantage of owning the property by paying the requested figure as opposed to renting, which, could be increased or their tenancy terminated by any new owner. The whole set up appears a little sinister like the rest of the happenings in the past.

*

Frank phoned Simon at the factory asking him to bring all the up to date accounts, money in the bank both in the Fifth Column and DFF. The reason is Simon, we are discussing the purchase of some property, this put Simons mind at rest, for a moment or two, he wondered if they were checking up on him in view of his previous hic-up but if they did they would find he had done nothing wrong, he had learned his lesson.

Simon collected all the papers together and went straight to his father's house; Bella was pleased to see him. Mr Blake spread all the papers out on the table and got busy with pen and paper, he and Simon spent several minutes going through the accounts. He looked up from the account sheets, smiled and said, "Your Company is in a very healthy state, if you would like me to work with your solicitor I will do so willingly, I feel sure my colleague at the bank will arrange the mortgage."

Dan suggested that they should go ahead with the purchase of the old cinema, both Fred and Frank agreed with him. "Right Mr Blake, we will leave you to deal with the money and the legal side of the business as we have in the past but I will phone our solicitor to tell him we are going ahead and Mr Blake will work with him." "Simon, we will leave you to deal the paper work but keep us up to date, okay?" That evening Fred telephoned Lance to tell him that they were going ahead with the purchase of the cinema, he replied, "Fred, I look forward to the next few weeks."

CHAPTER 18

Sam made arrangements to check the progress of the children now several weeks have passed since the operation. The local hospital has been very cooperative in putting the facilities at his disposal. The first four that he checked were exactly as he hoped to find and replaced the plaster cast with a lightweight bandage, which, made the child feel a little more mobile but they were instructed not to start trying to walk without help, otherwise all the good work would be undone. The two nurses lectured both the children and the parents on the do's and don'ts, and emphasised the importance of taking care, as this is the critical time of the healing process. The hospital was very kind as it allowed the children to collect and take home the elbow crutches on loan but they had to be returned.

Everything appeared to be going well until the fifth child arrived, his foot had not healed in the position as Sam hoped, fortunately the bone had not knitted properly so he was able to manipulate and put another full plaster caste on to maintain the correct position, he was at a loss how the bone had not knitted, which, was a good thing under the circumstances. He had two children to replace with a full plaster caste, he was disappointed but the nurses were of the opinion that two out of seven was very good but Sam did not feel that way.

The nurses were delighted when Margery picked them up and took them back to her house for them to stay the night. Plans were made for Sam and the nurses to deal with the remaining two children the following morning and he also wanted to check on the two that he had to replace the plaster caste. The nurses got themselves bathed and dressed up and Dan got ready to go out for dinner but unbeknown to Dan, Margery had planned with Mary to join them, just as they were about to leave the door bell rang, it was Mary and Fred all dressed up and ready to go, Fred just looked at Dan and smiled.

The following morning the two remaining children were seen and Sam was delighted with their progress and the children were overcome when he put just a lightweight dressing on their foot but here again the nurses insisted that they take care and they were given instruction how to use the elbow crutches. Sam met the two who he had put back in the heavy type of plaster caste, they were a little disappointed but they were persuaded to be more careful this time. After a discussion with the nurses

Sam agreed to allow them to borrow a pair of elbow crutches, the nurses instructed the children and their parents how they were to be used to keep the weight off the foot, otherwise it would never heal. You have only yourselves to blame that the foot did not remain as it was positioned during the operation; you have been putting weight on the foot.

*

Simon spoke to Fred when he arrived at the factory; the purchase of the cinema is going ahead smoothly, the bank has deposited the money with the vendor's solicitor, it now only requires his signature to complete the deal. The solicitor is amazed the way the consortium keeps increasing the offer to purchase the building; the last offer is almost double the asking price. There something sinister going on, in fact the situation is becoming explosive, why do they want this building? Mr Blake assures me that all the necessary insurances are in place.

Fred told Dan all that was happening with the sale, this consortium must know that the currency and gold has been removed from the building. I realise that land is at a premium but even if they demolished the cinema they would not recoup their outlay from the sale of the land. Lance telephoned Fred enquiring how the property sale was progressing, he was really amused when Fred told him that the consortium was throwing money at the vendor in an effort to get him to change his mind and sell the property to them. Fred, "I wish I had a fortune-teller's glass ball," "Fred chuckled, so do I."

The company solicitor telephoned Fred to tell him that the completion date will be delayed as the owner was attacked yesterday and had his left arm broken and he is left handed. His solicitor is going to arrange for two judges to attend his office and witness the vendors signature writing with his right hand, he, will be very pleased when the sale is completely wrapped up. The vendor is receiving unsolicited phone calls during the night, just to disturb his sleep.

*

Mary and Fred have become proud Grandparents to a baby boy whom they call Terry; he was born a very healthy child weighing 5lb. To Fred's delight, his family and friends say that Terry is a smaller version of Fred. They are baby-sitting this evening to allow Salina and Arne to join

Lillian and Richard for an evening out. The real reason for their get-together is to discuss the future of MBM Displays, Mary, Bella and Margery are prepared to hand over the reins, they are finding it difficult getting in and out of windows as in the past. Gwen cannot cope with her baby daughter and work, she has decided to discontinue window dressing and become a full time mother but she enjoys helping on a Sunday in the craft shop.

The four of them visited a restaurant, which is owned and run by a friend of Arne. The evening went with a swing, the food was excellent and the restaurant has a wonderful atmosphere but when the owner joined them for coffee and drinks, Arne said, "Why do you look so miserable?" Lee looked up, "Business is so bad that the overheads are eating into my capital." "Have you tried advertising, offering special food on different nights, why not advertise on the local radio, or would you like us to organise an advert on the local cinema screen?"

"How much will it cost?"

"We will stand 50% of the cost until your business turns around."

Lee was called away to deal with a customer, Lillian turned to Arne, "We are not an advertising agency Arne," Richard said, "We are now, I think that advertising agencies have a very rosy future." Salina suggested that they should enquire if they could rent the area on the stage behind the screen in The Fifth Column building and open an advertising agency, we could practise advertising on the screen. The four of them sat discussing their new venture but they must keep their interior decorating and window display business under control, they would need the capital to keep them afloat until the agency takes off.

MBM made a formal request to Dan and his directors, applying to rent a space in the old cinema as they had discussed in the restaurant. It was all kept very formal and on a business footing, Arne and Richard were called to a meeting in the boardroom at the factory; they went along, armed with all their plans and expectations for their future advertising agency. The directors were very impressed with the business approach displayed to back up their request. The three directors agreed to MBM's request and offered their best wishes in the venture. "The rent for the area will be calculated on the square footage you will require," said Dan with a smile on his face. "Now to enable you to get started, you can take over the area you need and you can delay any payment for three months, that should give a good breathing space but we expect you to take out

Public Indemnity Insurance from now." Arne and Richard could not believe their good fortune, they agreed readily.

Arne and Richard set to work on the planned advert and they agreed to include the two girls. The first step is to photograph the Chefs working away in the kitchen, which must be in a clinical condition. The camera will continue scanning the bar and the restaurant with people seated at the tables eating and drinking. In the background a cultured voice will be heard describing the special offers served in luxury surroundings, introducing Lee as the owner and headwaiter, he will ensure the customers receive the best of attention. The restaurant's address and telephone number will be shown at the bottom of the screen throughout the advert.

The advert will gradually fade but as it does so Lee is shown waving and the background voice is saying that Lee looks forward to your visit to his restaurant. Obviously, the photography and the message it portrays will have to be repeated and altered many times before we all agree. The message must be very powerful as it will only be shown for approximately 50 seconds and in that short space of time you have to convince the customers that it is where they should eat. That is how Arne and myself thinks it should be filmed, Salina and Lillian both agreed that they should go ahead and when they see it on the screen a vote can be taken. One thing we must stress to the photographer, permission is obtained from the people seated at the tables for us to use their picture in the advert.

CHAPTER 19

Lance received a message from his office telling him that Mrs Hester had returned from her holiday in Germany. The following morning he caught a train to Newcastle to visit Mrs Hester as he had been instructed to do by his boss Ken Lee. Arriving on the doorstep, he rang the doorbell and a tall, slim attractive young lady opened the door, "Are you Mrs Hester?" "I am," Lance showed her his pass "May I come in?" She stood to one side to allow Lance to enter, he was shown into a beautifully decorated room, French windows, which opened to a well laid out garden, obviously it is being attended to by an excellent gardener, very professional.

"Mrs Hester may I suggest that you take a seat as I have some very sad news to tell you." Her face was expressionless, "Your husband died in the course of his duty as an Intelligence Officer," her facial expression never changed. "I have been expecting this to happen, he was such a violent man with an uncontrollable temper and on many occasions on a night out he would pick a fight with someone during the evening. One instance he put a man into hospital with a broken jaw and his attack was unprovoked. The police called and told him that he would be charged with causing bodily harm but for some unknown reason the charge was dropped."

"You might be thinking, why isn't she crying or showing some remorse on the death of her husband, I have nothing left for Horace. I have ended up in hospital three times over the last two years with him taking his anger out on me, apart from being taken into hospital, he is always hitting me on the slightest pretence, his food is cold, the custard is lumpy or his favourite shirt is not in the cupboard ready for him to wear, in fact, I think he has become a schizophrenic. My holiday in Germany was spent making arrangements for my return home to live with my parents; I intended to leave Horace, I cannot stand any more of his bullying."

"I first met Horace at a college in Germany, he came to the college from England to study and learn the German language. I was just a teenager, we became very friendly and as it progressed we spent several weekends together and I became pregnant. When I told him that I was pregnant he went berserk, he beat me saying that I had been cheating on him and the child was not his. I was admitted to the local hospital and

91

was kept there for three weeks; I had three broken ribs, one of which had punctured my lung and several broken fingers that were caused by him slamming the door on my hand as I tried to get away from him. He had used my stomach as a punch bag. I lost the baby. Sorry to go on like this but you can understand my feelings towards Horace. When he took me to the hospital he told them that I had fallen down two flights of stairs, which I had to agree."

"My family were up in arms when I told them that I intended marrying Horace and move to England. The family have taken over the hotel, which my uncle Hans parents had owned but both of his parents were killed during an air raid and the building badly damaged. My family took the hotel on and they have rebuilt it and it is now a flourishing business that is why they want me to return to Germany to help them. They are very concerned for my safety."

Lance sat patiently listening to her story, he felt so sorry for her; he must have been difficult to live with. "One thing I must ask you, would you like the authorities to make the funeral arrangements?" "Yes please, I would be most grateful." "Would you like them to help with sale of this house if you still intend returning to Germany?" "It isn't our house, it belongs to a financial consortium based in Switzerland, and we have lived in this house rent-free ever since we arrived in England."

"Have you any idea why he was given this house rent-free?" "I have no idea but he received a lot of visitors, when they arrived I was pushed out of the room and Horace ensured that I was out of earshot. I thought he was an intelligence officer for Germany but it appears that he was employed by Britain. She smiled for the first time, perhaps for both sides; sorry I said that, it couldn't happen. When I did ask him how we were living in this beautiful house rent-free, he went into one of his tantrums. He started shouting and told me to mind my own business but when I insisted that as his wife I should know, he just started hitting me, look; these bruises are from a severe beating about four weeks ago. I feel sure that my uncle Hans and my cousin Otto will help me, I will only be taking a few of my personal possessions and I shall leave the rest."

Lance suddenly remembered what Fred had told him about the purchase of the Fifth Column building, it is a Swiss: consortium that is trying to out-bid Fred and his fellow directors for the property. He gave her his card and told her that the funeral will take place here at the local crematorium. "Thank you for coming to tell me about the death of my husband, I do hope that I have not come across as a hard faced bitch."

"Not at all, listening to your story I feel you have experienced a most unpleasant marriage and I feel very sorry for you. You have my card, if you have any problem at all, ring my office and your problem will be dealt with straight away." Before leaving, he called next door to thank the lady for telephoning his office.

Arriving back in his office, he compiled a complete report of what had taken place and sent it by messenger to his boss Ken Lee marked urgent. After completing the report, the office girl brought him a cup of coffee into his office, he leaned back thinking what had transpired over the past forty-eight hours, his brain stopped working and he fell asleep. The ringing of the telephone woke him; it was his boss, telling Lance to report to his office the following morning.

*

Mark called a meeting of the "Daisy Charity" trustees. Sam had attended to seven of the applicants but the remaining thirteen have been X-rayed at their local hospital and the plates were sent for Sam to study. After discussion with their doctors, it had been decided that they were unable to help all of them. Eleven of the applicants are elderly, in fact, three are retired and their own doctors did not think that they would benefit from the operation; it would be very difficult to manipulate the bones at their time of life. The remaining two children are aged three and four, it was agreed that at that age the operation could be carried out successfully but not just yet, as the coffers are nearly empty.

"Obviously you will be writing to the unsuccessful applicants Mark, when you do, make no mention that the decision is age related, otherwise we shall receive a lot of criticism but that unfortunately is the situation" Mark agreed," I will write to the eleven unsuccessful applicants advising of our decision, telling them that it is regretted but their own doctors discussed the cases with the surgeon and based on that discussion it was decided that we couldn't undertake to operate on them. It is disappointing to have to write with their decision, which makes your application unsuccessful. However, modern medicine is constantly progressing, if there is chance of the operation being made successful at a later date, you will be contacted."

Now gentlemen, the two young children whom we think will benefit from the operation; do we go to their local hospital or do we bring them up here? What ever is decided, bear in mind our lack of funds and I do not think the public will respond again so soon after their last cash boost. Dan said "We could contact their own local press, asking the readers in their immediate locality if they would help to finance the child's special operation, putting the child's photograph in the paper. Better still, I will ask the editor of our own local paper to contact the editors of other papers and tell them the story; I think it might work because the news from this charity has made an impact on his circulation figures." I have received several more application letters from various parts of the country requesting help. Mark told them that he had written back asking for the full details of their deformity and if possible a photograph and also their age. When I receive this information, I will advise any suitable applicant that their name will be put on the waiting list. The ones who are not regarded as suitable by Sam, I will write to them as I am going to the previous eleven people.

CHAPTER 20

The company solicitor notified Fred that the purchasing of the old cinema now known as The Fifth Column has been completed and all the legal requirements have been met, D.F.F are now the new owners of the Building and the Freehold. Mr Blake has arranged all the necessary insurances to cover all the eventualities of the business from today. Fred passed on the good news to both Dan and Frank, while speaking to Dan he asked him to meet the next day in the store, to carry out the interviews with the two applicants who have replied to the advert offering the balcony to rent as a café.

They met as planned at 9.30, the first applicant was due at 10.30 and they thought it would give them time to make sure they were both singing from the same song sheet. The company executive arrived and they liked his pleasant manner straight away and it appears that he represents a small local catering company with their eye to the future. He proceeded to show them some rough drawings, which indicated that they intended putting a lot of time and money into their project. They planned to level the floor and make the projection room into a kitchen to enable them to serve any meal requested. He went on to say that in view of their expenditure, they would like to have a long-term lease set up legally, both replied of course this would the solicitors deal all with. Dan asked him who owned the company, the man just smiled, the bank owns most of the company at present but my friend and our wives own the small remaining amount at present but we have great hopes for the future. Fred could not restrain himself, "My friend here and our wives started like that, I feel sure you will succeed." They shook hands and promised to write to him in a few days. When he had left, Dan turned to Fred, "The next applicant who we will meet this afternoon will have to be good" and Fred just nodded

Fred and Dan were ready to receive the second applicants at 2.30 to discuss the renting of the balcony. Three men came marching in, Fred went to introduce Dan and himself but the man just brushed him to one side, "Where is the balcony to rent?" Fred just pointed; the man started talking to his colleagues, totally ignoring Dan and Fred. He turned to them saying, "Money is no object as we are one of the leading catering companies in France and we want a completely free hand. We will want to keep the store open two late nights each week until 10 o'clock, to make it a viable investment." "I am sorry but the store closes at six each evening." "In that case, you will have to arrange staff to work late." They went around measuring saying how the projection room will have to be taken apart. Dan told them that their application will be considered, kindly leave your companies address to enable us to contact you. "To hell with him, Fred said, No way is he being allowed in this building."

That evening they visited Frank and put him completely in the picture and the question of tenancy was discussed at great length but the first applicant had got Dan's vote before he had even met the second one. All three decided that the local catering company would fit in better with their own set up. So, the local company was advised that they can go ahead making plans and as with Jenny's case, they would be given two months rent free from the day they open to give them the opportunity to get established before having to worry about rent. The second applicant was advised that their application had been unsuccessful, thanking them for their time.

*

The board meeting chaired by Dan had been called to receive the past months trading figures from Simon after introducing a special furniture promotion, hoping that the falling trade figures have been halted. Simon handed each member of the board a sheet depicting the past months sales in figures and in graph form, there were smiles and laughter and the promotion had paid off. "The Buckingham Suite" had proved to be popular and had halted the downward slide of trade; in fact, the graph displayed a slight increase, "Well done lads."

The next item on the agenda is an application, which has been received from French Television Company, asking for permission to make a short Documentary Film of the Fifth Column and the basement. A spokesman for the TV Company said that the discovery of the basement and its contents has caught the public's imagination. They think that the documentary will achieve very good ratings in the viewing charts.

The TV company claims to have researched the building itself, the cinema was built in 1894, designed and built under the watchful eye of Frank Matcham. This building is a smaller version of The Grand Theatre in Blackpool, which was built the same year; they both have the footprints of Frank Matcham all over them.

The elaborate decorated ceiling and the two boxes one either side of the screen and the balcony are decorated with ornate scrolls, curves, or other symmetrical ornamentation often referred to as baroque. According to the French company, The Fifth Column was the forerunner before the building of the much larger theatre. I am not in the position to say that these facts are true but they are just as the spokesman for the French Company stated when applying for the permission to go ahead with their plan, if access is granted.

If however, we do decide to give them access to this property, we will expect them to make a substantial donation to the Daisy Charity." Fred came in suggesting that they mull this over in our minds before making any decision. Frank and Dan knew the road that Fred was taking. After the meeting Fred telephoned Lance telling him of the French TV Company's request. "Thanks Fred I will pass this information on to my boss, Ken Lee, he will have the company investigated and I will come back to you. Incidentally, we could not trace the French Catering Company who applied to convert the balcony to a café. The plot thickens Fred."

*

Dan visited the local newspaper office and asked to speak with the editor; he came to his office door and invited Dan in. Dan then explained the situation regarding the two three-year-old boys who unfortunately had been born with a deformed foot. It can be corrected but they will have to wait, as the coffers of the charity are almost empty. The seven children that have been operated on and have been closely monitored, these cases have just about exhausted the funds; the books are available to any one wishing to examine them. I would like you to speak to the editors of the local newspaper in other towns, to print an article and a photograph showing the children hoping that the public will donate some money.

The editor leaned back in his chair. "Have a cup of coffee," he smiled at Dan, "Yes, I will speak to the editors; in fact, I know most of them personally." They sat drinking their coffee. When Dan had finished he got out of his chair and said, "Right Ted, I will leave you now I have passed our problem over to you." They shook hands and Dan left.

Several weeks later, Ted telephoned Dan asking him to call in his office. He told Dan the editors to whom he spoke had published the child's photograph and explained why they were asking for donations. "The result for one child was very good but the other one had a very poor response. The editor concerned is going to repeat the article but this time he is going to clearly show the deformed foot in the picture. He has written an article telling how a neighbouring town has responded and the operation is going ahead due to the reader's generosity but our boy will have to wait until the bank balance of the Daisy Charity has built up. He made the point that the "Daisy Charity" does not receive any government funding and it is dependant entirely on the generosity of the public."

The editor rang Dan one week later telling him the repeated photograph had pricked the public's conscience and made them reach for their wallet, so much so, the editor will be sending you a substantial amount of money to allow the operation of the second child to go ahead.

Samuel was elated when told that sufficient money was available for both boys. He can now go ahead to hire an operating theatre and pay for the overnight stay for the children and their parents. Mark contacted the small private hospital near Chester and offered money for the hire of their operating theatre, in this instance the charity is in the position to pay any costs involved.

The owners of the hospital wrote back to Mark stating that they will allow Samuel to use their operating facilities on this occasion but they cannot allow it to become a regular occurrence. The sterilisation of all the instruments and also to ensure that the theatre itself is sterile is very costly, which, we did not charge you for on the previous occasion. However, we will offer you the same facilities as before but we cannot promise any help in the future.

The next step is to encourage the editors to advertise for some people to provide transport for the children and their parents. The editors went ahead with the advert in the papers and they were overwhelmed with the number of offers received, as with Ted, the articles in the newspapers relating to the children's deformity has made a distinct impact on their papers circulation. The two operations went ahead and appeared to go well; the two nurses came to assist Samuel and stayed with Dan and Margery, to avoid the tiring daily travel from Leeds. The nurses again thought they were on holiday as they were made so welcome and they accepted Margery's hospitality and stayed with them for further week.

CHAPTER 21

The funeral of Horace Hester was arranged at a small crematorium outside Newcastle. Quite a few attended the funeral; Ken Lee sent two of his agents from another part of the country to represent Horace's office colleagues. They managed to get a few photographs of the people present without being spotted. Mrs Hester's uncle, Hans Kayberg, escorted her and he had two men walking behind him as if they were his minders.

The clergy made no mention that Horace had been an intelligence officer. It was surprising the number of people who spoke to Mrs Hester; it was obvious that they knew her, not just strangers offering their condolences. After the funeral service they all retired to a local hotel where a finger buffet had been arranged. Hans escorted by his two minders approached the two agents and tried to engage them in conversation. He asked how long they had known Horace, they replied saying, "they had only had dealings with Horace quite recently. They explained that they have a business dealing with cameras for the film industry, Horace called to enquire about a camcorder and what discounts were available as he had joined a photography club."

When they arrived back in their office, they sent their boss, Ken Lee a full report and promised to send the pictures to him at a later date. Ken passed a copy of the report to Lance asking him to report to his office as he had some more information, which Lance would find to be disturbing.

Lance went to Ken's office, as he walked in. "Sit down Lance. I had Hans Kayberg investigated. When he applied to enter this country to join the German Embassy as an envoy, there were doubts about him being a suitable person to have in this country and take up his position. Now, this is the upsetting part of the investigation. The application made by Hans was discussed at great length, all the relevant details and information that had been gathered was forwarded to the Home Office as it was up to them to make the final decision."

" Eventually, the go ahead was given for Hans to enter the country and take up residence in the Embassy, the final decision was taken by two very senior Home Office officials. One month after the decision had been confirmed, one of the officials and his wife were killed in a car accident, six weeks later the second official was found dead at the bottom of his stairs. The inquest said that he had been drunk and had fallen down the stairs breaking his neck." Lance turned to Ken, "The more I hear these stories the more I become a little nervous for the people around the store." "What are they up to?"

The exhibition in the basement of the Fifth Column store is still attracting a lot of visitors, the adverts in the various newspapers have created a desire to come along and see for oneself. A coach company contacted Bella asking if the basement could be opened specially on one Wednesday afternoon to receive a small coach party. Bella and the other two were more than happy to accommodate their request and the exhibition benefited from a weekly coach party who always spent money in the craft shop on the way out. Margery was very surprised by the number of people asking if they had a tearoom and toilets, she discussed this with Bella and Mary; we must have a meeting to bring this point up.

The requested meeting was arranged with the directors of DFF, the owners of the building (their husbands). Frank, Fred and Dan were completely in the dark what to expect. Bella started the ball rolling by asking how much room could be obtained by the removal of the cold store room, which is now disconnected and not in use. It just stands there empty and taking up a lot of space. Margery then took over from Bella; she explained that the basement is becoming so popular that a local coach firm would like to make a permanent visiting arrangement on the Wednesday afternoon each week. The thing we find lacking is toilet facilities and as they are mainly elderly people who arrive on a Wednesday they regard this facility as a necessity and also they are asking the way to the tearoom, the caterers who will be operating the balcony can not object as the basement is entirely separate from the store.

Fred looked at Dan and Frank. "How the dickens can we find the room to accommodate their request?" Mary made the point that the numbers are not that great, the ladies facilities could exist with just one cubicle and the gents could have one stall and one flush toilet. Fred and Dan spent two days wandering around the basement wondering how to find the space required to meet the girl's request. The space taken up by the cold room could be utilised by converting it into a tearoom but it would only accommodate three tables at a pinch but then they would want a preparation room.

Fred suggested they had a word with Richard and Arne and see if they come up with a better solution. They went into the store and found MMB working away in their unit on the stage behind the screen. They explained their problem to them, they both agreed to have a look around the basement; Richard picked up a large surveyors tape measure and followed them into the basement. Arne turned to Dan, "Do you mind if you leave us to walk around and Richard and I can argue and when we have decided on an idea, we will give you a shout?" Dan turned to Fred, "Come along Fred we have been dismissed," this caused a lot of laughter, the bosses pushed off.

*

Dan and Fred were looking around the store, they stopped to speak to the manager Alan and he told them that trade was picking up. While they were talking to Alan, The young man walked in who had been given the go ahead converting the balcony into a café. He greeted both Fred and Dan, "May I have a quiet word with you both?" "Surely, come into the office." All three went into the office and when they were seated, Dan said, "Now what is the problem?" He replied, "We really appreciated your offer to create a café in the balcony but unfortunately we cannot undertake to do that, I will explain why."

"As you know the floor will have to be levelled and according to three different contractors it will take a lot of structural ironwork, which will involve the local planning office. In view of the work involved and the three estimates for doing the job it is way out of our league. Thank you once again for giving me the opportunity but I must say no." Dan said "I cannot say I am not disappointed because I am but I admire your frankness, no contract has yet been brought up and no signatures attached, we both wish you every success in your business in the future." The young man got up from his seat shook hands with them both and left. Fred looked at Dan, "That is a disappointment but I did not realise there was so much work involved."

Arne came out of his office, seeing Fred and Dan he called "Have you minute to spare?" "Certainly." They both went to Arne's office, as they got seated Richard walked in. Arne looked at them, "We have spent a lot of time trying to come up with the answer to the girl's request and we have several reservations. The cold room can be removed but it is built with steel girders on the sides but here comes the snag, the girders across the top supports the ceilings. The cost of removing and replacing with RSJ's could be _very_ costly and with a job like this the planning office would get involved and they are quite picky about such a structural job like this. We would not recommend going ahead with this alteration."

"The one suggestion we have to offer is there is a large area at the back of the cinema; someone had the foresight of leaving sufficient room to convert to a car park sometime in the future. We suggest that a single storey unit be built behind the cinema in the large yard; it will still leave room for a car park if you wanted one at a later date. It would be a purpose built unit incorporating all the facilities required, a tea room with all various counters and preparation room, infact, it could be made just as you want it to be. The toilet situation would be straightforward, they could be finished with tiled walls and ceiling to save on decoration, it could be made into a plush facility. The stairs from the basement can be turned to come out in the new building, Richard and I have come to the same conclusion, the new unit would only cost a little more than messing about with the basement which would never be to your satisfaction."

" Richard and myself can deal with plans for you to submit to the local planning office and I cannot see any problem, I feel confident that you would get the go ahead." Richard said, "Not only would the basement benefit but also access can be made from the store to the tearoom or the toilets." Dan agreed, "That it sounds a very good idea but could you come up with some figures to give us some idea of the final cost, I appreciate that the figures would be approximate. We are most grateful for your expertise and help. One thing bothers me, would the new stairway affect our present stairs?" "No Dan, as the girls pointed out, most of the visitors are elderly; we would suggest a new staircase with rails and a lower tread to make it easy for the elderly to climb the stairs to enter the tearoom or the toilets." "Right lads, you go ahead with the plans but do not forget to give us an approximate figure."

*

The plans were drawn up and all the family were invited to join Dan and Margery to inspect and offer any suggestions, one or two minor adjustments were made. "Right lads, carry out the alterations to the plans and then we will submit them."

They were all taken by surprise how quickly the planning office passed the plans and were given the go ahead, Fred could not understand how quickly they have been approved. He contacted Ian, the decorator asking if he could recommend a builder. Ian suggested Gerry Latham who had just started his own building business; "I am not sure whether he could finance such a project, I will ask him to pop in and have a word with you Fred." Two days later Gerry called into the store asking to speak to Fred. The office phoned around and when found him, they told him that a young man was waiting to meet him. Fred immediately left the factory to make his way to the store; before he left, he telephoned Dan asking him to meet him at the store.

Gerry was getting a little jumpy, wondering what these people were like but when Dan and Fred walked in and shook hands he felt completely at ease. They all went into the office where all the plans were spread out on the table. "Now then Gerry do you think you can handle a job like this?" asked Fred. "Oh! Yes, although I have only recently started my own business I have contacts with all different tradesmen, I have access to an excellent bricklayer who will help me, I help him on jobs doing the joinery work and another friend who is a qualified electrician, so you can see we can work as a good team."

Gerry asked if he could take a copy of the plans home with him, to study what is required. "One thing I can see at a glance is the entrance to the facilities from inside the store will need to come six feet into the store for the stairs from the basement through the floor boards, otherwise it will mean tunnelling from the basement," remarked Gerry. "Good lord you are right, we missed that one Fred, and I am surprised the planning office has not queried that."

Two days later Gerry arranged to meet Dan and Fred in the store; "Yes my colleagues and I are confident we can do a first class job" Dan told Gerry that when they first started their own business they experienced cash flow problems, which caused all sorts of problems; we could help you if you wish. Would you like us to pay you weekly or monthly the cost of materials plus your labour costs? Do not think for a minute that I am being patronising but this way it will save you money by not having an over draught for which the banks charge a lot of money." "That is a very generous gesture Mr Green," "Gerry, my name is Dan and he is Fred, okay?"

" Have you given any thought to rerouting the staircase into the store? We can discuss that at a later date." "When do you intend making a start?" "I hope to start by getting the footings in one day next week; we can then get the okay from the council after the footings have been inspected to start the building." "That is quick," "I have a friend with a mechanical digger, so that makes it easier and quicker, the concrete will be poured straight into the trenches from a wagon. Bingo, the footings are in."

"One thing I would like you to think about is the colour of the tiles for the toilet area, I realise it will be a while before we get that far. The reason I mention this, is because different coloured tiles are being manufactured and I have found that the wives of the business men for whom I have worked, played hell when they have used plain white tiles, they said that they are old fashioned," "Yes Gerry, we will pass the choice of colours to our wives. Even if they choose and then do not like them when the job is completed, we shall still be blamed said Dan chuckling away."

CHAPTER 22

Dan and Margery went to dinner with Fred and Mary. During the course of the evening the question of coloured tiles came up for discussion, "Ladies, the selection of the coloured tiles is your responsibility, if they are wrong, you are to blame." Fred was having a real belly laugh, "Bella will be included, pity that Frank is not well enough to join us."

Mary said, " She did not want to stand behind the counter selling cups of tea and cooking food when the unit is completed," "That goes for me too said Margery," Dan looked at Fred, "That is what they call support." Mary made faces at Dan. Mary suggested that they contacted the local catering firm who was unable to take on the balcony conversion due to the very high costs; he and his staff are local which is a good thing.

"What a wonderful idea, I will ask the office girl to write him and ask him to call into the store." Margery turned to Dan, "You do not refer to it as a rented space these days, it is called a "Franchise" and I bet the catering company will jump at the chance." They all agreed that it was an excellent idea, no staff problems or entering a field, which we know little about.

Several days later, Robert called into the store; fortunately both Fred and Dan were present in the store. They called Robert into their office and the plans for the unit were all laid out on the table, Dan pointed out the size of the tearoom area, which will give plenty of room to stamp your own personality on the café. "Now then young man, would you like to take out the Franchise on the tearoom? I do not know how it works but I will find out."

"The tearoom would be yours entirely, to equip with all the electrical gadgets you need for cooking or drinks, in fact, you could treat it as your own as you or your wives will be in charge," this brought a smile to his face. "Gerry is making a start on the building next week, when he gets to the interior; you should get involved to decide where you want the counters, preparation room or whatever you need. Do get involved before the stud walls are erected."

" I would say yes today but as a matter of courtesy I must discuss it with my partner and our wives. "May I ring tomorrow?" "Certainly, there is no rush and we have not mentioned it to any other company." Several days later Robert telephoned requesting permission to bring his partner and their wives to have sight of the plans and the lay out of the store.

Fred told him to come along and bring them with him it will give you some idea what is required."As I said before, the electrical equipment for making meals or drinks will be your responsibility." The four people arrived; Fred escorted them into the office and laid the plans out on the table, "If you have any questions you will find me in the store."

Half an hour had elapsed before they emerged from the office and they went up to Fred, "At the moment we would say yes, we would welcome the challenge. However, we would like to see the layout as the building is going up." "I have already told you Robert, I would suggest you come along and weigh it all up before the stud walls are erected in place." "Great, we will be in touch again Mr Wharton, is it okay if we pop in from time to time as the building is going up?" "Of course, any time, you are most welcome."

*

Gerry called into the store to advise Fred that he would be making a start on the planned extension behind the cinema the following morning. Gerry and a surveyor spent the morning placing pegs and indicators for the depth of the footings, as required by the building regulations. After lunch Gerry's friend came chugging around the corner driving his mechanical digger. The driver set to work and they both worked late into the evening to complete the trenches and the base ready for the cement.

Gerry was up early and back on the on the job knowing the large lorry with a revolving drum full of cement would arrive at 8.30am ready to pour the cement into the trenches and a wide part of the base. The driver manoeuvred the vehicle to pour the cement into the various parts of the footings to save using the wheelbarrow and shovelling but some shovelling was necessary to level off. During the day Gerry telephoned the planning office asking them to inspect the concrete footings, hoping they would call the next day. He could not start the brickwork until he was given the official go ahead.

He was kept waiting two days before the planning officers came to check the footings, they spent a full hour wandering round and checking every detail against the plans. Gerry was a little apprehensive when he explained the variation to the submitted plans with regard to the stairway. He explained that they had decided to bring the stairs through the floorboards into the store rather than tunnelling and using ironwork to support the ceiling of the staircase. Both of the officials agreed that it is a much better idea rather than disturb the original footings.

Gerry took the officials into the store and introduced them to Fred, there was the usual round of handshaking, Fred ushered them into his office and the office girl brought in refreshments. Fred asked the two officials if they could foresee any problems in the building now they had studied the plans. "When you are ready to connect to drains you must make an application as a planning officer will need to be present when you open the main drains, we have checked that all the necessary pipes were put in place before the cement was poured in, so it should all go well."

They wandered back outside to look at the building again, three men walked up to one of the planning officers and said, "What is going on here?" "Building an extension, why do you ask?" "Just curious, has all the planning permission been obtained?" "Yes, I am here in the capacity of a planning officer to check that the plans are being adhered to; this does not concern you," with that, the three men walked away. He turned to Gerry "Do you know that man?" "No, never seen them before." Fred saw a tall blonde man talking to Gerry and the officials." Were they being nosey Gerry?" "Yes they wanted to know what we are doing and if planning permission has been obtained."

Fred did not make any comment but he returned to his office and telephoned Lance telling him that our friends have been around. He told him what conversation had taken place. "Fred, we shall know what they are up to one day." When Gerry was alone putting the tools away the same man came up to him and said, "Here is my telephone number, give me a ring when you are going to break through the cinema wall and I will make it worth your while." He went into the store, he found Fred and told him what the man had said, "It is odd," said Gerry, Fred just smiled.

CHAPTER 23

Mark received a telephone call from a Mr Nash asking if he could meet up with the trustees of the Daisy Charity, the meeting was arranged for several days later. When Mr Nash arrived, he introduced himself to all of the trustees as Bill Nash and Margery had organised tea and biscuits to create a social atmosphere

"The reason I wanted to speak with you is because my little granddaughter has been born with her right foot at a 45% angle, she is now eighteen months of age and I have been recommended to enlist the help of Samuel Stromsburg, who, I am told is the best orthopaedic specialist in the country. I would like him to advise on my granddaughters condition with the prospect of correcting her deformity." Mark explained that, as the bank account of the trust is almost empty; he could not foresee an early appointment.

He turned to Mark, "Would it be possible for me to speak to him? Have you his phone number? I can give him a call and perhaps we could meet for lunch." Mark wrote Sam's telephone number on a card and passed it to him saying "It might be difficult as he lives in Leeds." "Not at all Mark, I own a Woollen Mill in Batley and I live in Dewsbury, it could be very convenient."

It was arranged for Samuel to meet Mr Nash in Dewsbury for lunch, Sam walked into the restaurant, when he mentioned Mr Nash's name the head waiter said, "Kindly follow me sir," he took Sam to a table where a man was seated, he rose to his feet and introduced himself as Bill and you are Sam, "Do you agree?" "I most certainly do Bill" They ordered their meal and a drink and then they started chatting. While they were eating Bill told Sam the story about his granddaughter's problem. "Mark must have told you that we are unable to undertake any more operations for a while, as the trusts coffers are almost empty. We have carried out nine; I think that is the figure, anyhow, hiring the x-ray machinery and then the operating theatres it has cost much more than we had bargained for." "Sam, money is no problem, whatever cash you need I can supply."

"Sam, have you ever thought about getting a mobile clinic incorporating your own X-ray machinery, operating theatre and a sleeping area for the child and its parents, making it a complete self-contained unit?" "My goodness Bill, the trust could never think about such a project from the cost point alone." "Sam, raising the money is no problem. Let us go into the lounge for coffee."

"How much would such a scheme cost Sam?"

"I wouldn't hazard a guess at the moment Bill,"

"You find out and I will meet the cost."

"Bill; do you really mean that you would pay for a mobile medical centre to help a child in any part of the country." They had just got seated when several men walked into the lounge, when they saw Bill they walked over to join him, "Okay if we join you?" "Certainly, pull up a chair. Let me introduce you to the finest orthopaedic specialist in the country, some would say in Europe, Sam Stromsburg."

Bill then related what they had been discussing over lunch regarding the mobile clinic; "We are not sure at this moment if it is a practical proposition." One of the group said, "Of course it is possible but you will need to get the mobile clinic purpose built, Sam would have to be the main person advising on the layout, it is he who will be the one working in it." Another member of the group said,

"If you go ahead, I feel sure my Masonic Lodge, St John's, will make a donation towards the cost of the instruments,"

"Lions will make a donation," said another and so it went on, each pledging a donation from the various organisations to whom they belong. Sam turned to Bill saying,

"Are the people in Dewsbury and Batley always so generous?" Bill nodded his head;

"Yes Sam, in spite of the jokes about Yorkshire folk."

One of the group asked Sam if he could spare some time the following day,

"Surely" said Sam,

"Right, meet me in my office, my name is Ray Gibbs, here is my card." "Can you make it tomorrow? You can, good. I will ask my brother-in-law to come along, he is in the coach building business, if he is unable to cope with such an undertaking, he will know a company who can and he will be able to give some idea of the cost before you go too far."

Sam arrived home so excited, he went through every little detail of the meeting with his wife, she told him to simmer down and she poured him out a drink. He still could not contain himself, he had to ring both Mark and Fred, they too were delighted with the outcome but both said, "We will wait to see if it comes about."

*

Sam visited the office of Roy Gibbs as had been arranged, when he arrived he found that coffee was all laid on, ten minutes later Roy's brother in law came into the office, he was introduced to Sam as Bob Fraser, "We have never met but I have been told about you when you helped a friend of mine. Roy told me a little of what you are interested in having built."

"The trailer will have to be quite long and built to the maximum width allowed on the roads in this country. I would suggest an eight wheeled based pantechnicon for a smooth ride, which will protect its contents while it is being towed. Approaching the idea this way, the mobile can be towed to a hospital site and remain until you are satisfied with your patient's condition. I cannot foresee any problem with obtaining permission from the various hospital trusts to park in their grounds."

Bob laid a large sheet of paper out on the tabletop, "As I understand it you will need three compartments. The far end to be the operating theatre with a personal door and this unit can be hermetically sealed when sterilising the theatre prior to an operation. The next compartment is to accept the X-ray machinery with special lighting and finally, the sleeping area for a recovery room and provision for the nurse to be able move around the bed. A small bedroom for the parents to stay overnight, with their child and tea or coffee making facilities."

Sam turned to Bob, "Do you think you could work out an approximate figure to pass on to Bill"? "You will have to allow me a few days to come up with a figure, as I will have to work out the sizes of the compartments." "When you have designed a layout, would you mind if my two nurses have sight of your plan?" "Certainly Sam, they might see something that we have missed."

"Hold on Sam, we have missed something. A fresh water tank and a holding tank supported in a cradle underneath the trailer to take the water from the sink and the flush toilet. The holding tanks are so designed that the contents can be pumped out at any caravan or boating site, which is very hygienic. The fresh water tank can be topped up from any normal tap."

"Thank you for your time Bob, will you contact me when you have had time to look into the problems posed with such a project? When you are in Liverpool, why not call into the "Daisy Charity" shop and they will show you round, I feel sure you would enjoy the visit." Sam shook hands with Bob and Roy and left still on cloud nine.

CHAPTER 24

The family were invited to attend the Fifth Column on Sunday afternoon at 2pm. As they arrived, Arne, Richard and their wives jokingly showed them to their seats, the seats being the two rows that were suggested that should be left facing the screen. The screen displayed the large lettered DFF with the elderly gentleman wielding a mallet; it was just as it was shown on the first day the Fifth Column opened for business.

Richard stood in front of the family, "Arne and myself have spent many long hours producing what we are about to show you, in answer to the question shouted out, It is not a blue film," this caused a lot of laughter and clapping, someone shouted, "Why not"?

The picture on the screen gradually faded until the screen was blank, the screen came to life displaying large lettering, THE BIRTH OF DFF FURNITURE, and this was accompanied with the soft playing organ music, the music faded as the film came up on the screen, it showed men walking around in a forest, a well cultured voice took up the story of explaining that the men were looking around to select trees to be felled. A mechanical saw is used to cut down the selected trees and the trunks are then dragged off into the woods to the sawmill. The voice explained how the trunk was being cut into planks length wise and how they would be stacked to allow them to dry out and mature, normally they would remain stacked for about a year, the one thing he did point out, the planks are usually painted on the ends to prevent them drying out too quickly and splitting.

He went on to explain that various businesses would purchase the planks but in this case, several would be delivered to the DFF factory. The film showed Fred in the design office with various designs and plans, hanging from the wall the machine shop was the next step where the planks are machined into the many different shapes and sizes for the different pieces of furniture. Frank and Sam were filmed working on the machines or marking out the timber using templates to ensure correct sizes.

Roy is shown working in the cabinet shop, assembling the furniture as it arrives from the machine shop, once the furniture has been put together it is carefully scrutinised to ensure that it is up to DFF's high standard, when it has been accepted. The polishing shop is the next stop; here again the item is inspected after being polished. The manager of the despatch department is shown putting corrugated cardboard around the furniture to ensure that they reach the customer in pristine condition. The final film shot is of people sat in a dining room with several pieces of DFF furniture around them. The theme of the film is to show how proud DFF is of their products.

When the film came to the end, in large lettering it was shown as M.B.M. ADVERTISING AGENCY: Telephone Number: 222. 333. The voice repeated the telephone number and thanked every one for sharing the experience of visit to DFF Furniture with him. The end was greeted with a loud round of applause; Richard stood up. "It is hoped you enjoyed our efforts?"

"Now the reason we invited you all was to gather any criticism, in fact, any thing you might think might help to improve the presentation and we would welcome your comments. The film is available for DFF to purchase or they could rent it, if rented, we would up date from time to time," this was met with jeers and boo's and of course a lot of laughter. "You may remember the film was our offering on our first visit to the cinema." Dan looked around and he was surprised to see Alan seated next to Betty the chief cashier, he must regard her as family, I wonder if she still intends getting married next year, Dan wondered about that some time back "I found it very educational, some parts of furniture construction are most interesting, in fact, I bet some school teacher would enjoy showing this film to his class. As for renting the film, we must discuss that very carefully," said Dan, again much laughter.

Arne stood up and told them that their first effort was put together to help a friend of theirs whose restaurant business was losing money. As an experiment we put an advert together showing what goes on with such a business, the advert only lasts for fifty seconds. We used the same format as this one, showing what goes on in the background. It is surprising the amount of information and impact one can create on the screen in that short space of time. We approached the local cinemas to get this advert to be shown on their screens during the interval, we achieved success in both directions. The cinema made extra cash for showing the advert and the Restaurant benefited with a 15% trade increase, so it has encouraged us to expand in the advertising business. Fred came in, "Have you boys thought about making a training film, I feel sure some employers would welcome that?"

*

Gerry and his team started to lay the bricks on the extension as soon as the planning officials had given their approval that the footings corresponded to the plans, which had been submitted and approved. One week later, they had completed the brickwork; the fitting of the steel girder to support the building above the opening to the new extension took much longer and was more costly than they had planned due to the extended hire of a crane.

However, Gerry went into the store and told Fred that they intended to break through the wall into the extension the following morning. Fred asked Gerry to leave it until lunchtime, as he wanted a friend to be present. "Certainly." Fred telephoned Lance and he arranged to be at the store during the morning, in fact, he said he looked forward to visiting again. Fred suggested to Gerry that he should phone the number left by a gentleman who wished to be present to witness the break through. Gerry went into Fred's office to make the call, when he got through; a gruff voice said, "Yes, what do you want?" Gerry was taken aback with the man's attitude at the other end of the line. He told the man about the wall being taken down the following day; his manner changed completely. "Thanks I will pass the message on." Fred asked Gerry for a copy of the telephone number which he would pass on to Lance.

The following morning, Lance arrived about eleven o'clock, he and Fred had a long discussion as to what these people are up to, they have talked this over many times but neither can find a suitable answer. Gerry's team covered the entrance to the extension with heavy dustsheets hoping to keep the dust down to a minimum within the store. They made a start by erecting the acro's to support while gently removing the centre stone bricks and then they continued to work each side to where the extension walls are tied to the main building

It was while one of the team was working away using a pneumatic drill that four men walked into the store and made their way to where the wall was being dismantled. They tried to look in to see what was happening but they could not see very much because the entrance to the porch was sheeted to protect the store from the dust. The men walked outside hoping to get a better view but they could see nothing, they turned around and went back into the store, Fred suggested that the building team broke off for a cup of tea, which he had organised. This move was Lance's idea to take every one away from the wall and as he had expected, two of the men walked behind the sheeting and they were interested in the cavity between the walls, they inspected each side. The two men who carried out the inspection behind the sheets came out; spoke to the others and off they went. Gerry drank his tea and wandered around to the rear of the building, he was followed by one of the men who pushed a £5 note into his pocket, and he went back into the store and asked Fred "What on earth is going on Fred?" "Sorry Gerry, I cannot tell you, we are in the dark too, still you are five pounds better off."

Breaking through the wall was complete; Gerry telephoned the planning office, they promised to pay a visit the following day, the biggest job now was to remove all the rubble from the extension. Gerry realised that he and his team would have to work late into the night to fit the new door leading from the store into the extension. Although they had the framework and the door prepared, it had to be completed properly to ensure the store is made secure, to be doubly sure, Gerry had arranged a night watchman to remain on the premises overnight. This was to safeguard the store from any intruders and to satisfy the insurance cover. The window at the rear is boarded up not glazed at the present time. One thing that Gerry had not been told that the whole building is still under complete camera surveillance inside and outside for other reasons, Ken Lee had insisted this was carried on, he regards the Germans of having a sinister plan hidden somewhere along the line.

*

Alan, the store manager, telephoned Robert advising him that the extension is ready for him and his colleagues to call in to the store and discuss their plans as to where they would like the stud walls to be erected. The plan is that the staircase from the basement will enter the porch and then go through the porch way into the new extension area, Male toilets on the left and Ladies on the right and in each case they are to be tiled from floor to ceiling with wall mirrors above the four wash basins. At the far end of the extension it will have a large Double Glazed window with a personal door, which can be used for deliveries and marked as a fire escape in the event of a fire in the store.

The layout Robert will be concerned with is where the counter tops and the preparation rooms are positioned, bearing in mind prior agreement had been reached on the positioning of the pipes for the water, gas and sewerage before filling in the footings and of course the drainage inspection manholes. Gerry told Fred that he is still waiting for the decision on the colour of the tiles for the toilets. Fred agreed to have a word with the ladies to make a decision with regard to the colour of the tiles within the next two days; in fact, we will visit the tile depot tomorrow, select and arrange delivery. Gerry smiled, he knew that Fred would have to ask, not tell.

The planning officer arrived as promised, this time there were three officials each armed with a copy of the plans, they appeared to be concentrating on how the brickwork is tied into the original wall and if the correct size and strength of the supporting steel girder shown in the plans had been used, no short cuts They inspected the tying inside the building and the outside, they then entered the store and said that they were prepared to sign and stamp the forms to allow the building to proceed but not before they had a cup of tea.

Robert and his colleagues arrived but they were a little hampered because not all of the rubble had been removed, however, they planned the preparation room and counter to be at the end of the extension facing the entrance door coming from the store, then they could watch the customers walk in, which pleased Gerry. He had intended to talk them into using that area, as the water will enter the building at that position, that is, apart from the supply to the toilet area. They measured the area and they planned with Gerry to give maximum room to site quite a few tables but still giving the diners plenty of room between tables.

They all agreed where they wanted the stud walls, which pleased Gerry's team, now they can work on the inside. When the plasterers have finished, Gerry then comes into his own as the joiner; the final workman will be the painting and decoration. Robert's wife wanted to check that the entrance into the café was separate from the toilet area, she was assured that the customers will have to enter through a glass framed door from the toilet area into the café, after being shown the position on the plans she was happy.

CHAPTER 25

Samuel telephoned Mark asking him to arrange a meeting of the Daisy Charity trustees as he had some excellent news that they too will be excited about. It is to explain what came out of the meeting with Bill Nash. One week later they all met up in the charity shop and Sam and his two nurses arrived.

Sam addressed the meeting relating all that had been discussed with Bill Nash, firstly, telling them why Bill had contacted the charity; his granddaughter had been born with a deformed right foot and he wanted me to investigate in the hopes that something can be done to help the child. She is eighteen months old so she is in with a chance, at that age the bones should knit well. I explained to him that the coffers were very low and his response was that money was no problem, he would donate the necessary money for the operation, "Again" he said, "Money is no problem."

I have contacted a friend of mine in St James Hospital, Leeds and he has arranged for the child to have the foot X-rayed and he will phone me when the film is ready for me to study and make a decision. Bill insists that I carry out the operation, I agreed but the donation from him must be paid into the charity account as I am working purely as a charity worker, this made them all smile.

While we were having lunch, he turned to me and said, "Have you ever thought of buying a mobile clinic?" I told him that pigs don't fly. "The outcome is, he has entered into a contract to have an eight-wheeled mobile clinic built and he will meet the cost and it will have Daisy Charity painted on the sides of the vehicle." Dan said, "Sam, I will underwrite the cost of the operation until we have sufficient funds in our account but I might add, not the cost of a mobile clinic," this raised a chuckle. "Mark may have mentioned to you, the idea of having eight wheels is to provide a smooth ride to prevent any damage to the interior or its contents while being towed to wherever the destination might be." It was muted that we should contact the various hospital trusts to arrange parking for as long as is necessary, while we help a child whatever part of the country it might be.

" I have been promised a copy of the suggested interior layout of the mobile clinic; we can then discuss the layout ourselves." The trustees sat around looking at each other, Goodness! What a terrific idea and what a generous man to offer the finance to fund this project. It will be wonderful for any child in need of help. "Fred has checked at the backyard of the cinema and there is room to park the vehicle when not in use. Bill or his friends will supply the cab and driver required to tow the clinic to the designated hospital. It all sounds wonderful but we must wait, as some people say, don't count your chickens before they are hatched. Several of Bill's friends have pledged money to furnish and help with the cost of the X-ray machine, instruments and lighting equipment. The offers sounded quite genuine, well, ladies and gentlemen, that is what was discussed at the meeting; let us hope it all falls into place."

Charlie said, "How about water supply and calls of nature?" "Thank you for asking that question Charlie. Two tanks will be fitted in a cradle underneath the van, one for fresh water and a holding tank for the toilet and drainage from the sinks, the holding tanks can be pumped out at a Boatyard or a Caravan site. I have been advised that it is all very hygienic and the tank is sealed to prevent any unpleasant odours, are you happy with the answer Charlie?" "Yes, very much so." Meeting finished, tea was served, so it turned into quite a social atmosphere and everyone was excited about the project. Sam said, "I was told to tell you, in spite of what people say; Yorkshire folk are not tight with their money." This caused quite a laugh.

*

Lance reported to his superior Ken Lee, about the four strangers looking around the extension at the Fifth Column, explaining that they only appeared to be interested in the cavities between the walls, I wonder Lance. "Will you come to my office tomorrow morning as some interesting things are happening?" Lance travelled to Ken's office as his boss had requested, the secretary told Lance to go straight in to Ken's office as he is expected.

"We discussed some time ago how several units similar to the one in Liverpool but on a much smaller scale have come to light, well, there has been interest shown in those, perhaps because they cannot find what they are looking for in Liverpool. The units in the south have been found in old disused buildings, in two cases sheds have been used on garden allotments, the other allotment owners had no idea to whom the plots belong or when they were last worked."

"Now Lance I have the news for you. A man calling himself Otto Kranz entered this country two days ago, I think he will be joining Hans Kayberg in Liverpool, this man was Hans senior officer in the field during the war and he was going to face charges at Nuremberg as a war criminal along with the other monsters but some important American official got the charges quashed, how, no one seems to have the answer but why has he come to this country. If you do have any dealings with this man be especially careful, he is a vicious wicked man. Lance; pass that to any of our agents who might be working on the case. I have sent all the details to your office but I have a copy and a photograph for you here, just in case you wanted to dash off to Liverpool."

"If it is okay with you Ken, I would like to go back to my office and really study the man's details, is it an up to date photograph?" "Yes Lance, it was taken as he got off the ferry, you notice that he did not fly but he was still spotted. He is being followed and the last report was that he has taken a room above a bookshop in Charring Cross Road; we are checking to whom the shop belongs. As soon as I have that information I will forward it on to you."

Ken's secretary contacted Lance telling him that Otto had left London and had visited Leicester for two days and he then spent two days in Nottingham. In each case, he was met at the railway or bus station with a car and treated like royalty then taken to several addresses in each city, details and photographs of the people he contacted are being sent to your office and to The Fifth Column c/o Fred Wharton's office as I was not sure of your plans. Seane Flannery owns the bookshop in London where Otto stayed on his arrival, this man was a prominent member of the Mosley Black Shirt group in his younger days, obviously he is still very friendly and loyal to the Nazi movement, which seems to be raising its ugly head once more, and Semitism is creeping back in some parts of Germany."

Arriving at the Fifth Column store Lance was given a telephone number to ring urgently, he went into Fred's office to make the call, it turned out to be another agent who informed Lance that Ken would be joining him later that day. Lance delayed his lunch until Ken arrived and then they went off together. While eating lunch Ken told him "Otto was seen arriving at Lime Street Train Station, Liverpool yesterday afternoon, and a Mercedes car was waiting for him, he got into the car and was whisked away to the address where Hans Kayberg and his followers are staying. This is the reason I thought I would like to meet you; it is a funny old business Lance. This man should never have been allowed to enter this country. A few years ago, if a person was considered a threat to the national security they would not have been allowed to enter the country but now, no one seems to care."

After they finished eating they drifted back to the store. An agent of his handed him an envelope saying, "Your secretary thought you might need the photographs", this surprised Ken. "Many thanks Ned." They went into Fred's office, they were just about to sit down when Fred walked in. "Hope you do not mind us using your office," "Not at all Lance, would you gentlemen care to join me in a scotch?" "We certainly would Fred, neither of us two are driving today, we have decided to stay in the city for a couple of days, as again, we are a little puzzled." Dan walked in, "Yes please Fred, I will join you" and this caused both Ken and Lance to smile and pleased to see how comfortable Dan and Fred are together. Lance noticed that Dan was limping, "Are you having trouble Dan?" "Yes Lance, my boot is built up three inches and if I over do it my leg muscles become troublesome and really ache, still, I am luckier than a lot of people." "What a wonderful outlook, when a bomb exploded taking a part of my face with it, I felt like committing suicide but now I find it a wonderful world. Each time I look into the mirror while shaving, I just wonder, how my wife can still regard me as her good-looking husband. Dan, apart from shaving I avoid mirrors."

They sat chatting away about the mystery that still surrounds the cinema. "When the gold was taken away I though they would go with it but no." Fred got up and recharged their glasses, "This is a good scotch Fred" said Lance, Ken piped up, "The free ones always are" and this caused laughter. Let us have a look at what my secretary has sent, with that he opened the large envelope and tipped a pile of photographs on to the table. Ken pointed to one man, "This is Otto Kranz, he is a vile man and he is hated by his enemies and by his own men." Dan picked up one of the snaps, "Good lord, do you recognize him." Fred pondered for a moment or two, "Yes he is one of the French TV men who applied to film a documentary of the basement, good heavens, look Lance and do you recognise him? They wrote only last week asking if their application had been successful, the reply address is a Box Number in London"

Fred jumped to his feet, "We are all going mad," with that he refilled the glasses, "Don't worry Dan we will get a taxi home; we can pick the cars up in the morning." They all sat sifting through the photos for the next hour or so, it was uncanny, and several of the snaps were of people who had been seen wandering around the stores.

Ken related to Dan and Fred all he knew about Otto Kranz and that he has now entered the fray whatever they are looking for, I am giving you this information because he is such a dangerous man. I was telling Lance that I could not understand why he has been allowed to come into this country, unless a trap is being set of which I am yet to hear about. He escaped being charged in Nuremberg, so I cannot see him being punished by us in this country but you must be very careful, I am not trying to frighten you for your family but do take care.

CHAPTER 26

Samuel Stromsberg received a telephone call from Bob Fraser telling him that he had completed a suggested layout for the mobile clinic ready for him to study. "May I pick you up in my car and take you to Liverpool and visit the Charity shop and meet the trustees. This will give every one the opportunity to study, criticise or agree with the proposed layout. By doing it this way you can point out why this has been put in this position or in that position, do you agree? Perhaps we might get some useful suggestions." "That is a good idea, in fact, I could use a day out of the office." "Right Bob, ring back to tell me the day and date and we will make it happen, we are all retired so we can fit in to suit you. However, I would like a few days notice to enable me to advise the trustees."

The date arranged Sam's first call was to collect his two nurses, who got in the back of the car and settled down, "We have brought an overnight bag as we were not too sure about the plans." Sam just smiled a knowing smile, "Is Margery expecting you?" "I did ring her last night to expect us." He called at Bob's office and he was on the doorstep waiting in the bright morning sunshine, "Good morning ladies, Good morning Sam. I have not completed the full cost of the project yet, I phoned Bill yesterday and told him but he said, don't worry Bob, when you have everything in place, go ahead."

They motored to Liverpool and went straight to the Charity Shop.

When Bob had been introduced to the trustees he was given a tour of the exhibition in the basement and he was very impressed, "I like the idea of having to pass through the craft shop to get out again," every body smiled, "Could it be money?" He was taken along the passage way and taken up into the store via the new stairway, Fred had arranged to hold the meeting in one of the larger rooms, he had pinned a large sheet of plywood to the wall to enable Bob to pin the blown up plan of the mobile clinic interior on the wall.

They all expressed their admiration of the detail shown on the plans. Bob went through step-by-step starting with the operating theatre then the X-ray department, the recovery room and accommodation for the child's parents, if they wish to stay with their child overnight. Bob lightly touched on the freshwater and the toilet facilities. "No doubt, Sam will have told you that at the present time we are working on the basis of having an eight wheeled chassis, this is being worked on by the stress and comfort engineers, you will appreciate, every care must be catered for to safeguard the equipment while the vehicle is being towed." Charlie came in with a question, "Could you alter the sleeping area for the parents be increased, bearing in mind the parents will come in all different heights and sizes?" "You are right Charlie but the child has the first priority, if there should be any problem I am sure the hospital will help out." "As I understand it, the vehicle will be towed to some part of the country and permission obtained from the Local Hospital Trust to park on their premises."

The discussion carried on for quite a while but the general consensus was one of agreement, they all came to the same conclusion. It was vital to get all the details correct, even Sam who knew exactly what had to be done, agreed with the outcome of the meeting. Dan said "It is a wonderful opportunity for children in need of help, which on completion of the clinic we will be able to give. I can speak of this from my experience of being handicapped throughout my life. Bob, when you next speak to Bill, kindly thank him for such a wonderful offer, also tell him, we do not think Yorkshire men are tight with their money," this caused uproar. "Yes Dan, it will suit his sense of humour."

*

The MBM Advertising Agency was really taking off and they found that they needed more space; they put in a request to take over the workshop the girls had started off with when they first started the business using the room at the factory. Dan and Fred were only too pleased to see the room being used again; it had long benches against the wall and power points, which proved to be ideal for Arne and Richard who turned it into a studio to produce short advertising films. Bella, Margery and Mary repeated their previous statement, they were each finding it difficult to cope with getting in and out of windows these days, so they had left it all with their daughters and sons-in-law to carry on the business.

The advertising is taking precedence over window displays as many of the stores are now employing their own window display teams rather than pay freelance operators. Lillian has suddenly found she has the flair for writing adverts coupled with a suitable slogan, which has become invaluable to the company. The problem is, whether it is a film or a printed article, it must create an impact to the prospective customer and achieve an increase in the sales turnover of the company who have commissioned their work.

Salina, Mary's daughter, had become so wrapped up in her work that Mary is being taken for granted as a full time nanny to Terry her grandson. He is now two years old and has become a real handful and certainly keeps his grandma on her toes. When they go shopping he always creates a rumpus if he is not given an ice cream. Mary is beginning to find that she is unable to make time for herself; she has stopped meeting Bella and Margery for lunch because Terry becomes such a nuisance at the table and he spoils the luncheon for every one else. She loves Terry dearly but she realises that she is now being taken for granted, every one else has the time to plan outings but now she is unable to do so. After all these months, she feels that Terry is getting too much for her to cope with.

Fred had noticed that Mary had become a little irritable and jumpy during the past few weeks and he was very concerned, however, before he could mention this to his wife. Mary told him that she would like a serious talk with him. His heart fell to his boots, my god, is she not well and not told me her problems; I have been too busy looking after myself, he felt guilty. Mary could see Fred was upset, "Don't look so worried, it is not that serious." She told him how she felt by not being able to make arrangements to go out with the girls with her being the permanent nanny."Right my love, I will tell Salina that you are not available for the next two weeks, we will go to Scarborough for a holiday, I will ring the Royal Hotel and arrange accommodation and you pack the cases in the morning. Salina will kick up but we have a life too, Mary, Terry is a wonderful child but we raised Salina and now it is our turn to enjoy life."

Fred telephoned Salina telling her that he was taking her mother away for a two-week holiday for a rest. "Could you not take Terry with you?" "No love, I told you I am taking your mother for a rest. Will you take Terry with you in the morning or leave him with Arne's parents; your mother will want to shop and pack tomorrow morning, goodnight love."

*

Mary got up the following morning feeling a little guilty at pushing Salina off but excited to have time to just do whatever she wanted to do, she telephoned Margery to pop in for a coffee, she felt like a child just let out of school. Margery noticed the difference in Mary when she called round; she looked at the suitcase on the floor, "Come on Mary what are you up to?"

Mary made the coffee and when they were sat down she told Margery how life had been getting on top of her, not having any time to herself, she then told her of her discussion with Fred and his response.

"We are going to Scarborough for two weeks. Why don't you join us?" "Yes I will go and start packing," "We must sort out the hotel first I will ring Fred and tell him to make the booking for two couples." When Mary phoned Fred and told him to book for Dan and Margery, Fred's reaction was, "Great," "Does Dan know about this?" "No, don't you tell him, leave that to Margery." When Dan arrived home, two suitcases stood in the hall. "What on earth are you up to Margery?" "We are going on holiday with Fred and Mary;" "Do you want to go on holiday Margery?" "When did we last have a holiday?" "Yes Margery, you are right we should go away for a holiday," Margery just smiled as she went into the next room, no opposition from Dan.

Dan phoned Fred; "Are you involved in this conspiracy Fred Wharton?" he laughed, "Just go with the flow Dan. I have booked the best rooms at the Royal, you will have to sell some shares," they both laughed at the joke between them from many years ago. "You never know Dan, we might get lucky," Margery walked into the room while Dan was laughing, "What are you two up to now?" "I will drive Dan, my car has a large boot and by the look of Mary's case we shall need a large boot," "Right Fred, about eleven, okay." "Why not pop round now for a drink," "Margery, Fred and Mary are coming round for a drink to discuss the coming holiday." When they arrived Dan had the drinks ready for them, Mary Looked at Margery, "They are just like children going on a Sunday school treat."

The following morning they loaded the cases into the boot of the car; there were some comments about hiring the crane, which Gerry had used for the RSJ girders. They arrived in York about lunchtime; they took a long break to enjoy a leisurely lunch, which, they thought was a good start to the holiday. They were fortunate with the traffic, the roads were quiet at that time of the day; they made very good time into Scarborough. As they pulled up at the front of the hotel, a young man came out to help with the cases and carried them into the foyer.

Fred had booked the rooms, Dan started laughing as the booking was also in Fred's name, "We should enjoy this holiday Margery we have wealthy friends." One of the porters carried Mary's cases into the lift,

Mary and Fred followed, the lift went to the top floor, as he opened the door of the bedroom, Mary just gasped, it was a large room decorated in delicate pink, French windows opening on to a veranda with a stunning view over the harbour. They unpacked their cases and put most of the clothes away, Fred suddenly realised that he should go downstairs and park the car, Mary said, "Take Dan with you and have a drink, I am going to enjoy the luxury of pampering myself for an hour," Fred just laughed and off he went.

Mary went into the bathroom and to her surprise there was an array of small plastic bottles containing shower gel, hair shampoo, body lotion and many other cosmetic preparations, with which to pamper herself as she had told Fred she intended to do. On the tray with the kettle were several different types of tea and coffee, tea, she had never heard of. Mary enjoyed her long soak in the bath, when she got out she put on her dressing gown and lay on the bed piled high with cushions. Looking across the bay she could see fishing boats returning to the harbour, some going out and boats taking holidaymakers out for a trip around the coast. She was completely at peace with the world and its inhabitants. When Fred returned to his room he found Mary fast asleep.

After dinner the first night, they decided they should take a long walk as they had all eaten and drunk far too much, they had been greedy, they each blamed the other for encouraging them to eat and drink. They just consoled each other that they were on holiday; in spite of promising to eat less, the girls knew they would find it impossible to resist the desserts. They walked across the bridge, which spans the Valley Gardens to the Spa and enquired about the available entertainment during their stay.

Margery had one planned visit on her list and that was Whitby, they ordered a picnic the night before, which they enjoyed the following day on the Pickering Moors. Margery and Mary walked up the one hundred and ninety nine steps to visit St Mary's church but Fred and Dan caught a bus and met them at the church, Dan could not walk all that way with his deformed leg. They came back down on the bus and then travelled back to Scarborough; they each agreed it had been a wonderful day out. Arriving back at the hotel, arrangements were made to meet in the bar after a shower and a change of clothes.

They met up in the bar for a drink before dinner, where again they were tempted to eat too much. When they had finished the meal they went into the lounge to enjoy their coffee, Fred and Dan had a brandy and the girls enjoyed a G&T. A member of the staff came into the lounge asking for Fred Wharton, Fred nodded, "You are wanted on the telephone sir" Fred picked up the phone, "Hello," It was Salina on the other end and she sounded hysterical, "Calm down, what is a matter?" "The neighbour, who was looking after Terry, took him to town this afternoon and they went into a supermarket, she reached for an item off the top shelf, when she turned round Terry had gone. That was six hours ago, in spite of people searching for him and a van with a loud hailer going up and down the street giving his description, he is still missing." "We will come home tomorrow, try not to worry too much; I feel sure it will all work out okay."

When Fred went back into the lounge and told Mary, she too, was very upset, "It would not have happened if I had been looking after him, we must go home tonight Fred." "We will have to wait until the morning, I had too much wine with the meal and this brandy with my coffee. There is little we can do tonight, that was not already being done." Dan looked at Fred; yes we are both on the same wavelength but hoping our thoughts are way off beam. Fred went to a telephone and rang Lance telling him that his grandson had gone missing. I am hoping this has nothing to do with what Ken told us. Obviously you will tell Ken but keep it very low profile, we are coming home tomorrow morning, and I should be in the store by three o'clock.

CHAPTER 27

Mary and Fred were up and dressed early. They decided not to disturb Dan and Margery and they went down to the breakfast room, they were surprised to see Dan and Margery sitting at the table, my word you must have risen early, Dan had brought their cases down and had left them in the foyer. Breakfast consisted of toast and coffee as not one of them had an appetite. Fred went off and collected the car from the garage and parked outside the hotel, Dan put the cases in the boot of the car while Fred settled the bill, this time there was no leg-pull. The attitude of the staff was one of understanding, how they were aware of the situation Fred did not know.

It was a sombre journey travelling back to Liverpool, here again there was no leg pulling as there is normally when the four get together, just a quiet respect for each other. Fred did not make any stop on the return journey; Mary wanted to get home as quickly as possible. On her arrival home, she went straight to the telephone to contact Salina hoping that Terry was with her but she was disappointed. Salina and Arne are very upset and they decided not to go to work this morning in case of a phone call, they would not be able to concentrate if they went. The neighbour who had been looking after Terry was in a terrible state; so much so, her husband had to ask their doctor to call and when he came he gave the man's wife a sedative hoping it would calm her down.

Margery went into Mary's house to keep her company and Dan and Fred went off to the store to meet Lance, before going into the store Fred called in to the Police Station to enquire if they had any news but they too had drawn a blank. When they arrived at the store, they were surprised to find Lance and Ken waiting for them. "Any news Fred?" "No I have just called at the Police Station and they have no news. I am worried about your last sentence when we met, you said, I am not trying to frighten you or your family," I keep thinking, "I hope not."

They decided to go next door for a coffee, they kept going over the possibilities, whether he just wandered off or has he been kidnapped. They quietly sat for a while and one of the office girls came dashing in, "Mr Wharton you are wanted on the phone," "Is it my wife"? "No it is a man's voice, he would not leave a message, he insisted on speaking to you." Dan stayed behind to pay the bill, the other three returned quickly back to the store. Fred went into his office as the girl had put the call through to there, he picked up the phone and a guttural voice said, "Is that Fred Wharton"? It is; do you recognise the voice of this young gentleman, say hello to your grandad" "Hello granddad are you coming to take me home"? "Yes of course I will son." The man at the other end of the line took the phone from Terry; "This young man will soon be back with you if you do as I ask."

"Saturday night, which is tomorrow night, my colleagues and I want to have access to your store for the night without any interference, we intend to scan the building to search for something that rightly belongs to us, no one, I repeat no one will remain in the store. We do not intend stealing anything at all, we just want entry to scan, another thing I want all your surveillance cameras turned off, don't try and be clever, we have equipment that indicates that they are all active inside and outside the building, you must deal with it. You will be the last person to leave the building. I will phone you just before you leave and check everything is as I want it and I will check the cameras with you as you leave. You do as I ask and I will arrange for your grandson to be returned home Sunday morning but you must do as I ask. If you fail to carry out my instructions, your family will suffer," with that, the phone clicked off.

Fred walked out of his office Dan, could see that Fred was really shaken and he had gone a ghastly grey colour and it was obvious that a nasty plan had been hatched. They went back into his office, sat down and then he related all that had been said, both Ken and Lance were taken aback, never did they expect a kidnapping, all three sympathised with Fred being put in such a position, whatever one feels, flesh and blood takes precedence.

*

Ken turned to Fred, "You will do exactly what he asks and can you contact your decorator as I have a plan. I want the decorator to replace three of the ceiling electric light bulbs with the latest high tech bulbs containing a camera they are undetectable, at least they are to our latest equipment. When he phones tomorrow night, just tell him that as far as you know all the cameras have been deactivated and just check before I leave. There should be no reading but should there be, you will have a handset with which you can switch the ceiling cameras off."

Fred contacted Ian and impressed the urgency of his call. Ian had never known Fred to sound so upset with begging in his voice. Ian dropped what he was doing and called into the store to meet up with Fred. "Ian, I cannot explain the reason I am asking you to do this little job but I am desperate," There was no need for Fred to qualify his request, it was obvious he was desperate by his manner and his body language. Fred explained what he wanted doing, the new bulbs will be here in half an hour; Ian went off to arrange his hydraulic lift to reach the ceiling. When the messenger arrived with the bulbs, Ian placed them in the position instructed by Ken.

Fred suggested that Dan and Margery had dinner at his house that evening and they could help him in allaying Mary's fears for Terry's safety. When I spoke to him, he sounded all right but he wanted me to call and take him home. "Before we go home, I think we ought to visit Frank and tell him that the store will be left unlocked when the staff leaves the building on Saturday night but I will personally make good the cost of the stock, should any go missing."

When told, Frank would not hear of it, "You would not allow me to repay monies when my son embezzled money from our company, I am prepared to accept my part in any action you take, Fred, I am sure without asking Dan he will follow suit." Dan just nodded. Fred went on to explain, "Ken has told us how vicious this man named Otto is and he will let nothing stand in his way to achieve his objective, he is responsible for many deaths and he should have been charged for his war crimes but that is another story, which, I will tell you another day." "I agree with your every word Fred"

"Good luck Fred, I only wish my health would allow me to take a more active part with your problem, do keep me informed and if you think I can help in any way do ring me. I am not just being nosey but very concerned, we have been through a lot together over the past fifty years and it is in such a situation as this, we know that we can depend on each others support."

Arriving back at Fred's house, Mary was anxious to know the situation, "Let me deal with the drinks for our guests" "They are not guests they are family, now Fred tell me." "Sit down and do not interfere, just listen." Mary was taken aback; Fred very rarely spoke to her in that tone of voice.

"Terry has been taken by the German crowd who says there is still something belonging to them in the building of the old cinema, we thought that when the gold and the currency had been removed that would end their visits but there must be something very important they want. I have to leave the store unlocked tomorrow night, the camera surveillance all switched off and they are going to spend the night looking for whatever they think belongs to them, by using their latest high technical inferred and imaging equipment. If I do as they ask, Terry will be home on Sunday morning. Don't! Look at me like that Mary, of course I shall do exactly as they want me to do, I want Terry back too." Mary appeared to accept that Fred had everything under control; Fred hoped so too.

Saturday morning Dan and Fred went to work in Dan's car, Fred was not happy about driving, he had drunk more Brandy than he should have the night before and did not sleep well. Each time he woke during the night he saw Mary standing at the window just staring out into the night but seeing nothing, he wondered if she slept at all. Friday night it had been arranged that Fred and Mary should dine at Margery's house with Salina, Lillian and their husbands, they felt they could support each other. Dan and Fred went out to lunch as normal but neither had an appetite; they just had coffee and played around with a cake. Ken had not passed on the happenings to his seniors, he felt they would rush in and as in the case of Horace, cause unnecessary deaths, as mentioned before, they are desk trained not experienced in the field.

*

As the hands of the clock approached six o'clock Fred started to get nervous, Dan went out to the car and waited for Fred join him. Two minutes past six and no phone call, Fred was really getting upset, his heart was pumping, he started with a headache and he had difficulty to stop shaking, he suddenly realised that years were catching up with him. Five minutes past six the phone rang, he almost jumped out of his skin, although he was waiting for the phone to ring, it startled him. The voice sounded to belong to the same man to whom he had spoken to previously, Fred told the man that as far as he knew all the camera's had been deactivated, check before I leave. Fred was clutching the monitor ready to switch the cameras off in the ceiling if necessary, hoping the perspiration from his hand would not affect the instrument. Hold on, our equipment is checking the whole building, yes according to our reading they are all off. You must leave now, leave the security lights on as normal but remember, DO NOT! Lock the door.

Fred joined Dan in the car and set off to go home, he turned to Dan saying, "What have we done to deserve this Dan?" "I cannot answer that question Fred but let's hope what we have done, is right and we get Terry back in the morning." On arriving home they found the others had arrived and were sat having a drink before dinner and the atmosphere was very tense. They sat around the table, Margery had gone to a lot of trouble to ensure it was a good tasty meal but instead of eating they just pushed the food around their plates, Margery was disappointed but understanding.

After dinner they all wanted to help clearing the table and washing the crockery, anything to keep busy. Fred started drinking heavily again, no one mentioned it, it was obvious that the pressure was getting to him, at ten o'clock the phone rang, they all looked towards Fred but he was unable to rise from his chair, he pointed to Dan, you take it Dan. He picked up the receiver and it was Lance on the other end of the line, there are eight men wandering around the store. "Is it okay if I ring to keep you informed of developments," "Yes, ring me any time of the night, do not disturb Fred as he is not feeling too well," Lance chuckled, "Too many cheers no doubt," "Something like that Lance."

*

The ringing of the telephone bell awakened Dan, he glanced at the clock and it was five o'clock, who on earth is ringing me at this time of the morning. When he lifted the receiver to his ear he recognised the voice of Lance, "Otto has called a halt to the search, it has been very thorough and they all look disappointed, now, they are arguing among themselves, in fact, Otto is physically attacking two of his own men and strangely enough they are not retaliating, are they afraid of him or does he rank so high that he is untouchable. I cannot see exactly what is going on, they have gone round a corner and the camera bulbs are static so we are unable to follow them with this type of camera and there is no sound recording.

" I have a copy on videotape of all the activity, or should I say nearly all, we could not manipulate the camera into all the nooks and crannies, this is for you and Fred to study in the hope that you will spot something we have missed. I do hope they keep their part of the bargain by taking Terry home in the morning, if not, we will raid Embassy House and deport the so called envoys back from whence they came. They do not appear to be Diplomatic Envoys; they are more like a Military Attaché trying to recapture something from the past."

"I appreciate it is Sunday but will you and Fred meet me at the store in the morning about ten o'clock, no doubt you will want to ensure that the store is secure?" "Yes, I'll come down but I cannot speak for Fred, it all depends if his head is still on his shoulders, it has been a very difficult time for him and he has looked to the bottle for help." Lance laughed and put the phone down. Dan and Margery sat up in bed and enjoyed a cup of tea, while Dan had been on the telephone his wife had nipped downstairs to brew up, what else does one do at a time like this, they then snuggled down and Dan was asleep in minutes.

*

Dan was fast asleep but he could hear a bell ringing in the background and it was not until Margery nudged him did he realise it was the telephone ringing, when he lifted the receiver the caller did not wait for him to answer. "Dan will you come down to the store and show us where all the light switches are and also reactivate the cameras to enable the surveillance team to watch the store from the support house, Dan looked at the clock; the hands were just touching seven. We have a big problem Dan, Ken had several agents on duty during the night and two of them are missing, one was stationed in a room across the road to cover the entrance to the store and the other was on duty watching the Embassy House. Otto has been seen attacking another member of his own team when they got outside the building, what a vicious man."

"Ken is hoping he is wrong but he is convinced they will be found in the building, will you help Dan?" "Yes of course, I'll be with you in thirty minutes," when he told Margery, she got out bed, "I am going with you." He telephoned Fred, Mary answered the phone, he passed on all the information he had. "We are just leaving to go to the store, I'll ring from there, and Margery is going with me." Dan was hoping that this hiccup would not put Terry's safety in jeopardy; the viciousness attached to Otto is frightening. Hans and Otto; are they pursuing something for their own personal gain or are they acting under instructions.

*

Margery decided to drive to save moving the cars around, Dan does not drive a car with a manual gearbox. She drove round to the back of the store into the car park, Dan went into the building switched on every available light and it looked like the Blackpool Lights. Ken walked up to Dan, "Thanks, for coming straight down, it is a mess Dan," Lance came to join them. Ken and his agents started to search the building, one of his men shouted that he had found a body, when they checked it was not one of the agents, they did not recognise him, Lance walked up, when he looked down, "Good god, this is the man Otto was attacking. The thieves are falling out, that is a good sign."

The search continued, they even went into the loft section; the cupboard had been removed from inside the projection room leaving the loft steps in place. The building was checked but apart from the one body nothing more could be found, suddenly they heard a man shouting, they all rushed to join him, he was pointing through the window into the extension, in there laid two bodies, how did they get in there, the entrance from the store was locked. Dan eventually found a bunch of keys in Alan's office and one of the keys fitted the lock. When they went into the extension, it was a sickening sight, they both had their throats cut but the killings could not have been carried out there because there were no pools of blood. Margery suddenly started to feel ill; Dan helped her into Alan's office, sat her down and gave her a glass of water. Ken telephoned his office and a black van came and took the bodies away, all in fifteen minutes, thus preventing it to become public knowledge.

They all filed out of the store and were waiting while Dan locked the door, as they were waiting for him, a car pulled up and a man leaned out of the car and put Terry on the pavement and then sped off. Terry looked up and saw Margery, he toddled towards her with small beads of tears in his eyes, Margery swept him up into her arms and they both had a weep. Dan held Terry while she unlocked the car and then sat him on his lap while Margery drove home.

Arriving home they went round to Mary's house, Margery rang the door- bell, when Mary came to the door. "A young man wishes to speak to you," with that Dan and Terry came from around the corner, Mary's face was a picture to behold, she could not wait to pick him up and he responded too. The noise downstairs awakened Fred; he came down the stairs carefully, he was suffering from a very bad hangover, depressed and really miserable but when he saw Terry it all disappeared. He telephoned Salina and Arne, they were round in a few minutes and it was another tearful reunion. As one might expect, it was again a cup of teatime, by the time they drunk their tea Terry was fast asleep on the settee. Dan told Fred of all the happenings at the store during the night, the killings and how Otto had reacted against his own. Lance has a copy of the videotape for us to watch, Fred sat looking at the floor for a while, he looked up, "What do they want Dan?"

CHAPTER 28

Sam Stromsburg managed to hire the operating theatre and the facility at a private hospital just outside Leeds; the cost to the Charity was quite reasonable. He spoke to the Radiographer asking her to take several X-rays from different angles, as the degree of deformity of Lucy's foot is a bad case, which was going to be quite a challenge to Sam and the prognosis a little uncertain. Sam had been upfront with Bill on the severity of Lucy's case.

Bill arranged to meet Sam and introduce him to his daughter Pat, Lucy's mother. Sam explained that Lucy would require a lot of manipulation and the recovery time will take several months, Pat, it will make you nurse and mother, there will be times when you have doubts but you will have to persevere and call upon your love of the child.

"Having met you and discussed Lucy's deformity Mr Stromsburg, I am happy to agree to you going ahead and try to help Lucy with the operation; it is obvious, that I will be very concerned but confident during the whole process." "You can rest assured I will take every care with your little girl and please call me Sam, I feel so old when I am referred to as Mister."

Lucy would not entertain Sam at first but after a short time she was sat giggling away on his knee, he certainly has a way with children. They sat discussing dates. Eventually a date was decided on for them to meet up at the private hospital, "I think we should meet there before, just for ten minutes or so, in order to get Lucy acclimatised to the surroundings rather than arriving and going straight into the operating theatre," "Yes, you are right," agreed Bill. Bill said that he would drive his daughter and granddaughter to the hospital. Bill turned to Sam, "You will have to put up with a lot of interference from my wife she likes to think she is in charge, just be patient with her Sam." Bill looked at his daughter and they both burst out laughing, "I have quite a challenge to look forward to then Bill?" "Little do you know Sam," Bill and Pat were still laughing with each other.

They met up at the hospital to enable them to look around and Pat's husband came along, when Bill introduced his son-in-law, Sam said, "What a small world, Rob Slater, he spent a week-end at my house when he and my son were at Leeds University, you didn't know he had been slumming did you?" Bill smiled, "Well I'll be blowed." Bill left with his family after a short stay, as they knew that Sam had a meeting planned.

In view of the child's age, Sam had arranged a meeting with a colleague who is a Paediatrician, Pat's family doctor and the Anaesthetist. "I want to thank you for giving up your time to discuss this case with me; I cannot pay you for your time as my work is now entirely voluntary." Sam attached the X-rays to the illuminated panel showing the sides, bottom and from the top of Lucy's foot, the doctor said, "There will not be strong bones to break, they must still be like soft grizzle," they smiled but made no comment, they were aware of the fact but grateful for his remarks. After much deliberation they decided not to put the child to sleep but use a local anaesthetic and they felt confident the child's recovery would benefit from not using gas.

Sam thanked them again for coming along, Sam stayed behind as he had asked his two nurses to come and look around to familiarise themselves with the operating theatre and the recovery area. The nurses were impressed with the general layout and they felt quite at home. Sam briefed them by firstly showing them the X-ray plates, which, he had purposely left on the screen, after looking and discussing the foot Sam told them of the decision to use a local for the operation, usually they questioned Sam's approach but in this instance they thought it right. Sam turned to one of them; "Does your friend still work at the Maternity unit? If she does, try and find out the blood group of Lucy Slater; ensure you get the correct information." Sam phoned Bill, "Can I visit you in your office privately Bill?" "Yes, make it in about half an hour then I shall be alone."

Sam took one of his nurses with him, they entered his office and Sam introduced his nurse. "I wanted to see you privately Bill, I want a blood sample to check that your group is the same as Lucy's. I did not mention it in front of your family as I did not want to alarm them but should we need any blood I know it is there on tap said Sam laughing." The nurse had taken the equipment with her, it was soon dealt with and she put the phial into her case and she had plans to deposit the phial at the hospital to get it examined and listed in a Blood Group, the charity will meet the cost. "Don't look alarmed Bill; it is a precaution I take before every operation on a small child"

*

Bob telephoned Mark but Sally, his wife, answered the phone and she told Bob that Mark was not well enough to take his call. She told Bob that Charlie had been helping Mark by taking a load of the Charity work off him; Sally suggested that Bob contact Charlie and gave him Charlie's telephone number. Charlie telephoned Dan and told him that Mark was quite ill, Dan immediately went to visit him, Mark, is Dan's uncle as he is his mother's youngest brother. He was very distressed to find Mark so ill, in ten days he had lost half his body weight and it looks unlikely that he will survive many more days; it appears that the family must prepare themselves for a very sad event.

Bob advised Charlie that the chassis of the Mobile Clinic is almost complete and he thought the Trustees of the Charity would like to visit the engineering plant in Halifax. Dan, Fred and their wives in one car and Charlie managed to transport the rest. They decided to have lunch before going to the works, Dan reminded them that the charity would not stand the cost of the lunch, this was met with a tirade of boo's, however, Fred and Dan paid the bill, between them.

On their arrival at the factory, they were introduced to the engineer who was to take them around and answer any questions they may have. The engineer said that the chassis was to have four axles fitted with two wheels on each stub thus making sixteen tyres in contact with the road surface. The most up to date suspension is being considered: bearing in mind the delicate equipment and instruments, which are to be protected while the Mobile Clinic is being towed to its destination.

"Any questions?" "Yes," Fred asked "What are all the steel straps trailing under the chassis?" The engineer explained, "The straps are there to create a cradle to hold the fresh water tank and farther along the chassis is a cradle for the holding tank to receive the sink waste and the flush toilet." "It is undecided as yet, whether the generator will be slung underneath the chassis as a permanent fixture or if Mr Nash is prepared to pay for hydraulic sliding gear. While in transit it will be under the chassis but on arrival it could be automatically operated to slide on to the floor to become free standing, this would alleviate any vibration and lessen the noise. If left in the cradle there would be a certain amount of vibration and perhaps a little unpleasantness from the fumes. Whichever way is chosen it cannot be manhandled, it is far too heavy; It has to be a very powerful generator to provide the power required for the lighting for the operating theatre and the X-ray machinery. This is one of the items being worked on in the drawing office; they keep coming up with different ideas but nothing has been finalised as yet." Mary turned to Margery, "Painted in the red oxide, it looks like a monster from the deep." The chassis looked huge.

They all came away from the engineering plant feeling elated; the construction of the Mobile Clinic is beyond their wildest dreams, they never thought a benefactor would ever finance such a project. Having listened to the engineer, they all realised that they must rely on what he said, as the engineering project; was way above their heads. Fred contacted Jack Green telling of their visit and suggested that he should photograph the chassis to build a newspaper article when it is completed. "I think a photograph and an article might help your paper." "Thanks for the tip Fred, I will contact the plant and ask permission to take my camera; the charity is still a good story."

*

Bill and his daughter met Sam at the private hospital just outside of Leeds to carry out the surgery on Lucy's right foot. Sam asked Pat to put the special child's pretty gown on her daughter, there was a tussle as grandma wanted to do it. The anaesthetist played around with Lucy's naughty foot, Sam had again used that word as a child always responded. Eventually, the injection was carried out and she was placed on a small trolley and wheeled into the operating theatre. When they got Lucy settled, a large sheet was positioned to obscure the view of the operation. With the sheet in place Pat was allowed to sit with her daughter while the operation was taking place but Pat had to be suitably gowned and wear a mask. Sam began the surgery but he became very concerned, as there were several small complications that had not shown up on the X-ray. Fortunately, he managed to manipulate the young flexible bones into the position he wanted them.

The operation lasted for one hour, when it was completed, Sam appeared; looking quite pleased and Lucy was wheeled into the recovery room to be carefully watched over by the two nurses. Sam turned to Pat, "The foot is in its correct position now but the child will find the plaster caste rather heavy but it is up to you now to ensure she does not put any weight on that foot, or try to walk, otherwise all our work will be to no avail." It had been a wise choice to use a local anaesthetic as they could hear Lucy chattering away, which is a good sign.

Bill was pleased to see them come out of the operating theatre and by the look on Pat's face it must have been a satisfactory operation. Sam decided to tell Bill and his wife the same as he had told Pat. "Lucy will find the plaster caste heavy but she must keep her weight off it for at least a month. After that time, I will get a lightweight calliper made to be worn several hours each day for another month, Bill, this is a crucial time to ensure recovery." Bill's wife said, "Don't worry Sam, I shall take complete charge of Lucy and make sure all your instructions are carried out." Bill looked at Sam and winked, Pat had to turn away, otherwise her mother would see her laughing and Bill had a job to keep a straight face.

Bill invited Sam to go with him to visit the coach building company, where the body of the Mobile Clinic was being built. Bob wanted Sam's advice on several points. When Sam boarded the vehicle, stepping into the shell, he was amazed how they had created so much room for each section and Sam was delighted. Bob told him that the clinic would be completed in one month's time, painted in cream and the sign writing on the sides, reading "Daisy Charity" in brown lettering, it will look elegant. When Fred learned that the Mobile Clinic was almost ready, he telephoned Jack Green as he is building a story around the vehicle for his paper when the handing over ceremony takes place.

CHAPTER 29

Lance contacted Fred asking him to bring Dan with him to meet for lunch tomorrow at 12 o'clock at the Adelphi; "Yes we'll be there." Fred phoned Dan to make the necessary arrangements. That evening Dan and Margery went to Fred's house for dinner, when they were seated, "What is it all about Fred?" "I have no idea Dan but Ken intends coming from London for our meeting, if he can get away." Mary piped up by saying; "It's no good speculating on what the meeting is all about, I bet you would be way off target."

The following morning they called a taxi rather than driving into the city, it is always difficult to find a suitable parking place close to the hotel but with the taxi it will take us close to the hotel entrance, which is a great help as Dan's deformed leg is becoming troublesome. They were very early for the lunch appointment so they elected to go to the bar for a drink and they had just settled in comfortable chairs, Ken and Lance walked in, Lance turned to Ken, "I told you we would find them in the bar."This brought smiles to their faces. "Thanks for coming along and I'm very pleased to meet you again, I'll outline the reason I wanted to tie up with you again over lunch, I don't want to spoil your drinks," said Ken. Dan was absolutely mystified.

They went into the restaurant and the headwaiter showed them to a table in the far corner, ideal for a confidential meeting; Ken must have arranged it this way. They ordered their food and Ken started, "The reason for this meeting, I wanted to speak to you both face to face. There is going to be a meeting in London to discuss the Fifth Column and the owners of a similar building in Birmingham will be there, I would like you to attend. There will be a senior Home Office Minister conducting the meeting." They agreed and the arrangements were made.

Mary drove them to the Lime Street Railway Station in her car and they caught the early London train, they both enjoyed the journey. When they arrived in London, they travelled by taxi to the address the meeting was to be held, Dan paid the taxi fare, he was convinced that he had contributed to the driver's welfare fund, this made Fred laugh. Standing on the pavement looking up at a magnificent building, it looked huge and its architecture so beautiful, they mounted the steps into a large elegant foyer, it looked more like the entrance to a hotel than a government building. As they entered, Lance was standing near the main door, he walked towards them, "Good morning, let us go into the restaurant as the meeting does not start for another hour." A light breakfast was being served; they both indulged themselves in the luxury, "I'm so glad that we paid our taxes last week," said Fred sweeping his arm round and gesticulating with his hand. Lance told them that Ken would be joining them for the meeting but he was not sure if this would be possible before it starts.

Eventually, they were called to go into the conference room where the meeting was going to be held, they entered through a large doorway with a six-inch thick beautifully carved wooden door and Dan was very impressed. The walls were covered with wooden panels; in the centre of the room was a long large table with one chair at the head and five chairs down each side. On the table at each chair position was a glass, bottle of water, notepad and a pencil. What really fascinated Dan were the three large cut glass chandeliers and the reflection from these lights shining on the highly polished woodwork on the table and the panelled walls.

When they were all seated, a gentleman walked in and sat at the head of the table. "Thank you gentlemen for attending this meeting, I realise these trips are not always convenient, let me introduce myself. My name is Peter Horn and I am a Member of Parliament and senior spokesman for the Home Office. The reason this meeting has been called is because of the loss of life in this country of our agents, it was not thought we would have to face up to such a situation in peacetime. Now, on my right is Lord Thames and on my left is Sir Henry Grainger, will you introduce yourselves," Fred and Dan introduced themselves as Directors of DFF Liverpool Furniture.

Peter Horn went on to say that "We have studied the reports we received about the happenings in Liverpool and Birmingham. It appears these two cities had been selected to put sleepers in during the war ready for the invasion of this country but thank God this did not happen. This must have been what Mr Churchill meant when he referred to the Fifth Column. We know that a substantial amount of money, armaments and clothing had been hidden in these buildings, the value of the gold and currency found in the roof area of the Liverpool building, amounted to one and a half million pounds based on today's values.

Now the nitty gritty, we are convinced that an Ex-Nazi organisation is operating in this country but we do not know if they are trying to find the wealth hidden in readiness for the invasion, or is it to find and destroy damning evidence pointing to high ranking people in this country, who were Nazi sympathisers. That, gentlemen, is the puzzle but it is fast becoming a dangerous puzzle. Ken told me this morning that Fred Wharton of DFF of Liverpool had his grandson kidnapped and returned after allowing the Nazi group the run of the building for one night, which, he did, who wouldn't, however, they searched the building, the outcome we do not know but thankfully the boy was reunited with his parents the following day. It is debateable, whether or not Fred should have kept this to himself. Fred thought, clever Lance and Ken.

The Birmingham building was discussed; several visitors have been seen hanging around during the night and quite recently attempts have been made to break into the building. The question of apprehending these people: Every time we have sufficient evidence to have them arrested or deported, something happens to remove the evidence or the person or persons have disappeared. Each time they seem to be one step ahead of us, which, we find frustrating. We have checked all the telephone lines in and out of my office, in fact, and the whole building has been subjected to an investigation. I ask you gentlemen; if you can find any information on these people, please send it in."

The meeting concluded, Dan and Fred walked out of the room and Ken and Lance caught up with them, frightening things going on aren't there. Dan turned to them, "Will you walk outside with me?" They looked puzzled but they followed him. When they were away from the main door, Dan turned to Ken and said, "Are you a gambling man?" "Why do you ask that, Dan?" "If you are, I will offer you odds of 100-1 that Lord Thames and Sir Henry Grainger are on the photographs taken of the German group the day that Daisy Charity Basement was opened to the public." "Good Lord, are you sure Dan?" "As I said I will lay you odds of 100-1." Lance turned to Fred, "Do you think Jack Green will still have those photographs?" "I'll find out."

*

The first thing Fred did on arriving home was to telephone Jack Green, "Hi! Jack, may I call at your house this evening as I want to discuss something with you which is too sensitive to talk about over the phone?" "Certainly Fred, I should be home about 5-30, come along then, my wife will still be at work so it will be private." Fred asked Dan to go with him, as it was he who is convinced that he identified the two same people who were at the meeting. They arrived early, they sat in the car until Jack arrived; he drove into his drive and called to them to follow him into the house. He opened the door, he shouted, "Look! At the mess." It was obvious that he had an intruder; he dashed to his dark room, OH! NO, everything had been tipped on to the floor and when he checked his draws containing his photographs, he found they had all been stolen.

They went into the kitchen; Jack produced a bottle of beer and proceeded to pour the beer into three glasses. "Am I to ring the police or are you going to tell me what is going on?" "Jack, what I am going to tell you is strictly confidential and I trust you to keep it to yourself." Fred told him a little of what was discussed at the meeting in London and finally told him that Dan was convinced that two members of the government present were on the photograph you took at the opening of the Charity Shop. "Sadly, we shall never know now you have had the photographs stolen." "Hang on; let me check the negatives I keep in the loft." Jack came jumping down the stairs, "These negatives are the same date, come into the dark room and see if any of these negatives are what you are looking for."

Jack spent quite a while going through the negatives; suddenly he said, "Are these the ones you want?" "Yes Jack, Bingo!" Jack sent them out of the dark room while he printed the film off; he came out of the room. "I'll open another bottle while the prints are drying off, cheers." Fred and Dan were getting a little anxious hoping that Dan's hunch will come to fruition. Jack came out of the dark room holding the prints, "Is this, what you were hoping to see?" "It is Jack, exactly what we wanted to see," Fred looked at the prints, "Your right Dan, it is Lord Thames and Sir Henry Grainger, what is our next move? I will arrange a meeting with Lance; I feel we have been taken for a couple of fools. I'll ring him tonight telling him we want to meet tomorrow as a matter of urgency." Fred telephoned Lance asking him to meet them the following morning explaining it is an emergency; he agreed to meet but was not sure that Ken will be able to leave his office.

Dan and Fred were up and off to the store early to deal with any mail or problems that Alan might have but he appears to be handling the store, staff and the people who rent space very well. He and Brenda seem to be fully in charge of the unit. It went through Dan's mind again, he felt sure that Alan and Brenda are becoming an item and a very capable couple they are too. Lance arrived at eleven o'clock as arranged and they were pleased to see that Ken accompanied him. After all the greeting and handshakes, they went into a private office, when they were seated, Brenda, the chief cashier, sent a young lady into the office to serve coffee.

Fred looked Lance straight in the face, "I felt sure you and I would be on the same side, especially after serving together on the Dunkirk Beaches and witnessing the atrocities carried out by the Germans." Lance looked completely puzzled, Fred turned to Ken, "You allowed my entire staff to endanger their lives and my own flesh and blood to take part in the charade of the Germans searching this building on the pretence of catching the so called Nazi followers."

Dan was taken by surprise at Fred's attack on these two senior Home Office Officials. "I am very nervous and upset that Dan and I have been put in such a position that we have become pawns in a power struggle and made fools of. I have discussed the situation with Dan and you can no longer expect any further cooperation from us or our staff."

Lance pushed his bright red flushed disfigured face into Fred's face, "What on earth are you talking about Fred?" "Ask Ken," Ken said, "I can honestly say, I have no idea which road Fred is trying to take us down." "When the meeting in London finished, Dan purposely took us outside onto the pavement to prevent being overheard by any bugs picking up the conversation. Dan told you that he was confident that Lord Thames and Sir Henry Grainger were on the photographs with the German group at the opening of the Charity Shop." "That is right Fred, so what are you getting at?" "When we visited Jack Green twenty four hours later, his house had been broken into and all his files containing his photographs had been stolen."

Lance looked up, "What the hell has that got to do with me, I have not mentioned it to anyone, no one Fred?" "How about you Ken?" he replied, "I certainly have not mentioned it to a soul, I was hoping you had the photo to pass on to Peter, how did they know?" Lance and Ken looked at each other, neither claimed to have the answer. Dan laid the photographs on the table, Lance suddenly became excited, "You are right Dan and they are pictured quite clearly." Ken sat looking into space, "How did they get to know Lance, we did not mention it to anyone?"

They spent the next hour discussing how Dan's 100-1offer was picked up. They decided to go out to lunch, as they were standing up, a crackling noise came from Ken's jacket, Lance looked at Ken, "That is it, was it switched on that day?" "Yes, it will have been, because they monitor me 24hours a day for security or if they need to contact me.

Lance, telephone Judith and tell her I want the name of the person who was on monitor duty that day." The lunch was enjoyed knowing each could be trusted. Ken's secretary phoned the information he had asked for. " I'm off, before I go, I will entrust the three of you with this secret, my boss is the Home Secretary, only he and you three know that. If anything should go wrong, he will deny that he even knows me."

CHAPTER 30

Margery received an early morning telephone call from Mark's next door neighbour, telling her that Mark had been taken into hospital during the night and Sally had gone in the ambulance with him. She woke Dan up, he immediately roused himself and got out of bed, while he was getting dressed Margery got her car out of the garage and when Dan was ready, they drove off to the hospital. They were walking down the corridor when they saw Mark's neighbour, they stopped to thank them for the phone message.

They were shown into a small room off the main ward, Dan was dreadfully upset when he saw Mark laid in bed with his mouth open and saliva dribbling from each side of his mouth, Margery gently wiped his face, he looked ghastly. A doctor walked in, "Are you a relative?" "Yes he is my uncle," "I am sorry to tell you that while his wife sat holding his hand she had a severe heart attack, she is in the next room and it is unlikely that she will survive the day out." Margery started to cry and Dan was devastated, he could lose both in a matter of hours but as with his parents, neither would have to grieve for the loss of their lifetime partner. They sat by Mark and Sally's bedside, after a while they decided to go home as there was nothing they could do.

Dan received the sad telephone call from the hospital the following morning telling him that both Sally and Mark had passed away during the night, he just went numb but it was obvious he should have expected this call. Dan contacted an undertaker and asked him to deal with all the arrangements and was given a date for the funeral for both Sally and Mark. Dan then contacted all the members of the family but his brothers Jack and Brian did not want to know. Sally and Mark had said many months before their death, no flowers but make donations to the Daisy Charity.

Dan and Margery were surprised, by the number of people in the church, all the seats were taken and people were standing at the back of the church, of course the two front rows were reserved for the family. Dan had not realised that they had so many friends. There were several families from their old neighbourhood in Springfield Street and they too were looking elderly. Dan was very pleased that so many people had come along to say farewell to Sally and Mark. Dan had insisted that the

DFF Factory and The Fifth Column Store should remain closed for the day as a mark of respect.

After the service and the burial, they went to a hotel, which, the undertaker had arranged to serve light refreshments. A gentleman came up to Dan, "May I introduce myself, my name is George Wright, I am Mark's solicitor." "Good lord, I would have thought we would have met before; Mark was a crafty little devil." said Dan laughing. "When the family is ready I would like to read Sally and Mark's joint will, I have another appointment in one hour." Dan went round and ushered the family into an adjoining room, which, had been prepared.

When they were all seated, George Wright said, "This is Sally and Mark's last will and testament; My golden pen and pencil, I leave to my nephew Dan Green. The house and the remainder of my estate after any debts have been paid; I leave to my Goddaughter Lillian. The solicitor turned to Lillian; I can tell you that there is quite a substantial sum of money involved, mainly in stocks and shares." Dan was more than surprised when he mentioned an approximate figure. Speaking to the solicitor later, it turned out that the first 5/- share that Dan had bought in Mark's name in 1938 was now worth a lot of money as he had never taken any dividend money, it had been reinvested in shares.

The only extravagance Sally and Mark had indulged in, was to buy a small three bed roomed bungalow, it was adapted for Mark to regain a little of his independence. The bungalow had a small flower garden, it became Sally's pride and joy and she would tend and nurture all the plants and flowers. She put bushes all around the garden to make it private. Mark would sit in the garden on a large cushioned chair, reading or sleeping. He thoroughly enjoyed just sitting there. He would sit, letting his mind drift back, thanking the Lord and realising how lucky he is to be sitting here because, as a young man he had been crushed by a falling crane in the dockyard and he was written off as dead but he survived. In spite of his handicap, he has led a very good life; this is due to his caring and loving wife Sally and financial help from his nephew Dan.

*

Ken telephoned Peter Horn on his private phone requesting a meeting in his office, no; on second thoughts can we make it in the car park. Peter was very intrigued but quite prepared to go along with Ken's request. The meeting was arranged for that afternoon, Ken was in the car park waiting for Peter to arrive and when he did arrive Ken got out of his car putting his fingers to his lips indicating that Peter should not speak. Ken put his hand over Peter's two-way bleeper and asked him to ensure it was switched off.

Ken explained to Peter what Dan had told them after the meeting in London and he was confident that two members present had been photographed with the group of Germans at the opening of the "Daisy Charity" in Liverpool and they would obtain the photos. Twenty-four hours later the photographers had been broken into and the photos stolen but fortunately he kept the negatives filed in the loft. Ken then pulled out the photos from his case and showed them to Peter, he looked at them, he cried out, "No not those two;" he went to his car to sit down as he was so taken aback. "Both of these gentlemen have been involved in every meeting held regarding this case and they knew our every move we made hoping to solve the problem. We now know, how these people kept one step ahead of us;" Ken could see that Peter was badly shaken.

"Make sure this information does not become common knowledge; we will feed them with false information hoping they will trip themselves up but whom can I trust. The agent on your monitor has disappeared, he must have been tipped off that he had been found out, again, by whom." "Peter your office must be full of these people," "Your right Ken; I must carefully clean it out."

Several days later, Peter Horn contacted Ken asking him to arrange a meeting with Lance, Dan and Fred attending. I would suggest Chester and it could be made to look like a shopping trip for the ladies. "The reason given for my absence is that my wife and I will be visiting a sick relative near Chester, does that sound right Ken?" "Yes, it sounds good." "No one should be carrying a monitor, if they are, it is to be unplugged, as switching them off does not always isolate them, they are so sensitive. You will note that I am showing my full confidence and trust in all four of you."

Two weeks later they all set off on the shopping trip to Chester, Pat; Lance's wife was quite excited at the prospect of visiting all the beautiful shops. The second evening they arranged to meet up at an old pub out in the sticks between Chester and Wrexham. After organising drinks and nibbles, the men left the ladies in a small lounge area seated in lush comfortable chairs with their glasses fully charged and an open bottle of wine on the table. The men went into a small adjoining room, which Peter and Ken had previously checked for any listening device

"Before I start this meeting, I would like to thank you gentlemen for coming along without any explanation being offered. However, the two gentlemen shown in the photograph are definitely suspect but they are regarded as very high-ranking officers. If I made a move at this moment in time, it could result in me losing my own job. To unmask these two traitors, we will have to build up an irrefutable dossier to prevent them wriggling off the hook. I have formulated a plan, which, I am going to explain to you but I do not want, or expect any of you to take part as it may be dangerous."

"I am going to call a meeting of the Security Committee at the Home Office; those present will include the two men in question. I will request reports relating to Birmingham, Liverpool and the smaller units we have found. After receiving these reports and discussing them, I will then proceed to outline my plan. I will let it be known, that on the copy of the videotape from our hidden camera, we noticed that they did not check the cold storage room, I am trying to organise a search of the room and try to find out what is so important to them. For the benefit of any gentleman who has not visited this building, the cold room was built in the main structure as it was a Pork Butchers Shop and the door to the cold room is just by the main door. The result of our search will not be available for several weeks as the technicians and their equipment are not available for three weeks at the earliest."

"Due to the cost involved and my reduced budget I am forced to lower the surveillance of the Liverpool building. The alarm systems on the doors and the security cameras have been removed. The owners were given the option of having the security systems left in place at their expense but they were reluctant to undertake such an expensive outlay."

Fred said, "I like the plan and if they make a move we shall know we are on the right track." Peter went on to say that he is arranging to have the locking device strengthened on the door, just to make things a little more interesting and a very trustworthy colleague of mine will set a camera to photograph all the people present at the meeting and record a sound track, which, I will put under lock and key.

Peter looked at Lance, "What have you in mind Lance." "You said you want to build up a dossier on these people, we have several photos showing them in the company of the Germans, going in and out of the Embassy House, Opening the Charity Shop, walking around the building with a copy of the building plans in their hands. There are also some films of them in the same company attending the funeral of Horace, who you may know was one of our agents. Incidentally, Horace's wife is the niece of Hans Kayberg." "Good lord, we already have seven photos, Lance will you collect them together and give them to me by hand, I do not trust the post," "Before I hand them over to you Peter, may I run them past Bill Russell at his engineering plant and ask him if any of these people were responsible for putting him under pressure."

CHAPTER 31

Gerry reported to Fred that the entrance into the extension from the store is now completed with the exception of the floor covering, for which we are awaiting delivery. "The toilets are almost finished; the tiling of the floor and walls will be completed by the time the lads go home tonight. I do hope the ladies like the tiles they chose now they are on the walls; No doubt they will tell you Fred. It would be a good idea, if you can arrange for Robert and his catering team into the extension to finalise the layout, we can then finish off the plastering and decorating."

"The serving counters and cupboards are being made at your factory and Roy has promised delivery tomorrow, that part of the job will be finished by tomorrow night even if I have to work late. I feel confident that the completed extension can be handed over to you in one week. The final step is to have the planning officer present while we couple up the waste and sewerage pipes to the main drains. I hope we do not get any trouble from them; they are usually quite keen when the main drainage system is opened"

"What colour do you want the walls painting in the seating and entrance area?" "The ladies will tell us, I will discuss it with them this evening." Fred telephoned Bella, asking if he, Dan and their wives could spend the evening with them, Bella's immediate response was, "Yes please, do come, the company will do Frank good, as you know he does not get out much since his heart attack." Fred put the sample sheets of the various colourings that Gerry had loaned him into his car, hoping he could get a decision tonight. He thought it would be better to choose the colour on site but when they looked at the patterns, all three were adamant that the colour should be Primrose, so that was it.

Once the decision had been made, Bella made a pot of coffee and Frank opened a bottle of whiskey, Mary looked up, "I wonder who will be driving home?" Fred told Frank a little of what was happening since Terry was returned home but the most important thing is the trading at the store is on an upward trend. "We must hope that when the tea room and the toilets are completed they will attract people into the store to socialise and end up buying."

During a quiet moment, Dan said, "Let us open the extension on the same day as the Mobile Clinic is handed over to the Daisy Charity." "Brilliant, it will be all tied up with The Fifth Column, thus keeping the name of our store in the public's mind, just think of the publicity we shall gain." Right, Frank opened his diary, "How about two weeks next Friday," they all agreed on the date providing everything is in place several days prior to that date.

Fred telephoned Dan, we have a hiccup! DFF have received a large order from one of our main customers and it has a time scale when it is required, this will mean that the table and chairs for the tearoom will be delayed; it is obvious that our customer must be given preference; and money from this order will pay for the tearoom's furniture, which, we are donating.

It was decided to call an emergency staff meeting, when they were all assembled in the canteen at the factory, Dan told them that the handing over of the Mobile Clinic and the opening of the tea rooms would be delayed and he proceeded to explain why. Charlie spoke up, "During the war, when the forces were desperate for canteen forms or desks, what did we do, we worked into the night to complete the order, why not now?" A chorus echoed through the canteen, yes, let us do that, strictly as volunteers, no payment; this was met with a lot of Yeah and No's.

Sam and Roy arranged everything and so the plan went ahead but after working several evenings they found the bottleneck was with getting the furniture polished. To prevent the trustees being disappointed the staff in the polishing unit worked throughout the weekend to clear the backlog. Dan had brought in several bottles of wine; the first bottle was opened as the final chair came off the ramp. Fred looked across at Dan, "Just like old times but we did not have wine then." The extension was completed with furniture, electrical and catering equipment all in place two days prior to the opening.

The day of the handing over of the Mobile Clinic into the care of Daisy Charity Trustees had been eagerly awaited and it had been positioned in the car park to the rear of the extension. It was a glorious day, cool but dry and sunny, just right for such an occasion. The reflection of the sun shinning on the beautiful cream painted mobile, with its brown lettering of Daisy Charity made it look magnificent. The car park was full of supporters and well-wishers and of course the Lord Mayor and his entourage were present, it is a wonderful opportunity for them to be seen supporting a local charity.

Charlie got on to the platform and thanked every one for coming along to support such a wonderful charity and he pointed out, that it is only through your donations that made it possible for our work to be carried out. I must give special thanks to Mr Bill Nash for donating the Mobile Clinic; (Charlie had to halt for a while until the applause died down) it is a wonderful gift to the children who are in need of help and many thanks for all the monetary gifts to supply the clinic with the medical equipment, which have been donated. The Lord Mayor then took over, thanking Charlie and all the trustees for all their hard work in creating such a wonderful charity, helping people to live a normal life after the operation. "I am proud to be the Mayor of such generous people," with that he handed the microphone to Daisy. Daisy stepped up and cut the ribbon across the door of the mobile clinic showing the operating theatre but people were not allowed to go on board. The lighting was switched on to illuminate the interior, which could be seen quite clearly, while standing outside.

Dan was taken aback when Daisy said, "All this is down to the brainchild of Dan Green, he comes up with these ideas and somehow we all think, it is we who first thought of it," Frank was seated in a wheelchair, he said, "Yes, Dan is a crafty devil," this caused some laughter. "It was Dan who got some friends to help me," Daisy lifted her foot showing it to be straight, no longer deformed.

"Now I am going to hand you over to the man himself," with that, she handed Dan the scissors, he was taken by surprise and he was a little lost for words, he had not anticipated this happening. He stepped forward and cut the ribbon across the door at the back of the extension, as he cut the ribbon he said, "I declare all our ventures open," he received a loud round of applause. "Ladies and Gentlemen, you may go through the Basement, along the passage way and up our new stairway to the store, then enter the Tea Room where light refreshments are being served all free of charge, Yes, free of charge, we have made this arrangement but some of you like me, may prefer to enter through this door. You have my heartfelt gratitude for all the money you have donated to the Daisy Charity, I often wish there had been help for me as a child but God has been very good to me, Thank You All." The cheering and clapping brought tears to his eyes. "Just one other thing, the Tea Room is to be renamed to be called Daisy's Kitchen."

The parents of the children who had been helped by the charity had been contacted asking if they would allow their child to wear a golden silk sash with "THANK YOU" printed on it. The parents raised no objections and several children mingled in the crowd, saying thank you to various people and telling them what a difference it has made to their lives.

*

Sunday morning, Margery and Dan were up having an early breakfast, today, it is Margery's turn on the rota to open up the charity shop and issue the entrance tickets. Starting at ten o'clock and she will be on duty till two. When they arrived, there were quite a few waiting to enter the basement, several would just wander through and wait for the cafe to open. The pattern of the morning visitors is normally groups of people or families and in the afternoon it would be individuals just meandering through to the cafe, no one minded, they had paid their entrance fee and they might be tempted to spend some money when they leave going through the craft shop, in fact, it appears to be just somewhere for them to go. Dan was wandering around and he looked at the cold room door, it is now six days and no one has risen to the bait, have we got it wrong?

Mary and Fred arrived to relieve Margery and they would be on duty until five o'clock, the person taking the morning duty prepares the evening meal for the afternoon couple. As Dan was leaving, Fred shouted to Margery, make it a good one tonight, I'm hungry now, Margery picked up an empty cardboard box and threw it at him, he ducked but the fun was appreciated. At three o'clock the basement got unusually busy, the people were queuing to buy their tickets to get in.

Fred looked across and saw a group of four men standing near the cold room door, the man at the front of the four had taken his camera out of its case and stood holding it, suddenly there was flash, a basement volunteer ran across and told the man that photography is not permitted and pointed to a sign stating that fact, the man apologised and put his camera back into its case. A man standing next to Fred said, "That is odd, it was the man behind him that took the photograph," Fred just smiled. The man at the rear of the group must have photographed the locking mechanism on the door.

Fred could not contain himself, he went to his office and telephoned Lance, before he could answer, Fred said, "They have risen to the bait and then he went to explain how they had gone about obtaining the photograph," "I bet Ken will be pleased to receive this news." "I will visit you tomorrow as I intend to meet Bill Russell and take him through the photos we have. Fred, make sure all the doors are locked, even if the catering staff and the basement staff hand you the keys and make sure that the security system is all activated, like telling Grandma how to suck eggs." They both laughed.

Darkness was closing in; Fred decided to bring his car from the rear car park and leave it outside the main door, as it always appears to be so pitch black in the rear car park. He decided to bring this matter up at the next meeting and have the car park illuminated for the customer's comfort and safety. Mary went outside and got in the car to wait while Fred finished locking up, Fred felt very uneasy. He double checked the security and the cold room door, as he was turning off the lights the uneasy feeling returned, he felt as if his every movement was being watched, in fact, he felt nervous for the first time since he was under fire when serving in the army, he just could not shake the feeling off. He stepped on to the pavement and locked the main door, he kept looking over his shoulder as he did so his unease did not leave him, the night was dark and it had an eerie atmosphere, he was so pleased that he had brought the car from the car park. He got into the car, Mary looked at Fred, "What on earth is a matter Fred," "I cannot give you an answer Mary, I feel we are being watched, I have such an uncomfortable feeling." "Drive me home Fred Wharton, we are going to Margery's for dinner."

While they were having dinner, Mary looked across at Fred, "Go on Fred, and tell him, I know you are dying to." Fred told them all about the four gentlemen who came obviously to photograph the locking mechanism on the cold room door, I passed this information on to Lance and then he went through the security routine asking me to ensure that all the doors were locked and the security activated, whether it was him going on I don't know but while I was locking up I had a most horrible feeling that my every movement was being watched and when I stepped on to the pavement it did not leave me. Dan smiled, "It has not put you off your food," "Nor his booze," said Mary. In spite of all their jesting, Fred had that feeling that something was not just right.

*

The following morning Lance arrived at the store at eleven o'clock and joined Fred in his office, Fred told him how he felt the previous evening. "You were right Fred there were three men wandering about in the craft shop; they were measuring and examining the locking mechanism on the cold room door. When they left, they locked the main door behind them with a key." "How the dickens did they get a key"? "You tell me Fred, the situation gets worse each day." "Incidentally Fred, I visited Bill this morning and he identified two of the men who pressurised him on the photographs, the main man was referred to as Heini.

Margery and Mary opened the Basement on the Wednesday afternoon to get ready for a coach party to arrive, the inclusion of the toilets and Daisy's Kitchen plus the novelty of the Basement, has created an attraction for the tour companies. One of their volunteers named Norma Watson arrived to help them, when Mary saw Norma she was staggered, the previous week Norma had bounced in to tell them that her husband Brian had been promoted to Sales Director with the large engineering works along the East Lancs Road but today she looked so ill and she had been crying, her eyes were red and puffy. Mary went up to her, "What on earth is the matter Norma, are you not well, perhaps you should return home." Norma started sobbing, "No, I don't want to go home."

Mary looked at Margery who just nodded, Mary put her arm around Norma's shoulders, "Come along, we will go for a cup of tea." As they entered the tearoom, Robert's wife saw how distressed Norma was, she poured out two cups of tea and placed them on a table in the rear corner of the tearoom away from the other tables. "Have you trouble at home Norma, with that she burst into tears again, can I help you in any way?" "Mary, I have landed in terrible trouble through no fault of my own, if I tell you, please do not tell a soul," "Of course not, if that is what you want."

"Last week-end I attended a charity conference, which was held at a Manchester Hotel, after the afternoon session we all went to our rooms and got changed for dinner, after dinner we sat around chatting and discussing the after dinner speeches that had taken place and of course every body were continually being introduced to members from other parts of the country. I was introduced to two gentlemen who said they were from the South Coast and they had dealings with the company by whom my Brian is employed. One of the men offered to buy me a drink, he brought it to the table and then introduced me to other members of their group, I drank my wine and I cannot remember anything else."

"The next thing I knew I woke up in a bed and I was completely naked with a naked man beside me. I jumped up and started to cry and shout but one of them put a cloth over my mouth and proceeded to show me photographs of me in all sorts of sexual positions and of me performing disgusting sexual acts. I was then told if I didn't do as they ask of me they would send the photographs to my Brian and his company. Whatever they put in my drink it put me out like a light. She started sobbing again, what can I do Mary?" "Are you sure the photographs are of you?" "As well as I could tell Mary but what I was suppose to be doing was awful." "Have you heard from them since." "Yes, I had to leave the keys to the craft shop door on the counter, then go into the Basement, after ten minutes go back and pick up my keys again?" "I cannot tell you the full story but do you trust me?" "Of course I do Mary." "These people are very dangerous, they have committed several murders, which cannot be proven. Will you allow me to discuss your problem with Fred and a very senior Home Office Official? You will be quite safe and we can sort out your problem." "Mary, providing it remains between us and it does not involve my husband or his employers." "To avoid any embarrassment, I will tell them the whole story without you being present." "Yes Mary, I will agree to that but bear in mind I will have to decide when we meet up as I have two children to take care of." Norma did feel a little easier having shared her problem with Mary.

Mary went into the store and found Fred in his office. "Fred can you find Dan and Lance and meet me in your office as soon as possible, please." They all went into Fred's office, close the door Fred, What I am going to tell you is strictly confidential. Mary started to relate Norma's story when Lance said, "Wait, I would like Ken to be hear this, I will telephone him, and while we are waiting for him to arrive, Mary, will you take these photographs and ask Norma if she can identify any of them." Ken joined them in less than one hour; they used Fred's office as it is away from the main sales floor. "Before I start, Norma has identified these two men; at the charity conference." "Good heavens, they are the same two who Bill Russell pointed out this morning." "I will start at the very beginning of Norma's story; Mary related every minute detail as Norma had told her." "Did she examine the photographs that were shown to her?" "She said not, as she was too distressed, which, is understandable." "I would gamble that her face has been superimposed on the photograph by computer. Ken then turned to Mary, "Would you be kind enough to take Norma to this address where she will receive a full medical examination. We must make sure that her body has not been violated and to ensure that she has not become pregnant, or that she has not become subjected to any sexual disease. Advise me of the date you are going and I will arrange everything to be dealt with very discretely. I am not saying she has a problem but we must safeguard this lady who has played an innocent part in this plot. Now we have identified the two men I will have them dealt with," a large smile crossed Ken's face. "Lance will you make arrangements to have the door lock changed and do not give Norma a new set of keys. I will meet you here in two days, okay," and off Ken went.

True to his word, Ken contacted Lance and he in turn spoke to Dan and Fred asking them to organise a meeting and to ensure the Mary and Norma will be present. The meeting was arranged and when the meeting started, Ken pointed out that Bill Russell and Norma had identified the same two men in the photographs. "My agents located these men and they were very quietly arrested and they are now in Scotland in a detention centre. One of them is Karl Krupp, his duty is to act as Otto's bodyguard, Otto will be wondering what has happened to him. Karl was the man who forced Bill to operate the furnace, which, turned out to be a terrible incident causing the unnecessary loss of three lives, this man is vicious and wicked. The second man is quite a mystery; we cannot quite understand what his duties are supposed to be."

Looking across at Norma, "It was just as I had expected, the picture of your face was transposed on to the terrible photographs by using a computer, it was such an amateurish attempt. The drug in the wine was not very strong but it did put you to sleep and you were taken into a bedroom and laid on a bed. One hour later just as you started to waken, you were administered with a strong hallucinatory drug. When you did wake up, you were convinced that you were naked; which you were not, in fact, there were not any men on the bed with you, the drug they used creates all sorts of mental delusions. One of the men arrested gave me the photographs and told me the full story, he is pleased to be under arrest away from Otto and Hans, he claims they are going mental, as they have failed to recover what they regard as their own. No one knows what it is they are looking for apart from themselves."

"Norma, you have nothing to fear, you were targeted to get a set of keys, as a safeguard you will no longer hold any keys. You can go home and carry on with your life." Norma, burst into tears while trying to say thank you. Dan said, "They are very wicked people to cause an innocent person such anguish."

CHAPTER 32

Ken rang his immediate boss, the Home Secretary on his red scrambler direct line telephone, "Can you talk?" "No, shall we meet in the car park," "Yes, park too close to my car, I can then argue with you, then we shake hands," okay? If it is imperative that we meet, I will palm a suggested meeting place." Ken went into the car park and parked his car very close to the Home Secretary's vehicle, as his boss came out of the building and went to his car, Ken moved his car to allow his boss room to open his car door, he apologised, no harm done, with that he put his hand out to shake hands. Ken was conscious of a piece of paper being put into his hand, which, he slipped into his pocket, they said cheerio and Ken drove off. He parked in a lay-by along the road, pulled out the piece of paper from his pocket and it read, Meet me at the Cow and Calf, Ilkley, Yorkshire; spend the week-end there with your wife. We have not met before, I will deal with introductions.

Ken and his wife Kelly arrived at the Hotel about four o'clock, they rested and later they changed and went down to dinner. They enjoyed the meal and Kelly enjoyed having Ken so relaxed, which, is so unusual for him. After dinner they went into the bar, Ken went to the bar and ordered a Brandy for himself and a G&T for Kelly, they sat down at a small table away from the crowded bar counter. Kelly was really beginning to enjoy herself. The Home Secretary walked in and went to the bar, having bought their drinks, he looked at Ken and walked across, "Don't we know each other?" "Not that I am aware of," said Ken.

"I am sure we met at the Woodbridge Golf Club a few months back, it was a competition sponsored by one of the Car Manufacturing Company's."

"Yes, I remember now, it was in the bar," they both laughed as Kelly said,

"Where else?"

"Firstly, let me introduce my wife Olga and my name is Nathan," "Ken got to his feet, this is my wife Kelly and I am Ken." "May we join you?" "Yes please do."

They sat down at the small table together and Ken and Nathan continued talking golf, Nathan said, "There is a golf club quite near and it has a Driving Range and practise putting grounds." Kelly and Olga were chatting away quite happily, Kelly turned to Olga, and "Do you like

Markets?"Yes, I love them," "Right, if these two little boys are going to play with sticks and a little white ball tomorrow, shall we go to Skipton Market?" "Lunchtime, I will take you to a Fish Restaurant by the canal bridge, we might have to wait for a table but when the fish is served, I feel sure, that you will agree it was worth the wait."

After breakfast, Ken and Nathan went into the car park, Nathan said, "I will drive and he went to an old banger of a car, Nathan laughed, this belongs to my Grandson, I left my car in my daughters garage, I feel confident that there are no bugs in this car," Ken replied, "Has it got an engine?" they both laughed loudly, in fact, louder than the joke warranted.

During dinner that evening, Nathan turned to his wife, "Ken has been telling me all about a store named The Fifth Column in Liverpool and in the basement it is completely stocked with guns, uniforms and food ready for the Germans if they had invaded this country during the war. It has been made into a tourist attraction and all the entrance money goes to the Daisy Charity and the funds are used to pay for medical help for any child born with deformed feet. Have we anything on next week-end?" "No," "In that case it might be worth a visit." "Olga turned to Kelly, will you be able to persuade your husband to bring you along?" "I think I might be able to persuade him, I have my ways," Olga's face formed into a large grin. "Nathan, if you are serious about going, the hotel I use is the Adelphi, it is central for the city and I found it very comfortable. The thing we will have to worry about is all the beautiful shops and stores that will encourage the ladies to open their purses;" this brought hissing from the ladies. "Providing everything goes okay, we will meet you in Liverpool next week-end, I am looking forward to visiting the Basement, from what you have told me Ken, you have stirred my inquisitive mind."

*

Friday afternoon Ken's wife was packed and waiting for the off, Ken found it amusing the way Kelly was preparing for a week-end away, she didn't care, she thinks it is about time they she had some week-end breaks. They went away last week-end and this was the first few days away for about six months, Ken is always working and no time for his home life. Kelly and Olga had discussed this problem last weekend and she too has yet to overcome the hours Nathan is working. It was now one o'clock and no sign of Ken, Kelly was getting annoyed, he had promised to be home by lunchtime to ensure that they would arrive in Liverpool by teatime.

The clock was striking two o'clock as Ken came dashing through the front door, sorry I am late, I will be washed and changed in ten minutes, he kissed her as he dashed past her, it all happened so quickly, she didn't get time to tell him off, instead, she just smiled. Kelly had a cup of tea ready by the time Ken came down the stairs all ready to set off, he sat down and chatted to Kelly, after a few minutes they were both happy with each other. They were up and off in a matter of fifteen minutes and if the traffic is kind they should arrive in Liverpool in about one hours travelling time but unfortunately the traffic was far from kind and it took them two hours. When they arrived and checked in Ken said, "Have Nathan and Olga arrived yet Kelly?" "Yes, I have seen their names on the register, they are in the room next to ours." On the way to their room Ken knocked on the door to say hello, Olga opened the door, "Come in we have just opened a bottle of wine, do come in and help us drink it," this caused some laughter, the laughter became infectious, after a couple of drinks they were giggling like young children, the wives were so excited to get away with their husbands for another week-end. Kelly was so surprised with the hustle and bustle of the city, she had not experienced such an electric atmosphere as she found in Liverpool and she loved it. There appeared to be so much going on, she would need at least a week to visit a fraction of the activities in the city.

They met for dinner at eight o'clock and it was decided to drink iced water with the meal in view of the drinking prior to the meal. They found the service excellent and the meal absolutely delicious, they were going to enjoy this weekend. They were just finishing their meal when Ken saw Lance and his wife Pat walk into the dinning room, Ken was a little surprised as he had not told Lance of his visit. When Ken and his party got up from the table, he said, "We must say hello to Lance," Ken introduced Lance as Major Goodchild and Nathan as a Home Office Official; we shall be in the lounge when you have finished your dinner. When Lance and Pat did finish their meal they decided to have their coffee served in the bar and so they joined Ken's party.

Ken told Lance that his party wanted to visit The Fifth Column and the Basement and Nathan was particularly interested in the layout and the interference from some people. Lance said, "May I suggest that I lead the way as I can guide you away from the city traffic." "Yes, we will be guided by you Lance," both Kelly and Olga found Pat easy to get on with, so the husbands are in for a lot of trouble, knowing how Pat likes shopping. Lance side lined Ken, "Is there any reason for this visit Ken?" "None what so ever Lance, the wives have dragged us away for a weekend, they are fed up with us working all the time. I will meet you in the car park in the morning and you can lead the way."

The following morning they shared the same table for breakfast, when they had all finished eating, they collected their coats and off they went. Ken and his party followed Lance to the store and they parked in the car park at the rear of the Fifth Column. They walked around the building to the Charity Shop and Margery was waiting for them, Pat introduced Margery to Nathan and Olga, Ken introduced Kelly to Margery. The Basement was opened up for them to enter and Nathan and his wife were fascinated with the layout, it was still as the Germans had set it up, the thing that Nathan found very difficult to understand is how it had been all constructed during the war.

After spending quite a while looking around, Lance then took them up the new stairs to visit Daisy's Kitchen where they all enjoyed coffee and home made cakes. Dan, Fred and his wife Mary walked in and were introduced. They were all chatting away, Dan took Margery to one side,

"Shall we invite them to dinner tonight?" "Yes, if Robert and his team can organise the catering, I will ask him." Margery went into the kitchen and asked Robert if he and his staff could put on a meal for them. "I will ask my colleagues," after a few minutes he came back, "How many people?" "Ten," "Yes we can do that for you." "I will go and invite them," when Margery invited them to their house for dinner they immediately replied, yes please. Margery went back to Robert and handed him the key to her house to enable him to go and make the necessary preparation for the meal.

Before they left Dan took them round the store showing them the beautiful decoration in the old cinema. They walked round to the car park and Dan opened the doors of the Mobile Clinic, as before no one was allowed to go on board, they were all very impressed and asked for the details how they could help. "I will tell you the full story tonight after dinner. We will expect you about six o'clock then we can have a drink before dinner."

When they arrived Dan suggested that they should put their cars in the drive to prevent any damage by leaving them on the main road and depending on the amount of drink consumed, they could always get a taxi back to their hotel later this evening and collect the cars in the morning.

They sat having a drink and Kelly said, "She had not been to Liverpool before and she finds the city really fascinating. They were all very impressed with the meal, Dan was really delighted considering Robert and his team had very little time to make the necessary preparations. After dinner, Dan "Related to Kelly and the other guests how the Basement was discovered and after all the publicity the members of the public wanted to visit the Basement. It was decided to open it to the public each Sunday, charging an entry fee, the money going to a charity, the choice of which charity was easy, my niece, Daisy, had her deformed foot corrected a few years ago and what a difference it made to that child, so that was our choice. Before we could go ahead with this project we arranged to rent the Pork Butchers Shop and built an entrance into the Basement and a Craft Shop by the exit, Kelly, you have no idea the fun we all had setting this up."

"One very important donation was made by Bill Nash, he ordered and paid for our Mobile Clinic, the instruments and the X-ray machinery was donated by various charitable organisations in Bill's town of Dewsbury. That is how it all came about Kelly." "Thank you Dan, it is a credit to you all. Before I leave tomorrow, I would like to look around the Basement and your store once more as I am most impressed with the beautiful surroundings and its layout."

The following morning they all met up in the Fifth Column, after looking around the store, they went into Daisy's Kitchen. They sat drinking coffee and talking among themselves, Fred looked up as six men walked in, Fred, recognised Hans, Otto, Sir Henry, Lord Thames and the other two were on the photographs who Ken thought were Members of Parliament. They ordered coffee, their talking got louder and louder. It was obvious that they were arguing and they started shouting at each other, it became very heated and looked as if they would come to blows. Robert came from behind the counter and asked the gentlemen to leave as they were upsetting the other customers. Without any objection they got out of their chairs but they were still arguing as they walked out of the restaurant. Kelly looked at Fred, "I see what you mean." Nathan sat observing all that transpired, hoping he had not been recognised as the Home Secretary

*

Charlie contacted the trustees of the Daisy Charity; he had received a letter from Bill Nash inviting the trustees and their wives to a luncheon in Leeds, the date of their choosing. They were all very pleased to accept the invitation; the date was arranged and agreed on. Fred and Mary shared their car with Dan and Margery, Charlie transported the other members and Sam and his wife had arranged to meet them at the hotel.

On arrival they were very pleased to meet Sam and his wife together with his two nurses. A sherry reception was held in a small room away from the dining area. Bill greeted them as they arrived, having done so, he stood and said, "I would like you to meet my daughter and her daughter, my Granddaughter Lucy, with the introduction made, Pat walked in holding Lucy's hand, Lucy was skipping as she entered the room. I want to thank you all for what you have created, from which, my little Lucy have benefited. She is now a happy healthy little girl with her deformed foot corrected," Lucy bowed; they all gave her a round of applause. "Bill, think how many children that have benefited and hopefully many more in the future, this have been made possible by your most generous gift of the Mobile Clinic. The clinic is going south next week to help four children, in fact, two of the children are babies," said Dan, this received a round of applause. They all went into the dining room.

CHAPTER 33

Nathan, Ken and their wives left to face the journey home later that day but Pat and Lance checked out of the hotel and accepted the hospitality of Mary and Fred. Lance contacted his office and advised his secretary where he was and his telephone number, should she have the need to contact him. He and Fred sat discussing the incident during their coffee in Daisy's Cafe that morning. Neither could understand the hostility and venom the six men showed to each other but they agreed that the situation is getting explosive. The Germans have never reported the missing two men who were arrested and taken to a prison in Scotland. It was if they had never existed, or is it they don't want to know, or, they don't want to been associated with them.

That evening Lance received a message from the man in charge of the surveillance camera, monitoring the store, focusing on the Cold Room in particular. He reported that several men had entered the Charity Shop using a key to gain entry; it was obvious they were only interested in the locking mechanism of the Cold Room door, when they left, they locked the door. Both Fred and Lance were disturbed, "Where on earth did they get the key?" "The problem is certainly coming to a head Lance."

Lance contacted Ken and explained the report from the surveillance house; good things are beginning to move. Ken phoned Lance back later telling him that Peter Horn, the Home Office Spokesman, is holding a security meeting the following day and he will casually announce that the technicians have been made available two weeks earlier than had previously been planned. They have been issued with precise instructions to carry out a full survey of the Cold Room, using their most up to date technical equipment. When I receive their report I will call a meeting to discuss their findings. "Lance, it will be interesting to wait and see if this information filters back, if it does, to watch the Germans reaction. This should force their hand, if they are still intent on searching the building. Make it more fun Lance, "Change the locks again but make sure this is carried out very discreetly."

Two nights later the Germans paid a visit to the Craft Shop, it became obvious that the purpose of their visit was again to inspect the locking device on the Cold Room door. One of the group produced a key and proceeded to attempt to unlock the door but the key did not operate the lock. Otto pushed the man to one side and he tried to unlock the door, he too, was unsuccessful. He threw the key to the floor and stamped his feet as he left the shop, another member of the group locked the door as they left. The man operating the camera managed to get a close up of the group and it was the same six people who had caused the unpleasant rumpus in Daisy's Kitchen the previous day. In the light of this report, Ken arranged to have a team of agents inside the store each night. The senior officer will have radio contact with Ken and he will take charge of the operation.

Fred received a phone call very late in the evening from Lance telling him that a small explosion had taken place in the Basement of the Fifth Column Store. The team of agents, Ken Lee had ordered to stay each night in the store, found that the lock had been blown off the door of the Cold Room. On checking they found six men in the cold room with a technical probing device, which, they were placing against each wall of the room. The men have been arrested, charged with breaking, entering and trespassing.

They were put into the Black Maria and transported to a secure Prison in Preston. When their details was being asked and entered on the charge sheet, Otto Kranz and Hans Kayberg both claimed diplomatic immunity claiming they were German envoys to this country but their claim was completely disregarded by the authorities and they were placed in separate cells. The Home Secretary contacted the War Crimes Commission, passing the details of the two men under arrest and requested an early reply.

The following day he received a message asking him to deport the two men to Germany, they will be charged with atrocities, rape and murder during the year's 1940 to 1945.

They feature prominently on the wanted list. It was arranged that the two men should be deported and agents to escort them until they are handed over to the commission. The Home Secretary ordered the release of Otto and Hans and arranged for their deportation, they were taken to Manchester Airport and put on a plane bound for Germany.

Although they were handcuffed to the agents, they were so arrogant and cocked a snoot at the agents but their attitude was short-lived, as they stepped off the plane they were placed under arrest by the German authorities. They will remain under arrest while the charges are prepared for the trial.

Fred had called to pick up Dan and they went to the store to check, what, if any damage had been caused by the explosion. They entered the store by the main door locking it behind them, at first sight, they could not see any damage in the store but walking down the sloping floor towards the stage, they noticed the force of the explosion had damaged the screen and some of the surrounding area. Fred jokingly said, "I hope your little pet has not been damaged." Dan said, "I will check the organ Fred. The organ is okay but the base of several organ pipes have become dislodged, we can soon push them back into place Fred." As they started levering them back into position, Fred noticed something hanging down from one of the pipes, he pulled it down and to their amazement it was two oil paintings one larger than the other rolled up in a cardboard tube. They checked the next pipe and found another two paintings, Fred continued checking and to his and Dan's surprise, they discovered two small chamois leather pouches, when they opened the pouches they could not believe their eyes, they contained Diamonds. They continued checking the other pipes and they found another four pouches making six in total.

"We must ring Lance and tell him we have found what the Germans have being looking for," said Fred. They went into Fred's office to make the phone call, he explained exactly what they had found and where. Dan and Fred checked what they had found and waited for Lance to arrive, he had alerted the security people. They showed the four paintings and five chamois leather pouches, each pouch had the name of a bank stamped on it and a person's name. "Pass me an envelope Fred," Lance selected a few Diamonds, placed them in the envelope and put the envelope in Fred's safe, "Why don't you take a few for yourselves," Fred declined, Lance smiled a knowing smile.

Ken walked in, he had a big smile across his face, "Thanks lads, we have cracked it at last." Dan and Fred left the office while Lance showed Ken the treasure that had been found, "God Lance! There must be a fortune here," the security people came in, counted the Diamonds, sealed and numbered the pouches and tubes containing the paintings, they handed Lance a receipt for the items.

Dan and Fred went home taking the pouch with them. They met up for dinner at Fred's house, after dinner Fred tipped the Diamonds out of the pouch on to the table, both Margery and Mary gasped, they had never seen the like before in their life. Dan told them how they had been found and he described the oil paintings and said that they will fetch a fortune at any auction. "Are you sure you will not get into trouble removing these precious stones?" "Strictly speaking, they were on our property," without any more discussion; they were divided into three and placed in Fred's safe. "We must make a point of visiting Frank and put him in the picture."

Later that evening Fred telephoned Jack Green and explained about the explosion and what they discovered hidden in the organ pipes. "Bring your camera along with you in the morning and you can photograph the pipes before they are pushed back in place and I will tell you exactly what was found. I promise you won't get beaten up this time," this made Jack laugh.

*

Two days after arriving in Germany, Otto and Hans were taken to a courtroom to hear the charges against them read out by the clerk of the court. "Nazi Officer Hans Kayberg, you are charged with ordering the killing of wounded Prisons of War, Murder and causing a lot of suffering to humanity. How do you plead," Hans shouted, "Not Guilty?"

"S.S. Officer Otto Kranz, you are charged with ordering the shooting and killing of Prisoners of War, Rape and Murder of a British Intelligence Officer two weeks ago. How do you plead"? Otto just scowled at the bench and shouted, "Nonsense, I am Not Guilty." The judge just smiled, you will both remain in custody while preparations are made for the trial, which will take place in the Nuremberg court as used years ago to try the Nazis leaders.

The date of the trial was set, on the day, Otto and Hans were brought to the courtroom, both handcuffed and under a heavy guard. The three judges sat on the bench adorned in their black gowns and wearing wigs. There were two teams of lawyers, one for the prosecution and the other for the defence. There were also a number of interpreters, as many of the witnesses would speak in different languages to ask and answer the questions in court.

The first witness called by the prosecution was Brigadier Smithson. He told how Hans was put in charge of removing the dead and injured from the Dunkirk Beach, after the allies had left. He related how his hair and face had been purposely targeted by an enemy flame thrower, his face was tended to by the British Medics to prevent infection but no treatment was offered or received from the Germans that is the reason for my badly scarred scalp and face but as it turned out, I was one of the lucky ones.

Brigadier Smithson went on to explain how the dead were collected from the Dunkirk Beaches and thrown in a long deep trench that the other prisoners had been forced to dig. As the bodies were put in the trench, one or two moved and the guards shot them. The injured were carried off the beach as they were unable to walk and they were shot and rolled into the trench. The walking injured like myself, had to stand and watch this atrocity being carried out and unable to prevent it taking place. The defence lawyer did not attempt to question the Brigadier but he did say that Officer Kayberg was only carrying out orders.

The next witness called to give evidence, was a retired German soldier, he told of similar situations as described by Brigadier Smithson. He still experiences nightmares of being forced to shoot prisoners of war; if he hadn't carried out orders he would have been shot. He was ordered to shoot injured prisoners of war, High Command would not accept prisoners unless they could walk and work. It was Officer Kayberg who ordered the slaughter of the helpless wounded soldiers. Several more witnesses were called, each relating the cruel suffering Hans Kayberg caused; in fact, they all painted the same picture.

*

Otto was the next accused called to the stand, he just glared around still with the arrogant look on his face. The first witness called by the prosecutor was a soldier who escaped when he was a Prisoner of War. He told how when he was in a Prisoner of War camp in France, the Germans said that the camp had become overcrowded, they were going to transfer three truck loads to another camp and I was designated to go on truck number three.

When we left the prison camp, we travelled for approximately thirty minutes, the truck pulled off the road and entered a wooded area after a further fifteen minutes the vehicle came to a halt. The prisoners were ordered to get off the truck; there were two guards at the rear of the truck, pushing and pulling the prisoners to get them off the lorry, I had become friendly with one of the guards. As I was about to jump down off the truck, he stepped forward and indicated with his hand behind his back to run for my life, which I did and made it into the bushes without being seen, I had not realised it but a Polish soldier had run with me.

We both remained hidden to watch what was taking place. The prisoners were forced to dig a long deep trench, when they had completed digging the trench, Otto shouted, "Thank you gentlemen," with that, the guards opened fire on the prisoners, some fell into the trench and those that didn't were just rolled in. I remained behind the bushes until the Germans had driven away, my friend had looked in my direction and nodded, then I made a move and walked through the woodland until I came to a village. I was interrogated by the villagers, eventually they were satisfied that I was, who I claimed to be but they could not help me to escape, due to the heavy presence of the German army. They supplied me with forged papers and insisted that I pretended to be deaf and dumb.

One morning there was panic among the villagers, one of the look out posts reported several German troop carriers coming towards the village. Otto arrived with a number of troops, he ordered his troops to search several houses, no one knew the reason for the search, six of his soldiers dragged two young couples out of a house to the village square, Otto walked up to them, pulled out his revolver and shot the two men and the two young women were put into the van and driven away. I have never forgotten this vicious man."

Several more witnesses entered the stand to give damming evidence against Otto, mainly how he treated the prisoners of war in the camp where he was camp commander, he would kill without flinching. There were many incidents told in court but there was one which really brought tears to the eyes of the females employed in the courtroom. It was when a witness was brought in by the prosecutors, he being pushed in a wheelchair. He told how he and his pals from a neighbouring French village got together and created havoc for the Germans by blowing up train tracks and bridges. One afternoon when we met up, we were ambushed, they chased us but did not shoot to kill, they had us completely surrounded and we were captured. They marched us back to the village square and all the villagers were made to come out and watch. Otto shouted, "The Third Reich will have no more trouble from these ten men," "I thought we were going to die but what followed was worse. He ordered his troops to open fire and they machine gunned our legs, they were mashed." Otto laughed as he said; "You will not give me any more trouble." He marched off leaving us crawling around on the floor.

All of the ten men were in the courtroom in wheelchairs. The defence lawyers put forward their case stating their clients were carrying out orders. The prosecuting lawyers said "The witnesses had put their case for them." The senior judge said, "Having listened to the prosecutors and the defence lawyers, we will retire and consider the findings. The two accused will remain in custody while we are considering the case."

CHAPTER 34

The date for the judge's decision was arranged. On the day, Otto and Hans were transported to the courtroom in an armoured van and handcuffed to their escorts. The case had created a huge international interest, the courtroom could not accommodate all the visitors and the photographers were refused entry, a large crowd of people were left outside the courthouse. The same three judges were sitting on the bench; the senior judge told Otto and Hans. "We have considered the case very carefully. We have taken into account the arguments put forward by your defence team, saying you were forced to carry out the killings and sufferings. This does not change the fact, that you are both cruel vicious monsters and you were responsible for many unnecessary deaths just to satisfy your egos. We have come to a unanimous decision that you are both guilty of murder and caused suffering to humanity. Therefore, you are both sentenced to life imprisonment and I shall insist that you serve the full sentence. I wish your case had come before me a few years ago; you would have been sentenced to be hanged along with the other Nazi thugs."

Otto's face changed for the first time from arrogance to despair, Hans was whimpering as he was taken away to serve his sentence. When the prisoners were taken outside, to be placed in the armoured van, there were crowds of people pushing to get near the prisoners and the police had difficulty keeping control. There was the sound of a gunshot at the rear of the crowd, the security guards dashed off to investigate. The prisoners and their escorts quickly pushed through the crowd and nearly tripped over two wheelchairs, as the prisoners passed the chairs, the air was filled with the sound of automatic gunfire and there was a lot of screaming and panic. When the chaos was brought under control, they found both prisoners had their legs shattered by gunfire and they were crawling around on the floor pulling their escort down. The escorts were questioned, how did they escape the bullets. They just shrugged their shoulders. When the witnesses returned to their hotel, they found ten men in wheelchairs sat round a large table with their wives celebrating, celebrating revenge. No one was ever charged for the automatic gunfire. The other four prisoners were taken to the local courtroom and the charges read out against them, both Lord Thomas and Sir Henry were charged with treason and passing secrets to another country, they will remain in custody while arrangements are made to conduct the trial. The other two were told that apart from trespassing the prosecutors' said they did not intend pressing any other charges, they both received a caution and were discharged.

The trial of Lord Thomas and Sir Henry is now going to take place at the Old Bailey, the defence and the prosecuting legal teams each have now prepared their case. The judge sat on the high bench looking down on the courtroom; the jury was eventually selected, in spite of the many changes by the defence team of lawyers. The first witness called by the prosecuting team was Peter Horn, the spokesman for the Home Office. He described how over the years they had been trying to catch people who were spies in this country. When we had accumulated sufficient evidence, a raid would be planned to arrest the person or persons but when they arrived to make the arrest they found that the bird had flown the previous day, they had been alerted.

This was not an isolated case, quite recently we fed both of the accused with false information and sure enough they took the bait and passed it on to the Germans, they took the action as we had planned, that is how we managed to arrest them. The defence lawyers tried to change Peter Horn's evidence but he told how he arranged the false information to be told during a security meeting, at which, both of these gentlemen were present. They definitely passed this information on and you will not be able get me to change my statement.

The next witness to be called was Ken Lee; he was a Senior Secret Service Officer. He told how the two prisoners were constantly in the company of the Germans; I submit six photographs showing them in the enemy camp on different occasions as evidence. They were shown to the jury and then handed to clerk of the court who numbered them and put them on the table by his seat. I would also like to submit several CCT films; you will see how they spent so much time with the Germans, it will also show they were present at the break-in to the Fifth Column Store. They were searching for some valuable items, which they were convinced, were in the store.

They were so vicious, they kidnapped the grandson of Fred Wharton, a director of the store and he was held hostage until Fred, did as they asked. They said his grandson would be returned the following day providing he left the store unlocked that night, which was a Saturday, he did as they asked and the boy was released the following morning but they did not find what were looking for, on one of the films you can clearly see the two accused taking part in the search. We were so definite that the two accused were guilty of passing on information, Peter Horn called a security meeting and announced that in ten days time our own people were going to use the latest technical equipment, to check the Cold Room in the Basement. This was passed back to the Germans and as hoped, it forced their hand. The night they were arrested, they broke into the store and had used an explosive device to blow the locking mechanism off the door and were caught in the Cold Room checking the walls using technical probes and both of the accused were present.

Many months prior to this incident, our people thoroughly searched the store because of the Germans interest in the building and in the loft thirty bars of gold and both British and German currencies were discovered. It was booby-trapped and it was only the quick thinking of one of our officers that prevented a disaster. The gold was removed, we thought now we would see no more of the Germans but it was not to be, they were still wandering around.

When the store was being investigated to ensure the explosion had done no damage, the investigation paid off, we found four valuable oil paintings and five chamois pouches containing Diamonds that had been hidden in the pipes of the organ, the explosion had dislodged the base of the pipes. The expression on the faces of the accused when they heard this, they looked at each other in dismay. The prosecuting councillor asked Ken to tell the jury about the Basement. The Basement was discovered by accident by the new tenants of an old cinema, a trap door was found which led down into the basement area below the cinema. When it was checked out, it was found to have been built to be used as a Fifth Column, ready for the invasion of this country during the war but thank God that didn't happen, how it had been built during war time is still a mystery. There was a long tunnel leading from the trap door, the first door on the right contained civilian clothing hung on hangers and on the right hand side was a long rail of German uniforms and leather topcoats. The next room had rifles, ammunition and boxes of hand grenades, at the end of the tunnel it was set up as a canteen with a table and twenty chairs placed around it. It was obvious that the Germans knew of some looted valuables being stored there and they appeared determined to find it. It was sad, to see our own country men helping them." "Thank you Mr. Lee, that will be all."

Each team of lawyers conducted their summing up facing the jury, defence first, followed by the prosecution. The judge too summed up the case giving guidance to the jury. When the judge had finished his summary, he asked the jury to retire to consider all the evidence and advise the clerk when they have reached a verdict, you will then be brought back into the courtroom, it is hoped that you will have selected a foreman, he will be called upon to deliver the verdict. The clerk said, "All rise" the judge left the courtroom.

One and a half hours had elapsed, when the foremen of the jury knocked on the inside of their room door, a junior clerk of the court opened the door and went and announced that jury was ready to return to the courtroom. "All rise," the judge walked in and sat down, "please be seated." The judge said, "Members of the jury, have you reached a verdict?" "We have your honour" the clerk walked up to foreman and was handed a slip of paper, the clerk then handed the slip of paper to the judge, he read it and handed it back to the clerk. The clerk then said, "The prisoners will stand." The clerk then said, "Members of the jury do find the prisoners guilty of the charges of being traitors or not guilty?" The foremen replied, "We find both prisoners guilty as charged." "The Judge looked up, "Is that the verdict of you all?" "Yes your honour, it is a unanimous decision."

The judge faced the two accused and said, "You have been found guilty, the law still allows hanging for treacherous acts but the prosecution have not pressed for the death penalty. I sentence you both to 15 years imprisonment and I will ensure you serve the full sentence." Both of the prisoners clicked their heels and gave the Nazi salute, the judge was appalled. "I hold you in contempt of this court, your sentence will now be 20 years imprisonment, with no appeal for parole until you have served 15 years and you will be stripped of your titles." Both prisoners slumped back on their chairs.

*

Charlie called an emergency meeting of the Trustees for the Daisy Charity. When they arrived and were seated, Charlie addressed the trustees. "The operations that have been requested will have to be put on hold for a while, the Mobile Clinics visit to the Southern Counties has exhausted our bank balance and the donations have dried up. I spoke to one of our regular donators; he told me that his household expenses have risen so sharply, with which, I must agree, his family must come first. Ladies and Gentlemen, it looks as if we will have to suspend operations for a while. Having told you about the money, I must say how proud we all are of Sam, the wonderful operations he has carried out, I know he will be disappointed," he looked at Sam and he nodded his head. Dan said, "Don't despair Charlie, I am sure there is always a silver lining."

After the meeting, Dan suggested to Fred that he should ask Maurice, Sam's nephew, if he knew of a professional jeweller who would appraise three diamonds and being paid with a diamond, "What a wonderful idea Dan." When Fred approached Maurice, "He just smiled; did they fall off the back of a lorry"? "Something like that Maurice." Two days later Maurice telephoned Fred asking him to call in his Flag Shop. Fred called and was given a business card with a telephone number written on it. He phoned the number and made an appointment to visit the jeweller.

Dan and Fred kept the appointment with the jeweller, when they entered the shop and introduced themselves, the jeweller introduced himself as Finn Scholar, "Tell me, are you the Fred Wharton who saved Maurice's life in France?" "Yes, I am." Finn said, "Let me shake your hand." "Now, how can I help you?" Fred put three diamonds on the table and said,

"Are they valuable, if they are, the money will go to the Daisy Charity? Sell two and the other one is yours, for your trouble."

Finn picked up the stones and used his eye magnifying glass to study them. "These are beautiful stones and they will command a good price on an open market." Fred said, "Sell two, the third is yours. If you do sell them, make the cheque out to Daisy's Charity, if you have any difficulty, just phone and we will sort another way."

The next day Fred received a phone call from Finn telling him that he had sold their two diamonds for a very good price. "I have made the cheque out to Daisy Charity as you asked and I will send it to the secretary, asking him to say it was from an anonymous donor, okay?" "If I brought a diamond to you, can you make it into a diamond ring for my wife?" "I can do better than that; I can make the ring to your wife's own design." Bella, Margery and Mary, having each selected their own stone, arranged to visit Finn Scholar the jeweller. He spent a considerable time with each girl showing them the various designs and settings. They each decided on their own individual design, Finn said, "What a challenge you have set me; I will contact you when I have them ready." Mary asked the cost, Finn said, "We will discuss the cost when the rings have been made and you are all completely satisfied." When they collected the rings, their daughters were very envious, they too went to visit Finn and again he was faced with a challenge, as they wanted a more modern style.

Charlie called another meeting, "Dan was so right there was silver lining and we have received a considerable sum of money from an anonymous donor. Samuel, you are not out of work after all." Dan made a point, of asking the amount on the cheque, when told the amount, he was staggered. Dan and Fred visited Frank to put him in the picture with regard to the diamonds. They told him they had each given a stone to their daughters, Dan said "He was going to give one of his stones to his sister Ruth and her husband Charlie, will deal with getting it mounted. I will keep one stone to pay Finn for all his work, the remaining two I will sell and give the money to the Daisy Charity, I am hoping this will ease my conscience." Frank and Fred both burst out laughing. "I will give one to my daughter-in-law Gwen and you can have the remaining two," said Frank. Fred joined in, "I will keep one for my grandson's future wife, as with Frank, you can have what is left, with one exception, I will retain one to cover the cost of our 50 years in business celebration next year." "Fred Wharton, you are as crafty as ever." They decided they should have a drink to toast each other; all three were laughing again.

CHAPTER 35

Dan's Sister Ruth called to visit him, bringing with her a Newspaper cutting for Dan to read. There was an article relating to the air raids during World War 2. It was during two such raids the planes dropped land mines, which demolished Springfield Street and many adjoining streets. This caused a terrible loss of life, in the two raids the death toll was in excess of fifty souls, Dan's parents were casualties and his wife Margery lost her father during the first nights raid. The undertakers were not in the position to cope with such a tragic loss of life.

The local authorities had decided to excavate a deep hole and bury this large number in one grave and a religious leader from each denomination said a prayer at the funeral.

The houses have now been rebuilt and where the communal grave was, bushes and flowers have been planted and making it a memorial garden beautifully laid out with an appropriate plaque. The memorial garden was to be officially opened by the Lord Mayor in two weeks time. Dan thanked Ruth for calling to show him the newspaper article, we'll be attending, and we will meet you at the garden.

Dan and Fred with their wives caught a taxi to the memorial garden and met up with Ruth and Charlie. Dan and his two sisters Ruth and Mary went around looking for their brothers, they felt sure they would attend but could not find them. The ceremony started, the religious leaders of all denominations each saying a short prayer and followed by a general hymn sang to the music played by the Salvation Army Band.

The Lord Mayor stood up, "Ladies and Gentlemen, citizens of Liverpool, I am proud to be the Mayor of Liverpool; the people of Liverpool withstood the wicked onslaught from the German bombers during World War 2, the town and docks were virtually flattened. We lost many loved ones, friends and our homes. The people we are remembering today would be proud of our resilience. Here we are, houses rebuilt and this beautiful memorial garden acknowledging and still mourning our loved ones. It is hoped that you will find comfort sitting in the gardens to remember them. We still have our wonderful city of Liverpool remembering our tragic loss. Ladies and Gentlemen, I duly declare the memorial gardens open and if any person is caught damaging the vegetation or the seating forms, they will never forget their punishment, I promise you that." He was loudly applauded.

The crowds of people started to disperse, some stayed behind looking around and remembering the loved ones they lost, the service had brought memories flooding back and tears. The Mayor walked across to speak to Dan and Fred, "Is the Charity still coping with the number of operations being requested?" "We have been very fortunate with donations recently and we are managing to keep solvent and able to give help where needed." "You should all feel proud of such an achievement."

*

All the excitement was now beginning to die down at the Fifth Column and the uneasy feeling of "What is next?" was difficult to come to terms with. In fact, now the Germans have been apprehended and what they were looking for has now been found, life was now returning to some normality. Fred and Dan felt there is a vacuum in their lives but never the less, very glad that the problem has been solved and the constant threat removed. The kidnapping of Terry was still a sharp reminder of how vicious and determined the Germans were to find what they regarded as their own. The valuables they were looking for, when found, were taken over by the British Government. Dan wondered if they might receive some reward for finding the treasure on their property, no doubt they would be notified. If that is the case, Daisy Charity will benefit.

Fred suggested that a meeting should be called at The Fifth Column and explain to all the staff what had been going on at the store. Frank and Dan agreed and thought it a very good idea. It was arranged that all the staff working in the store and the workers at the DFF factory should also be invited to hear exactly what had been happening, it was also agreed that the meeting will take place at the store after it has closed, the staff can claim overtime payment if they so wish. The date was set, some of the staff was a little apprehensive about their future; all sorts of rumours have been running around regarding the meeting.

The evening of the meeting, tea, coffee and snacks were arranged, as some of the staff had an early lunch. Fred got to his feet, "Firstly, let me ally any fears regarding your jobs, I have heard the rumours that have been running around since we suggested a meeting. It has nothing to do with your employment. The reason for this meeting is to explain all that has been going on over the past year. As you all know the Basement was found, which had been set up as a Fifth Column for when the Germans invaded, Thank God this did not happen. I must admit, when I was on the Beaches of Dunkirk, I honestly didn't think we could stand up against such a powerful force but we did, of course we did and we triumphed, we are British." This brought a round of applause.

"To come back to the reason for the meeting, we feel, the company owe you an explanation of what has been going on with the secret service people wandering around. It appears that apart from the Basement being built, a substantial amount of money had been deposited in the building, two German Officers named Otto Kranz and Hans Kayberg ransacked various Jewish homes and Banks in occupied countries and they had hidden the stolen property in this building. The officer who had hidden the property had died without disclosing where their spoils had been deposited.

That is the reason why the Germans have spent so must time wandering around this building trying to locate the loot. It is not common knowledge at present but I will tell you. When they blew the locking mechanism off the Cold Room Door, the explosion dislodged the base of the organ pipes and that is where the loot had been hidden, we found five small chamois leather pouches containing Diamonds and four very valuable paintings, these items were taken away by the Government security people. Incidentally, the value of the currency and gold found in the loft some months ago, amounted to approximately one and a half million pounds based on today's figures." The staffs were delighted to gain the knowledge about the loot being found before the public and there were sighs of relief knowing their jobs were safe.

*

The newspaper photographer Jack Green's editor, really pulled out all the stops, using Jack's photographs showing the locking device hanging off the Cold Room Door and the base of the dislodged Organ pipes showing where the loot had been hidden and saying what the loot consisted of. He had taken photo's of the interior of the Cold Room and of the equipment the German's had been using when checking the walls of the room. There had been six people arrested but the names of the six had been with held at first but the names soon became common knowledge. There had been so many names banded about, it was decided to name the six arrested to clear the air. The editor used every trick he knew, in an attempt to create a big impact and substantially increase his newspaper circulation, this, he achieved.

The paper followed up with the story of the arrest of SS Otto Kranz and Nazi Hans Kayberg and how their deportation to Germany took place. This had been requested by the War Crimes Commission for them both to face charges of atrocities during the World War 2 and they had been arrested as they stepped off the plane on to German soil. They had been initially charged but their trial will be held in Nuremburg, the date to be advised. Several editors rang Ted, Jack's editor, asking from where he was getting all this information; he claimed that he didn't know where his staff were obtaining the information. Fred was feeding Jack with all this information to repay him for his help in the past.

Ted, the editor, was creating such an increase in the papers circulation, the owner of the paper suggesting that Jack should go to Nuremburg to cover the trial and obtain as many photographs as possible. Jack was delighted to be given this opportunity, such a challenge but one thing he did not know, was that photographers would not be allowed in the courtroom, however, he reported the trial in full. He reported the vile atrocities that had taken place and he managed to obtain several good photographs outside the courthouse and he was delighted to get a good picture of the ten men in wheelchairs. They claimed to have achieved their revenge, as least it was assumed it was they, who were responsible but they were never charged for machine-gunning the prisoner's legs. The papers owner and the editor were delighted with Jack's contribution; he had given them enough material to attract readers for about ten days on this one subject.

Jack's contribution not only attracted the readers, it also increased the number of people visiting the basement, looking at the lock hanging off the door and then going through the passage to the stairs to see the dislodged Organ pipes. One of the big attractions was a blown up copy of the newspaper covering the trial of Hans and Otto and their punishment. The public demand became so great, that Tour Companies made arrangements for their coaches to visit on certain day's, the volunteers were only too pleased to open up. Robert and his team in Daisy's Kitchen, had difficulty in dealing with the increased number of visitors. They never expected to get such a thriving business when they took over the kitchen Franchise but they were delighted how things are working out.

*

On his return from Germany, Jack Green phoned Fred to arrange a meeting. When they met up, Jack showed Fred photographs, which he had taken before and after the trial of Otto and Hans, "Do you recognise this man, pointing to a man in one of the photographs"? Fred replied, "Yes Jack but I can't put a name to him but I have a feeling that is the man who persecuted Bill Russell, telling him to get his ovens working if he valued his wife's health."

"May I take these photographs and run them past Bill at his engineering plant, he may be able to put a name to this man," "Okay Fred, you can take them as I have several more. "This man accompanied by three other men visited Otto and Hans before the trial and they made daily visits to the hospital after the trial and each day they were picked up by a large black Mercedes Car. There must be some influential people looking after them."

"When I tried to book a flight home, I was told that there were no seats available on that particular flight but the same Mercedes Car pulled up at the Airport and four men got out of the car and as they approached the check in desk, they were just waved through to board the Manchester plane."

Fred went to visit Bill Russell at his engineering plant, when Bill spotted Fred he went straight over to meet him, they shook hands. "Now Fred, what can I do for you?" Fred pulled the photographs from his pocket, pointing to one man in the photo, "Do you recognise him Bill." "Do I remember him Fred, he tried to attack me, and it was only the intervention of the two agents with shovels that prevented him striking me. He is a horrible man, his name is Heine Spiers and he was the man in charge of cremating Horace Hester's body. Fred, if you have any dealings with this man, you must be very careful. I wonder why he is returning to this area, I understood he was arrested and in a prison in Scotland, I wouldn't think that there is any more treasure to be found in Liverpool or Birmingham." Fred was very surprised to be told that Heine Spiers had returned to this country. Fred went back to his office and telephoned Lance explaining his conversation with Jack Green and Bill Russell, he said, "Not again Fred. I will ring you back later." Lance rang Fred later that evening, "Fred, when Heine's plane landed, a Mercedes car was on hand and he was taken to the Embassy House on the outskirts Liverpool."

*

Lance arrived at the Fifth Column store the following morning, he found Fred in his office and told him, in view of the recent information, Ken Lee, intended to continue camera surveillance, inside and the outside the store just for a while longer. The number of agents living in the house used to observe the cameras is to be reduced to two. They will watch the store during the day and the happenings during the night will be recorded on film, which can be studied the following day.

Dan, Fred and Lance went out to lunch, they didn't like turning their backs on the meals served in the Daisy's Kitchen but they did not want their conversation overheard. On their return to the store they could not believe their eyes, Heine and three colleagues were wandering around the store. Fred said, "Let's go up onto the balcony, from there we have an uninterrupted view." Heine appeared to be interested in the architecture of the building, studying every nook and cranny, Fred looked at Lance, he just shrugged his shoulders, and they were both completely puzzled. Lanced turned to Fred, "Is this a red herring, or are they up to something. Incidentally, the treasurery is considering a reward for the diamonds and the painting found on your property, the percentage being discussed is very small but considering the total value of the items found, it could be a sizeable pay out."

CHAPTER 36

One of the furniture salesmen working in the store approached his manager, "Alan, who are those people wandering around?" "I have no idea Gordon, why do you ask?" "I saw them in the Three Legs of Man last night; my mates and I often drink there. They were in deep discussion with a man who is employed as a fire investigator for a private company. Not only were they talking but the big man laid a plan of a building on the table they were sat round." "Thanks Gordon, keep your eyes open watch where they go." As Alan said that, Fred, Dan and Lance walked by, Alan called, "Fred, can you spare a moment?" "Sure" said Fred.

"Gordon is inquisitive about the four people wandering around the store, pointing to Heine and the three men with him," "Why Alan?"

"Gordon, tell Fred exactly what you told me." Dan and Lance joined Fred; they listened to what Gordon had told Alan previously. Lance looked at Fred and whistled,

"Why, a fire investigator?"

"Gordon, do you go in the pub often and is the man in question in the pub most nights?" "Yes, whenever I have been in there, he is there also." "We will join you for a drink in this pub tonight, you can then point this man out to us, Gordon, do keep this to yourself please."

"I will."

Fred telephoned Jack Green, "Jack, have you a small camera with which you can photograph a person without their knowledge?"

"Yes I have Fred,"

"Good Jack, will you meet me for a drink in the Three Legs of Man at eight o'clock, you know where it is,"

"Yes, at the bottom of London Road." Lance turned to Dan,

"I am not scaremongering but have you got all your insurances up to date?"

"Yes Lance, Mr Blake was always a stickler for these to be kept up to date."

Dan, Fred and Lance went home for an evening meal, Margery made Lance very welcome, Mary was there to help Margery. After the meal, they told Margery that they were going on a pub-crawl. Margery said, "Okay but don't speak to any strange women." They called a taxi and off they went, Mary said to Margery, "I wonder what they are up to now?" It was five minutes to eight when they arrived at the pub; Fred was at the bar buying the drinks when Gordon and Jack arrived, Fred claimed that they were standing at the door until they saw him at the bar, this broke the tension, they each got their drinks and found an empty table to sit at. They were sat talking but Gordon could not see the man in question. Their conversation drifted on to the two football teams in the city and which had the better goalkeeper. Gordon kicked Fred's leg indicating a man who had just entered the bar that is the man. Jack got up to go to the toilet, as he came back, he nodded to Fred.

They stayed and had another drink, just as they were about to leave, another man entered the bar and went straight up to the Fire Investigator. They found a table and sat talking in a low secretive voice. Fred nodded to Jack, he went off to the toilet again and Gordon made a reference about Jack's weak bladder. When he returned it was obvious that he had taken the necessary photographs. By this time Gordon's pals had arrived, so off he went to join them and Jack said goodnight and left the pub.

Lance, Fred and Dan just sat there looking at each other suddenly they burst out laughing. "Come along" said Fred, "I have a bottle of a good Malt Whisky we can do justice to." They went outside and walked a little way to the taxi rank. When they arrived home, Lance turned to Mary, "We didn't find any strange women to talk to."

"Is that the only reason you have come home?"

"No," said Fred, holding up a bottle of Malt Whisky.

*

The following morning Jack Green called into the store, he handed Fred several photographs he had taken as Fred had asked him to, he gave Lance two sets and these were much larger than the ones he had handed to Fred. Lance spoke on the phone to his superior, Ken Lee he promised to send the photos by courier. Just as the store was about to close its doors, Ken Lee walked in, Lance was very surprised and thought, something must be serious, they both arranged to stay at the Adelphi Hotel. During dinner, Ken told Lance that his team had checked the photographs and found that the police know both men. "The fire investigator has been questioned on several occasions regarding his reports, the insurance companies feel sure the reports have been made leaning towards the claimants, thus enabling the insurance claims to be met and paid out in full. His name is Rob Wilson and his companion is

Nick Brown and in the past he has been imprisoned for carrying out arson attacks."

Lance, "I am a little worried, what is being planned? Are they planning a reprisal, because of their officer friends being arrested? I have decided to keep the full team at the camera surveillance house as before and not withdraw any agents as we were planning, this will give twenty four hours coverage." They both sat looking in their coffee cups, hoping that perhaps they could find the answer in the bottom of the cup, Lance, jokingly said, "Should we drink tea, then we could study the tea leaves?" "Lance, I wonder, what their next move is going to be? there is no doubt that the German called Heine is involved, in fact, he appears to be the instigator of what is to take place but how come he is here, when he was arrested and taken to Scotland. Incidentally, I have spoken to Peter Horn and he is arranging to have the movements of those involved watched and reported daily. We all thought that when Otto and Hans were put away that would be it, we shall see."

*

Charlie Oates called a meeting of the Daisy Charity trustees. He commenced the meeting by telling them the various sums of money he has received as donations; we have been most fortunate in receiving sizeable sums as anonymous donators who don't wish to be named. The bank balance is now in a very good shape, we can now undertake to arrange for the Mobile Clinic to be towed and parked in the grounds of a Hospital in Exeter. By using this parking spot it will enable us to offer our services to six very young children in the surrounding area. Mary asked, "Where has all this money come from?" "Mary, I am not at liberty to tell you but I can assure you it is all legitimate. If Bill Nash was here, he would be insistent that it came from a Yorkshire Man." This always gets a good laugh. "Do you all agree? I must have an agreement before arranging the cab to tow the clinic to its destination and contact the parents of the children giving them an approximate date, the definite date will be confirmed later."

It was agreed to go ahead and book accommodation for Samuel and his two nurses but Sam took on the responsibility of approaching the hospital in Exeter to get the children x-rayed prior to their visit with the mobile clinic, this is to save time with the operation programme. Sam visited the hospital to meet the children and their parents and of course, the term, naughty foot was brought into the conversation, which tickled the children. He had view of the x-rays while he was there and by doing it this way he know if he would come up against any problems. On checking the x-rays he visited the hospital to enlist the services of the anaesthetist, the reason for this was because one or two of the children will need a longer operation and this will necessitate the careful eye of a fully qualified anaesthetist and the charity will have to meet the cost of the services of such a person.

*

Several days after the visit to the Legs, Alan was checking how the furniture was displayed, he saw Gordon, can spare me a minute Alan, "I saw that crowd altogether in the Legs last night, I think Fred ought to be told what transpired." "I'll give Fred a ring and then you can speak to him." An hour later Fred and Dan walked into the store and found Gordon, "Now Gordon you wanted to speak to me." "Yes, I was in the Legs last night and the fire investigator and his pal were there and really drinking heavily and they were laughing and joking. The man you referred to as Heine, walked in with his three mates, ordered drinks then sat down at the same table and started talking to them. Heine passed an envelope over and later in the evening as Heine was leaving he picked up, what looked like a war time kaki services gas mask bag and they went off laughing."

"Thank you for telling me Gordon but please do not mention it to any one else, I promise, I will put you in the complete picture when our little problem is overcome." Both Dan and Fred were very concerned, wondering what have they to put up with now and where is the danger spot, is it the store or the factory. They went to visit Frank and Bella and told them exactly all they knew about the new threat; they considered it only right, because he too had money invested in these businesses.

Returning home Fred decided to telephone Lance, he apologised for ringing him so late but Fred told him they were very worried about the situation. "Fred, we knew that Rob Wilson had got this bag to hand over and that Heine had taken it with him to the Embassy House. His every move is being monitored. I am sorry, I cannot tell you the target, I do not know but where ever it is they seem to be very pleased with themselves. I will contact you immediately I have any more news.

Dan and Fred were upset by the possible chance that their businesses were again being threatened through no fault of their own and yet they were being penalised. They decided to have dinner at Fred's house; they felt sure Mary and Margery will be able to feed them, as these arrangements are always being made at short notice. Fred kept walking up and down the room after dinner, he just could not settle, he felt sure what ever is going to happen, will happen tonight. Fred was awakened at three o'clock in the morning, it was Lance telephoning, "Fred, the cameras have picked up four people walking around inside the store that is apart from our own agents, as they are wearing special headgear."

"The intruders have been wandering around and they have been placing small incendiary devices in various parts of the building, planning to create a fierce fire in the store. Fred, you will enjoy the funny part, the camera people pinpointed all the spots where the devices had been placed partly hidden and when Heine and his associates left the building laughing and joking and shouting, "We have arranged your reply Otto." Our agents then went round defusing the firebombs but leaving them in position. Ken Lee will love this result. They had put six of these devices throughout the building, the result will be interesting, especially when Rob Wilson compiles his report, which he will have already written up, it will make interesting reading."

Fred thanked Lance for phoning him, "Shall we visit the Legs tonight, on the off chance that Rob and Nick would go to the pub and be joined by Heine." "I'll not be able to get to the store before five o'clock as I have a meeting this afternoon, yes; I think it could be an interesting evening." When Lance arrived, he told Fred that he would meet them at the Legs as he had some reports to write, I must go and book into my hotel now, I will meet you later about eight o'clock.

Dan and Fred called a taxi and arrived at the Legs about seven thirty and sat at the same table, as on the previous night, hoping Rob and Nick would choose the same table as the previous night. Lance joined them as planned but Dan was beginning to think they had chosen the wrong night. However, a little later Rob and Nick came into the pub together and sat by the same table. They were sat reading the local evening paper and discussing something, which Lance could not hear clearly but they appeared to be in high spirits. Rob was just turning to another page of the newspaper when Heine and his pals walked in and sat at the same table as Rob and Nick.

Lance looked at Fred, "Here we go." They started talking and the conversation appeared to get serious, suddenly it erupted. Heine jumped to his feet and grabbed Rob by the throat, Nick joined in fighting off the other three men, it became a proper Public House punch up, so much so, the Landlord called the police. The fighting was still going on when the police arrived; all six were arrested and carted them off in the police van. The case was reported in the local newspaper. They were all charged with breaching the peace, the magistrate bound them over for one year and they were to be released. If they should break the peace again within one year, they will face imprisonment. When they sat on the chairs waiting to be released, Rob said to Heine, "Why did you attack me without explaining the reason?" "Not one of the fire bombs worked." "How could that be?" said Rob, "Nick uses that type in his business, they become undetectable after a fire."

*

Lance received a message from Ken Lee, telling him, when Heine and his three friends were released from the court, they were collected by car and taken to the Embassy House. One hour later, all four came out of the house carrying suitcases, got into the car and were driven to Manchester Airport. Another agent took over then to shadow them; he watched them go to the check in desk and then go through the various checks and boarded a plane for Germany. Had Heine become disillusioned, or had he been instructed to leave Gt Britain, by the person, or persons who was at the back of the attempted arson attack to set fire to DFF Furniture Store, I wonder.

When Lance finished his conversation with his boss, he immediately telephoned Fred telling him the news.

"Thanks for letting me know Lance but what will they try next?" "Incidentally Fred, the small holding that was discussed, it was a shed on an allotment site, do you remember?" "Yes, I do." "That was burned down last night." "Is Rob Wilson dealing with the claim?" With that Lance rang off laughing at the prospects of that happening.

CHAPTER 37

Dan was working in the store when one of the office girls called him to take a telephone call. When he picked up the phone, he found that it was the solicitor who had dealt with the purchasing of the Old Cinema. Sorry to bother you Mr Green but I have had a phone call from a gentleman asking if your store was for sale? "Not that I am aware of" replied Dan. "The man is very interested, he considers it to be in a very good position and will become an ideal spot as a distribution depot for his company." "What company is it?" "I don't know."

"Thank you for ringing me, I will pass the request to my other directors but I feel sure they will be of the same mind as I, not to sell." Dan asked the office girl to phone around to find Fred, ask him to meet me at the store. Dan sat in his office looking round at the highly polished wooden wall panels and the DFF styled furniture. No, I would not want to give this up. While he sat day dreaming, there came a knock at the door of his office, Come in, Fred walked in Dan shook his hand and said, "I am Chrip, I believe you are Grubie?" They both started laughing at their nicknames being used but that was back fifty odd years ago. Dan explained to Fred about the offer.

Fred suggested that he should telephone Lance; he might have some undercover news from the secret service people. He did contact Lance but he said that he had not been told of any person or persons connected to Otto, Han and Heine being on the move. "I will speak to Ken Lee, asking him to make enquiries and I will come back to you, don't tell me Fred." "Here we go again."

The next telephone call Fred made was to Frank, his reply was, "What are they up to now? If it wasn't for the fact, that our venture into the Fifth Column has been so successful, I would say that it has caused us nothing but worry." Frank laughed, "It is profitable and my recent bank statement tells me so." Fred asked Frank if his health is improving,

"On the last appointment my specialist was pleased with my progress, Bella has denied me all my favourite food and has hidden the biscuit tin but she tells me it is for my own good. I have lost three stones in weight but I still have one more to lose. Cheers Fred keep in touch." Fred put the phone down and joined Dan in his office for a cup of tea.

Lance telephoned Fred telling him that he will meet him the following morning in his office within the store. When Lance arrived, he found

Dan was there also. " Fred, it appears the man making the overtures to buy this building is an elderly gentleman named Klaus Gunter. He was one of Hans and Otto's senior officers," Fred looked up, "How did he avoid the Nuremberg Trials?" "Klaus helped the allies leading up to and during the trial but the allies did not know then, it was he, who was instrumental in helping senior Nazi's to leave Germany and go to countries that would accept them and he arranged bank accounts for them.

South America was the popular and easier country to gain residency due to money being available. Klaus was eventually charged but taking into account his help, he was treated very leniently and he was sentenced to five years imprisonment, of which, he only served three years. Klaus must have breathed a sigh of relief when sentenced; his friends were hanged for their War Crimes."

"May I make a suggestion, ask your solicitor to arrange a meeting to discuss the offer? Invite them here to discus their proposition and what they are looking for." The solicitor made the necessary arrangements for the prospective buyer to visit the old cinema (Fifth Column) and meet the directors. Frank wanted to be present with Dan and Fred; Lance asked if he could be present.

Several people entered the store, or a better description would be, they marched in. The leader was very impressive, over six feet tall well built, thinning blonde hair and his eyes were striking and they looked like pools of water with sparkling blue centres. When he looked at you, his eyes bored right into your brain, at least, that is how Fred described it. He introduced himself as Klaus Gunter and very briefly introduced his colleagues. They all went into Fred's office.

Klaus looked around, "I know what you paid for this building and it is obvious you have spent a lot of time and money cleaning and painting. Let us not fool around, I will offer you double the figure you paid for this building. The reason I want this building, is to set up a chain of building units in this country and I feel this building will make an ideal distribution centre." Dan said,

"We were considering offering you a unit to rent."

"No, I want it all, if necessary, I will pay you three times the amount you paid and I will even allow the Mobile Clinic to remain in its parking spot."

"This offer will have to be put to the directors and our accountants at a future board meeting for consideration. Kindly leave your contact address or telephone number," this was handed over by one of his group. Klaus shook hands all round and left the building. Fred looked at the others open mouthed. Dan said, "We will have a meeting to discuss the offer but as far as I am concerned, No Sale."

A meeting was planned to be held in Fred's office at the factory, away from the store. Those present were Dan, Fred, Frank, Lance and his boss Ken Lee. Dan opened the meeting by expressing surprise that Klaus would offer three times the figure they paid for the building. Ken said, "Our people cannot trace any German Building Contractors planning to open units in this country." The discussion was going on when the phone rang, Fred answered, it was their solicitor and he told Fred that the man enquiring to buy the building was the same person or persons who tried to gazump them when DFF first bought the property. Ken stood up,

"The decision is obviously yours but I am a little nervous of what is behind this offer. The gold and currency was found and then the valuable paintings and diamonds were discovered, so, what are they still looking for." Dan said, "It is a unanimous decision, the offer will be refused."

Dan telephoned his solicitor telling him that they have no intention of accepting the offer made to buy the Old Cinema. "We have held a meeting and it was decided, whatever offer they come up with, we are not interested in selling now, or in the future." The solicitor chuckled, "Dan, it looks like being an interesting next few weeks, the building must be built with golden bricks," "According to the money offered it must be." Dan offered the solicitor Klaus's telephone number but he said he already had it.

"If this is your decision, I will speak to him, firework night is not until November Dan," they were both laughing as he put the phone down.

The solicitor must have phoned Klaus, he phoned and told Fred that he must be mental to refuse such a generous offer. Fred replied, Klaus, "It is not I but you, who is mental, to offer such a sum for our building. Perhaps it is what the building contains," "What do you mean by that; it is a building in the ideal position we were hoping to find." "If you walk down the next street you would find a building similar to this one and a lot cheaper," Klaus rang off.

That evening Fred and Mary went to Dan and Margery's house for dinner, during the meal Fred related the details of Klaus's phone call. Mary suggested they took the offer and invested the money; she winked at Margery, who said, "Just think of all the shopping we could do." Fred smiled at Dan; they both knew they were kidding. Dan pointed out, the number of the family, would become unemployed, even if we gave them money, it is not the same as working and earning your own wage. They all agreed, that is true, not one of our family could sit back and not work, we are a working family. Mary looked at Fred, "What is bothering you Fred?" "I went downstairs at the store and saw Alan and Brenda at it on the small table, should I do anything about it?" "No, just mind your own business." "What do you think Dan"? "What do I think? Sell the table?" The room erupted with laughter, it continued for quite a while. "Okay, fair comment," said Fred.

The decision not to sell the building was buttoned up and they were all hoping that would be the end of it but it was not to be. Several weeks had elapsed, one morning Klaus walked into the store by himself. He went to the office and asked to speak with Fred. He came out of his office, walked up to Klaus and shook his hand.

"Are you still reluctant to sell these premises to me, even if I offered you four times the price you paid for it.?" "Your offer was discussed by the directors and members of the family who are involved in the running of this company and I can tell you Mr Gunter, no amount of money would make them change their minds."

Klaus fixed his striking steely eyes, boring into Fred's eyes, "You will be very sorry you refused my offer" and he stormed out of the store.

Sam telephoned Fred asking him to join him at the factory, Fred went straight away, Sam was usually unflappable but he did not sound that way on the phone. Fred walked into the main office at the factory and three gentlemen wearing fawn warehouse coats faced him. Sam stepped forward, "May I introduce Mr Fred Wharton, company director." "What is all this about Sam?" "These gentlemen have arrived to check our safety procedure regarding the guards used on the wood working machines, in fact, the whole factory. They have received an anonymous complaint, that through our lack of attention to the safety rules, we are putting our workers at risk."

"Right gentlemen, you are at liberty to enter any part of the building and check the safety guards on the machinery being used. Do you object if Sam and I walk round with you?" "Not at all Mr Wharton," "Stop right there. I am known as Fred to every body in the factory." "Okay Fred, we will start in the timber yard and check the way the planks have been stacked." They spent the whole day checking all the machinery and they even checked the lunchtime food supplied for the workers in the canteen, which, they thoroughly enjoyed and finally, the electric appliances in the canteen. Their report gave the factory a clean bill of health; they made one or two suggestions but that was all. When Fred caught up with Dan, he related what had taken place, he just looked at Fred and smiled, "I wonder what next Fred we do have fun."

CHAPTER 38

Ken contacted Lance telling him that he had received a report from the two agents shadowing Klaus; they followed him to the DFF Factory. I cannot tell you any more at present but I will keep you informed. Lance contacted Fred telling him about Ken's message and promised to ring him if any thing further developed. Fred immediately asked the office girl to find Dan and ask him to get in touch, when Dan arrived, Fred related the message that had been passed down from Ken, "What now Dan"? "Fred, do we know of a good trustworthy man who would be interested in the job of night watchman at the factory, I bet some one would be keen to get the job." "I will ask Charlie, he is more in touch with what is going on around the city."

Fred made a point of visiting Charlie and Ruth and they were very pleased to see him. Fred knew he could trust them both. He told them all about the offer and that they were a little nervous with Klaus being seen near the factory. "Dan and I have decided to employ a night watchman at the factory, will you ask around and see if you can find a trustworthy man to fit the job. Charlie, you know whoever you recommend will be well looked after." "Fred, I have got just the man for you, he is a relation of mine, he is a retired fireman but he cannot manage on his pension, he has a pal who is in the same situation, if they are suitable they could cover the seven nights."

"Great Charlie, ask them to call in the store as soon as possible and we can sought things out. What I have told you tonight please keep to yourselves." "You know you can trust Ruth and I." When Fred told Dan he was delighted. Charlie's relation called into the store with his pal two days later, he introduced himself as Cyril and his pal as Bernie and they were both retired firemen. Dan and Fred had a chat with them and they agreed they would be a suitable pair, when offered the job, they were happy to accept. Bernie and Cyril were taken to Simon to get them included on the pay roll, Simon raised his eyebrows, Dan, whispered quietly, "I will fill you in later." It was arranged that they would start the following night. When they had left, Dan asked Sam, Roy and Simon to join them in the main office; Dan and Fred told them the complete story of Klaus's offer and the fact that people had been spotted on camera walking around and how Fred had been threatened. They also told them about the arson attack on the store and how lucky they were to prevent it, Roy smiled, "Was Nick Brown involved?" "I am not sure."

Ken telephoned Nathan, the Home Secretary, telling him that another Ex Nazi Officer is hanging around the Fifth Column store and constantly bombarding the owners with ridiculous sums of money to buy the building. In fact, the most recent offer is four times what they paid for the old cinema; Nathan whistled down the phone line, "Good Lord Ken, They must want it badly." "I will contact our secret service, instructing them to delve into Klaus Gunter's movements, if I think there is anything you should know, I will ring you Ken."

*

"Olga would be delighted for us to have another week-end in Liverpool, have you anything planned for next weekend." "No, if I mentioned it to Kelly, she will have her bag packed in five minutes, Yes Nathan lets do it, why not?" "Right Ken, I will see you on Saturday in Liverpool sometime after lunch, the same hotel as before." "Okay Nathan, I look forward to meeting you again, tell Olga, it is our turn to bring the wine, what is her favourite?" "A good red wine or Asti Martini, they are her choice but don't go mad on price, I am getting excited already, I have not had a break since our last weekend away, you know how long ago that is."

When Ken met up with Lance, he told him of the weekend arrangements, Lance replied, "Okay if Pat and I join you?" "Certainly, we would enjoy your company, we are planning to meet at the hotel after lunch on Saturday, Kelly and Pat are in for a surprise, they will think it is their birthday." Lance told Fred about the arrangements, he was surprised. "Shall I book a table at the hotel for dinner? A table will need to be booked, as they get very busy on Saturday nights, eight o'clock okay?" Fred telephoned the hotel and reserved a table for 10-12 people.

He had included Frank and Bella, hoping they would be well enough to join them. That evening he told Dan and Margery about the weekend arrangement and the girls were delighted, they were thinking that they stay at home far too much. Mary and Margery were plotting another holiday in Whitby but the boys did not know about it yet, they were waiting to find a suitable time to tell them. Lance had difficulty in containing his wife Pat when he told her of the arrangements; she began pulling her clothes out of her wardrobe, planning what she should pack.

The weekend came around so quickly, Lance and Ken were at a meeting on Friday afternoon and after the meeting several of those present suggested going out for a meal but Lance decided against going, saying, "He wanted to go home and complete some reports as he was going away for the weekend." Suddenly, Ken jumped up, "Goodness, I promised to pick Kelly up from the hairdressers, I had better go as well," so they both left the building.

This time, Pat made sure that Lance was ready to leave on time for her weekend, which is what she called it; she said, "She wasn't having him dashing in at the last minute, as he did the last time they planned a weekend away. They were the first couple to arrive at the hotel and they were fortunate as they were all neighbours, later, Kelly said, "She felt sorry for the people next door because Ken snores loudly," Ken just smiled and laid his head in his hand and snorted, "That ladies and gentlemen is the extent of my snoring, Kelly always exaggerates." They decided to have lunch and then spend some time visiting the shops and other interesting parts of the city, which, they thoroughly enjoyed but did not see a fraction, of what they would have liked to see.

They all met up in the bar of the hotel before dinner and the ladies were delighted to meet up again. The meal was excellent and there was a certain amount of excitement around the table. Dan was sorry that Frank and Bella had not felt well enough to join them; the atmosphere would have helped them to enjoy the evening and relax, this might have stopped them worrying about their poor health. During the evening, it was decided that they would meet up at the Basement; Daisy's Charity the following morning after Kelly and Olga had attended church.

The group all insisted on paying the entry fee to the Basement, as the money is for a charity. They spent quite a while looking around, they found it just as fascinating as on their first visit. Nathan wanted to see the locking device that had been blown off with an explosive charge and it was still hanging off the door of the Cold Room and the equipment the Germans had used to check the wall, hoping to find the treasure was still in the room. The equipment had been made safe and unusable but still attracted a lot of attention; Nathan was standing in one of the rooms, staring at the rails of German uniforms on the one side and civilian clothing on the other side. He turned to Ken, "Have you checked in the pockets of all these garments?"

"Yes, every pocket, even the trouser turn ups."

"That is interesting, trouser turn ups were not allowed in this country during the war, even if you had clothing coupons for a suit or a pair of pants." Nathan and Ken continued looking at every corner hidden behind any item but neither could understand why this building was wanted so much. He stood looking a the large Nazi flag, "I bet a collector would offer a good price for that flag, we are so lucky that flag was never used to hang outside the Town Hall Ken, I often wonder if Winston Churchill was as confident as he sounded, when he delivered his wonderful war time speeches?"

"Ken, will you take the party into Daisy's Cafe, I would like Fred to show me the displaced organ pipes where the paintings and the diamonds were found." Fred took Nathan into the store and showed him the pipes, "I bet the Germans were pig sick, when it was shown the treasure was under their nose all the time." "When Klaus threatened you, was there any venom in his manner?" "There certainly was, so much so, we have employed two night watchmen to cover the seven nights each week at our factory." "We had better join the party." Robert's team had created a wonderful selection of cream cakes, the ladies just could not resist trying them, when they had cleared their plates, Margery came out with the usual comment, I shouldn't have eaten that cake, they all agreed but they burst out laughing, they all agreed they were marvellous, it was suggested that they were none fattening, to ease their conscience. They all thought it had been a very enjoyable weekend and we must do it again. Mary told the ladies of their plan to take a few days break in Whitby, the other ladies all said, "What wonderful idea." Margery said, "Do not mention it, our husbands don't know about it yet," that caused laughter, "Let us exchange telephone numbers and start working on our husbands." They were laughing as they left the store to travel home.

*

The two night watchmen started at the DFF factory the following night together in order to sort out a routine. A camera system had been set up and radiotelephones were issued to Cyril and Bernie to keep them in contact at all times with the agents working in the camera surveillance house. Fred took them both to one side and explained that an arson attack has been threatened; you have picked the right people, firemen. "Can we suggest? In case of such an attack we would need several pieces of equipment." Fred said, "Give me a list and I'll deal with it." During the first night they walked round using their years of experience as firemen locating the likely spots to be targeted.

The night turned out to be uneventful but they achieved what they wanted by working together the one night. Two days later the people in charge of the cameras contacted Lance telling him two men had been seen walking around the factory, we managed to get a close up of their faces, the photos will be sent to you care of DFF. When Lance opened the envelope containing the photographs, it could only be Nick Brown and Rob Wilson the fire investigator. Fred went to the factory and waited for Bernie the night watchman to arrive. When he arrived, Fred showed him the photograph, Bernie said, "He is a crafty one but his pal always seems to get himself off the hook, reporting the fire had been caused by an electric fault or a lighted cigarette. I know the type of device Nick uses; it can be dealt with as a war time incendiary, using a bucket of sand but you must hit it before it ignites the surrounding area."

"Can you arrange for several buckets and a sack of sand in the morning and Cyril and I will call in at lunchtime, fill the buckets and put them in, what we consider to be the most vulnerable area." "Looking at the photo, they appear to be studying the camera, may I suggest that the camera is made dud but still showing a red light as if it is active and place another camera nearby to cover the area." "That is a very good idea; I will get it dealt with straight away."

*

Charlie had a very busy time clearing up all the loose ends. He contacted the anaesthetist requesting the cost of his services for assisting Sam in a difficult operation, when he was told the cost he immediately wrote out the cheque. He then confirmed the hotel booking for Sam and his two nurses and forwarded a cheque to cover the full cost of their accommodation. He wrote to the Exeter Hospital, asking them to confirm that the Mobile Clinic will be allowed to remain parked on their premises, while the operations were being carried out and allowing time to check on their patients a few days later before leaving. He sat back in his chair and breathed a sigh of relief, his face lit up when his wife Ruth came into the room, carrying a cup of tea. After drinking his tea, he started writing again. He wrote to the parents of the children telling them the date of their child's operation but the surgeon, Mr Samuel Stromberg will confirm the timing of the appointment. Finally, Charlie telephoned

Bill Nash to arrange a cab to tow the Mobile Clinic to the grounds of the Exeter Hospital, his reply was, "Kindly tell me the date you require the cab and it will be there?" "That is great Bill, thanks a lot." Charlie sat back in his chair and looked at Ruth, "I do hope the jigsaw is now complete."

When the Mobile Clinic arrived at the Exeter Hospital, Sam was there to receive it and pointed out the spot that had been allocated for its stay. Sam studied the x-rays once more and arranged to operate on two children each day, the two difficult ones will be split up, to one in the afternoon of the first two days. He feels this will give him a little longer to check on them before he leaves, he had arranged with the hospital, to allow him a room, to check on his six patients after one month.

The surgeons and the staff from the hospital were overwhelmed by the appearance and the facilities available on the one vehicle. One of the senior members of the group said, "I feel sure this is where the future of the NHS lies." One of the surgeons was very impressed with the operating table and the room available to move around and the x-ray machinery with the electricity supplied by the large generator. This is on a hydraulic slide from beneath chassis on to the floor behind the vehicle, this prevents vibration, and the engineers had spent many a long hour working how to avoid the vibration. Sam proudly told them, he was present to advise each step of the way, he was very surprised; he received a round of applause.

The first patient in the morning was a small child fifteen months of age and Sam was very pleased the way the operation went, the afternoon patient was one of the difficult ones, he was not too sure whether the child will benefit from the operation but he is quite prepared to try. He spoke to the anaesthetist and showed him the x-ray pointing out the difficulties they might encounter, he said, "You can but try Sam, I will watch the child very carefully while you carry out the operation." The operation went reasonably well and when he and the nurses put heavy plaster caste on the foot, he began to be a little more optimistic. One of the nurses stated, two done only four more to go. The other child, he thought he would have difficulty operating on, turned out to be a complete success. He carried out all of the operations to his own satisfaction. The nurses over the years have had trouble with Sam; if an operation did not go right, he would punish himself. He had previously arranged with hospital to allow him a room to check his patients after one month, he visited the hospital to ensure the promise still held and he said

"The charity will pay for the light weight castes he will use when the heavy one are removed."

*

Cyril got to the factory at nine o'clock and he put his snap box containing his sandwiches and his thermos flask containing tea in the office, all the doors were left unlocked in case they required access. He switched on his radiotelephone on and reported to the surveillance team that he was on duty. This was the routine he had been told to follow, Fred said, "Have we misread the signals Dan," "Maybe or maybe not." Bernie was on duty for the ninth night and he was doing his rounds when his telephone buzzed gently, he looked at his watch and it was three o'clock in the morning, when he answered his phone, they told him there was some activity in the timber yard, the intruder has placed something by the stack of timber on the right hand side as you leave the machine shop, he has smashed the dummy camera but we have him on the active camera.

Bernie eventually found the incendiary device and piled sand on top of it but while Bernie spent time looking for the one device, another had been put in place and it had ignited and a fire had started each end underneath a stack of wood. Bernie tried to control it but several other devices in the centre of the stack ignited, he called the fire brigade. He continued trying to contain the fire but unsuccessfully. When the fire service arrived, they soon quelled the fire, the senior officer said, "Had we been ten minutes later the whole yard would have gone up in smoke and possibly the factory with it."

Fred and Dan dashed down to inspect the damage caused by the fire, fortunately it was not as serious as they expected. They had lost two stacks of timber and the surrounding fence. Bernie explained how he had piled sand on the first incendiary but the others ignited, not giving him a chance to deal with them. Fred looked at the incendiary Bernie gave him; "This is the same as used in an attempt to create a fire in the store." Dan asked Bernie to clean the sand off and they would keep the fire bomb under cover for an exercise later, "Fred will you use Bernie's radio telephone and phone the camera surveillance team, tell them to watch where you put the device and keep a watch on it."

When the fire brigade were confident that they had controlled the fire and dampened down the embers they left. Fred placed the device on the ground near a stack of timber, he checked with cameras and they told Fred that they had watched him placing the device. The private company sent Rob Wilson to assess the fire damage; he arrived at the factory, introduced himself and produced the company's authorisation for him to carry out the survey. He left the office and spent two hours looking around for the cause of the fire. He spotted the device Fred had planted, he picked it up and put it in his haversack, he was photographed doing this and they sent a copy of the photo to Fred.

The following day Rob called at the factory and handed Fred his report. Fred opened the envelope and read its contents, after reading, he looked at Rob, "According to this report the fire was caused by someone tossing a lighted cigarette over the fence," "Yes that is my findings." "How about the incendiary device you picked up, did that not have bearing on the fire." "What incendiary," "The one you picked up," "I did no such thing."

Fred showed him the photograph of him picking the device up and putting it in his haversack. "Rob, are you going to tell me what is going on before I call the police." "My pal Nick Brown was offered a lot of money and I mean a lot of money to set fire to your timber yard and a big bonus if the fire engulfed the factory." "Who was the man who offered him the money?" "I do not know his name but his striking eyes; I was frightened when he looked at me." The police arrested Nick Brown and was sent to prison for the arson attack, the police had been hoping to get some concrete evidence to jail him again; he had eluded conviction for quite a while. There was not enough evidence to charge Rob with any offence but his company suspended him while they investigated his reports over the past year. That evening, Fred said, "Breathe deeply Dan and pour out the drinks, the insurance company will pay out for the timber loss."

CHAPTER 39

Dan and Fred sat enjoying a cup of tea in Daisy's Kitchen, Fred turned to Dan, "In eight months time our business has been up and running fifty years. I would suggest that we all meet up at Frank's house and discuss, what, if anything, we are going to do to celebrate." "Yes Fred, that is a very good idea, I feel sure the ladies will want to have their fingers in this pie." Bella was delighted to receive a phone call, asking if it was convenient for them to visit. "Yes please do come, we would love to see you," Frank got a bottle out of the cupboard, Bella said, "You can put that back, it is not going to be a boozy evening." When all the greetings were over, Dan started the ball rolling, "Fred has reminded me that DFF has been up and running for fifty years in eight months time, should we celebrate starting up the company."

Bella came into the conversation saying, "That man who is always telling us he designs beautiful furniture, what has he in mind for the suite called "Celebration." They all looked at Fred who burst out laughing, "What a wonderful idea, I will have to start thinking about that one." "May I suggest, we arrange with a hotel to provide a room, arrange a buffet and a DJ to provide the disco for the evenings dancing." Fred said, "We will provide an open bar." "Good Lord Fred that will cost a lot of money." "You may remember I kept one of the diamonds back, when it is sold, it will go a long way to help pay for the evening, in fact, it is such a beautiful stone and it might even cover the full cost of the evening."

"Bella, do you think you are well enough to join forces with Mary and Margery to organise the affair?" "Yes Dan, I am sure I am capable of doing that, it is not as if it is hard or heavy work." Dan looked at Bella; "I would like to think that the people, who worked so hard for us during the war, can be included. You can get a list from Simon's records of who were on the pay roll at that time but now retired. If however, they have passed away, invite the wives or husbands." "I am glad you said that Dan, These people helped us to where we are today." "I hope it is a beautiful stone said Frank, if not, I still have a spare one." This met with a lot of laughter.

"Right ladies, we leave this in your hands, when you have compiled the invitation list, kindly arrange a copy for Frank, Fred and I, just in case we feel someone have been missed off, then this can be discussed at our next meeting before the invites go out. In one month's time, we will meet up to discuss your progress. Fred will then be able to tell us about his celebration suite," Fred threw his arms in the air and they all started laughing and he joined in. The meeting over, Bella made a pot of tea but Frank took three glasses from the cupboard and proceeded to pour each a wee dram of whisky in each glass. All three toasted each other, here is to our continued good health, Dan said, "We will all drink to that."

After one month the meeting was arranged to be held at the factory, Margery spoke first; "We have finalised most of the arrangements but the Hotel have come back saying they want to increase the cost in view of the number of people who will be attending the function." "Why is it more expensive?" "The reason is, our party will have to take place in the Ballroom?" "Gentlemen, have you all gone over the list of people we think should attend?" "Yes Margery, we have added four names, you can have the lists back as the names are written at the top of the list."

They all agreed on a date for the celebration; "Kindly ensure that the date is confirmed by the hotel. Nothing is to be actioned until the hotel writes and confirms the date, Room, Buffet and the availability of the Disco. Do make sure the confirmation is in writing, the Buffet must be a varied selection of food to suit all tastes and religion." Dan visited Daisy again, she threw her arms around him and kissed him, she will never forget, it was he, who arranged her operation for her to correct her deformed foot. Dan asked if she would make the presentation to Sam and flowers to his wife at the party. "Uncle Dan, I will honoured to do that"

"He is such a wonderful man," "You are quite happy to carry out the presentation," "I have told you, I will be honoured."

The Saturday for the celebration came too quickly for the girls, they kept checking with each other, have we done this, have we done that and they were constantly on the jump. They found it was the little things, that gave them the headache but their attitude was, if we have missed something, tough! The evening arrived and as the guests came in and handed in their invitations at the door, Fred looked around, "Dan, Where have all these people come from?" On arrival they were offered a sherry or whatever they preferred. Eventually, things started to buzz, the DJ got his music going and as one might expect the open bar became extremely busy. Every one seemed to be enjoying themselves.

Dancing carried on for a couple of hours, the DJ announced an interval and the buffet is now available. They collected their food, Dan left it for half an hour before going on to the stage, the DJ handed him the microphone. "Ladies and Gentlemen, he waited for the applaud to die down, Thank you all for coming along tonight to join us to celebrate DFF being in business for fifty years. It is hoped you will continue to enjoy yourselves, on behalf of the directors, Frank, Fred and I thank for your loyalty and dedication in your work and tonight is just a little thank you. I am not going to continue taking up your time. Mr and Mrs Samuel Stromberg, will you both please come on the stage," Sam was taken aback and his wife had to push him on the stage. When they were on the stage, Daisy walked on, she said, "I am delighted, to have been given the opportunity of making this presentation," she then presented Sam with a solid gold wristlet watch. "Sam, this is a little appreciation from all the children you have helped to overcome their disability. Just read out what says on the back of the watch." He held it up, "To Sam, from the children you have helped to tame a naughty foot." He was so emotional he had tears in his eyes. Daisy presented his wife with a bouquet of flowers. The music struck up and fifteen small children marched on to the stage, each with a brightly coloured sash with bold lettering saying THANK YOU SAM. The children surrounded him laughing and giggling, at this moment he had find his handkerchief to wipe his eyes.

Sam and his wife walked off the stage with the children. Sam sidelined Dan, "This was your doing wasn't it?" "Yes, I had a little to do with it," "I bet," said Sam."Thank you very much, it was wonderful to see all those children march on to the stage, a few years ago they would have hobbled on to the stage, not walked, thanks again Dan." Ben Blake was the next to speak to Dan, "A very good night Dan and do you need any advice on paying for the party tonight?" "No Ben, when we get the bill, I will need you to advise me how to go bankrupt." Ben left Dan laughing.

The hotel had gone to a lot of trouble to make the Ballroom very attractive. Brenda spotted Garry, her partner when working on the form line during the war and it was she, who stole his cherry. She dumped her drink sodden husband on a chair in the corner. She then went across the floor and asked Gary to dance with her, his wife spotted how Brenda was behaving and she excused her and danced with her husband, problem averted. Fred saw what was happening and had to suppress his laughter. The man in charge of the bar told Fred, "If this lot keep drinking at this rate, the bar will run dry," Fred just laughed, "As long as your staff do not add their own drinks on it." "Fred, as if they would," they both looked at each other and laughed.

During the evening, Bella, Mary and Margery met up and they agreed the evening was going as they had planned and they were delighted in view of all the hard work and sleepless nights, trying to get things just right. They realised at midnight they will have difficulty in persuading the dancers to leave. The time of the evening was approaching midnight, a young man jumped on the stage, he was handed a microphone, he said, "I have only recently joined this company, if this evening is the recognition of the work force, I feel I have made the right choice of employers." This was followed by a rousing cheering and a chorus of, they are jolly good fellows, and the singing was followed by resounding applause.

Two weeks after the celebration, the local newspaper carried a full report of the "Celebration" night at the hotel, accompanied by a lot of photographs of the revellers. It also included a photo and a full report of Sam's presentation and all the children who have benefited from the peoples donations. On the same page the "Celebration Suite" was displayed, the advert created a demand to buy the suite, so much so, Sam and Roy had to switch the production line to meet the demand.

*

Maurice Stromberg telephoned Fred, "My father and I would like to visit the basement, we have heard so much about it but we have never found the time to visit." "Ring me, when you would like to come along and I will open up for you," "How about tomorrow morning Fred, we are both free then?" "Okay, meet me in the store and I will take you round." Fred made sure he was at the store early, the first person to approach him, was the manager, Alan.

"How did you think up the Celebration Suite. I have ten orders waiting to arrive from the factory before we can deliver," "Fred said why?" They could be delivered direct from the factory, and this would save all the handling." "Great! Will you organise that Fred?"

Maurice and his father arrived, come with me, I will take you through the original Pork Butchers shop. As they entered, Fred explained how the locking device came to be hanging off the Cold Room door and the equipment on the floor inside the room with which they were checking the walls. Maurice's father shuddered when he saw the German uniforms; he lost relatives in Auswhischz prison camp. He then showed them to the room containing the rifles and hand grenades, Fred took them through to Daisy's Kitchen and while they were sat having coffee,

Mr Stromberg turned to Fred, "I was impressed with how the large Nazi Flag had been made but it needs taking down and cleaned by a specialist, if it is not dealt with, it could disintegrate but it will need a specialist. We will engage the specialist, take the flag down and put it back on the wall after treatment when we get it back." "That is most kind of you, will you allow me to discuss it with the trustees" and when Fred told them what had been advised, they all agreed to tell Mr Stromberg to go ahead.

Fred contacted Maurice Stromberg telling him to go ahead with cleaning of the Nazi Flag; there was a long discussion on how to go about removing the flag from the wall. The flag specialist visited the basement to decide what ladders or steps would be required. They arrived on the Wednesday afternoon, three men arrived with the different types of steps and ladders, Dan said, "Surely it is just the case of removing the pins and folding it up," when he said that to the man in charge, he burst out laughing. "If you did it that way, it would just fall apart." Two hours later they had taken the flag down and packed it away.

The steps and ladders were removed, Dan called,"Fred come here." Dan, pointed to the wall, there was a large brown envelope pinned to the wall, Fred managed to reach it without any steps, it had an official seal on the flap, "Goodness, I do not think we ought to open it Dan," "Put it in the safe Fred and ring Lance." Fred telephoned Lance from his office, when he told Lance what they had found pinned to the wall, he replied, "Do not tamper with it and I will phone Ken." One hour later Lance arrived accompanied by Ken, they went into Fred's office, he took the envelope from the safe and as he was handing it over, Fred said to Lance, "You are my witness that I am handing this envelope over to Ken," "Of course Fred," "You all witness that I am opening the letter." Ken read one or two pages; he looked up and said, "MY GOD, these papers will rock the very foundations of the BRITISH and the GERMAN GOVERNMENTS

The End

Lightning Source UK Ltd.
Milton Keynes UK
19 November 2009